FALLEN

Withdrawn from Stock
Dublin City Public Libraries

FALLEN

A novel

Mel O'Doherty

Bluemoose

Central Library, Henry Street,
An Lárleabharlann, Sráid Annraoi
Tel: 8734333

Copyright © Mel O'Doherty 2021

First published in 2021 by
Bluemoose Books Ltd
25 Sackville Street
Hebden Bridge
West Yorkshire
HX7 7DJ

www.bluemoosebooks.com

All rights reserved
Unauthorised duplication contravenes existing laws

British Library Cataloguing-in-Publication data
A catalogue record for this book is available from the British Library

Paperback 978-1-910422-77-9
Hardback 978-1-910422-76-2

Printed and bound in the UK by Short Run Press

To a single child in an unmarked grave
on the grounds of an Irish convent.
His name is Legion.

And he asked him, What is thy name?
And he answered, saying
My name is Legion: for we are many.

Mark v. 9

On the pillar by the low gate it read: *Our Lady of Lourdes Grotto. Ballyredmond. Blessed and opened May 9th, 1954, The Marian Year.* Wooden rosary beads were wrapped about the Madonna's praying hands; they looped down almost to her feet. At the base of the pedestal were potted chrysanthemums and violets, and closer in there were single-stemmed lilies and roses. The Madonna's head lay there on its side, facing out towards the gate and the road, her nose beaten flush with her cheekbones and her mouth beaten clean of its lips; the stone chippings on the petals looked like soap flakes and bitten fingernails.

Children went around the village accusing each other and eyeing up teenagers; men and women stopped each other on the paths and flicked their heads up towards the grotto and spoke through their fingers. The priest said in Mass that the person who did it had no road back from the eternal fire and old women edged out on the pews with their eyes pressed shut and nodded over their rosary beads.

He thought of those women now. It was thirty-odd years ago he'd sat and watched them, watched their hands tremble and their bodies bob minutely in some rhythm of hate and age. And it came to him then, for the first time, sitting there. He paused and arced his hands over his food. "It must have been her," he whispered. He gave slow pendulous shakes of his head and pictured his mother kissing him goodnight and rubbing his cheek and heading off up the road in the dark with a hammer in her hand.

He took his plate and cup to the sink and walked up to the top of the village and stood at the little gate of the grotto and

Leabharlanna Poiblí Chathair Baile Átha Cliath
Dublin City Public Libraries

when cars went by behind him he'd hold one hand with the other like he was praying, then he'd break and hook his thumbs again in his pockets. The Madonna was different now: an avid replacement with bigger eyes, her head tipping to one side with her arms cast out and open from her robes. He looked at her for a long time, then he turned and walked towards home and did not look at the cars passing by on the road but watched their lights drift across his clothes and vanish over and over.

I

1

They walked up the avenue with their flagons of cider swinging in bags off their shoulders and the sun stuck in the trees over their heads and flung chips of light at their feet and in the leaves and in the dirt. They sat on the steps of the house and opened their flagons and they stared down the land to the dead pines way off, tipping towards each other or slanting away, branchless and black; they looked to him like nails driven askew by some inept god. The grass rolled and swayed.

Michael touched the acne at his temples and forehead, then ran his fingers over it like it was braille. The eczema on his neck was itchy from the sweat of walking so he dipped his head back and rubbed it against his collar. They picked their ears and noses and they spat in various ways. His eyes were sore for he slept little and he rubbed them with his finger and thumb and kept them closed to watch the patterns fizz and then fade to dark.

They lay on the steps on their elbows and they leaned over and took sups of their flagons and rolled back again and swallowed and they stayed like that for a long time and barely spoke. The trees in the avenue hissed in the breeze and then there was nothing at all, a weighty warm like the silence was breathing and his friend whistled slow and quiet and Michael knew he was going to say something.

"We could try the pub."

"We wouldn't get served," Michael said. "What ya think I come here for?"

"I don't like this place."

"No?"

"There's something wrong with old mansions. The size. The size of the emptiness. Something off about them. Old, I'd take. But the silence – I probably wouldn't come near the place if we weren't drinking."

"I like it. And I don't know why. I walked up that avenue one day – just probably out of pure curiosity and I came out from under the trees and there it was. Somerville House. Hidden, abandoned forty, fifty years before, according to my father."

"The vanished life. The silence here is – I don't know – seems like it's waiting."

"Nah. I'd say houses are happy in silence."

"No way. They're built for the opposite."

Michael looked off to the pines and took a drink from his flagon. He swished it about his mouth and the gas puffed his cheeks and he swallowed and burped. His friend leaned to one side and took a long drink from his own, then another short one, rolled back onto his elbows and sat up and patted the breast pockets of his jacket. Michael watched him.

"Why you do that?"

"What?"

"Pretend you have fags? Pretend you're looking for them? Pretend you forgot them?"

"I have some, langer."

"John, you pull one measly fag out of some pocket – you can have my full box with it. If not – you get nothing."

"Just gimme a fag, ya bollocks."

Michael reached in his jacket pocket and took out his cigarette box and took one and tossed it sideways without looking. John took it and lit it and stared down the land with one eye.

"Your old man says you come here a lot. To sleep even."

"Yeah. Sometimes."

"He sounded worried."

"I've never known him any other way. He might be joining me here soon, the way things are."

6

He knew John wanted to ask, but he did not ask, and silence came and they looked back down the land. A breeze picked up and a window behind them hummed in its frame and John turned over his shoulder to it and took the cigarette from his lips and replaced it with the flagon and took a long sup and wiped his lips and took a long drag on the cigarette.

"This fuckin' place."

Michael chuckled in his throat. He watched the hip-high weeds sway like they were counting off time. When they stopped they leaned eastward. He said, "You never told me why you were expelled from your old school."

"No?"

"Nah."

"What ya want to know?"

"Suppose how a fella gets kicked out of a private school."

John took a slug from his flagon, then he swallowed and he did not speak and Michael turned his head to him and waited. "A bastard," he said, after a while.

He came up off his elbows and lifted his legs onto the lower step and braced them with his arms and his flagon dangled on his shins. He looked at his friend and gave solemn shallow nods.

"I was one of those kids – grew up without a father. One day just decided to take it out on my mother. They used call me 'John the Bastard' in primary school – for a while at least – till my mother went in to the principal."

"Not easy."

"No. In secondary, years later, we're doing King Lear. Fifth Year English. Gloucester's illegitimate son, Edmund. *Now gods, stand up for bastards.* I heard some laughs. It hurts, deep, and you don't know exactly where. Is it you or your mother they're mocking? I came into English the next day, there it was up on the board: *Now gods, stand up for John Howard.* I knew the fella who did it. He winked at me as I took my seat. I got up and walked over and plunged my biro into his cheek. Two weeks

7

later I was in St Joe's, sitting behind you. What was that – six months ago?"

"Jesus."

"The last thing you want to be is 'a story'. I was a story. My mother made me a story and I hated that – hated her for it. We didn't speak for days after I got expelled. I come walking in the gate and she's sitting on the bench out front. 'Your grandfather wanted to give you to the nuns,' she says. I got the whole story then. How she got pregnant one night on a bench in Fitzgerald Park. Didn't even know the fella's name. Her father is trying to make her give the baby to the nuns in Blackrock, and she's refusing, just saying 'No'. And she's only seventeen and still in school. But that'd be her alright. 'No' meaning 'No fuckin' way'. She says to her father, 'You make me give my baby away, I'll kill myself.' So they didn't. She had me up on the third floor of the house one day in '68 with the curtains closed with a midwife from the Erinville. Within two years, both her parents are dead. She's nineteen and alone in a big house on the Western Road with her little bastard. Believe that?"

"God."

"Shame. I tell ya – worst thing. Lethal, even."

Michael's voice was gravelly when he spoke, rusted and old-sounding. "Ya," he said. "Must be."

"Oh, a right little trail-blazer, my mother. 'I could've given you to the nuns, John,' she said. 'And I didn't. I didn't. Remember that the next time you want to blame me for some prick in your class.' And she was right, of course. I said: 'Would you have, mother? Would you have killed yourself?' She said: 'You take a woman's child – they're already dead.'"

Michael rose from the steps and swept the back of his pants with his hand and walked up the steps and went inside the house and didn't speak.

When John went inside the candles were lit and Michael was sitting back in the windowsill with his flagon on his lap and one hand tucked under his thigh. "You finished your flagon already?" Michael said.

"Nah. Small bit left only. Left it out on the steps. Bit a warmth in the blood I'm thinking. Throw me over that vodka."

Michael reached into his pocket and took out a naggin and lobbed it to his friend. "Don't do the dog on it."

He opened the cap and took a short sip and clenched his face and coughed. They both laughed and their voices clanked vulgar and clean in the great empty room and they heard themselves away in the house a moment later and John took another sip and made no sound.

He sat on the windowsill next to Michael and they watched the candle shadows jigging on the walls like marionettes and Michael talked of Vietnam films like *Platoon* and *Apocalypse Now* and *Coming Home* and when the naggin was gone he smashed it against the fireplace and picked up a piece of glass and gouged something on a space of wall around which were any number of inscriptions and vulgarities and names, including his own. He turned and watched his friend through the grainy light, then he dropped his hand down and tapped the piece of glass against his thigh and carried on.

After a while he dropped the glass and walked slowly to the windowsill and turned and sat down and rubbed his knees with his hands then held them there and rocked gently and rolled his eyes dully over the floor, then he looked away to nothing at all. In the night he went and sat in a corner and pulled up his legs and tucked his face between them. He could feel the cool air from the hall down his left side; he watched his friend walk down the room and disappear in the dark and he heard him vomiting and muttering and then he returned and slumped against the wall and muttered things and wiped his mouth with his shoulder. Then the house went silent.

Michael sat at the window and watched a languorous morning drift across the grass and into the trees. He took a drink of flat cider and spat it at the window and watched it run and stall on the glass. He could smell the moulds of other rooms. He stood up and stretched and turned to go. In the night, they'd pissed in the fireplace and let it run under their legs and out around the warped oak and it welled in a hollow by the door. Now he stepped in it on his way out and felt its cold to his ankle. "Christ," he said, and he ground his knuckles against the bottoms of his pockets and walked out to the steps and sat down.

He thought of his mother. When he was a child he used to wake in the middle of the night to her long drawn-out banshee wails and his father's attempts at calming her; he'd sit up in bed and listen and wait for it to stop.

"Bad night," he'd say to his father at breakfast.

His father would jab his spoon sideways through his porridge and leave it there and look up to a space of ceiling and nod gently. "Bad night, Michael."

That was her gift to him, he figured; a middling, everyday unease. John came out after a while and stood there and blew into his fist and a fog reared up and vanished on his glasses. Michael could hear his watch tick. He rose and they walked down the steps of the house and headed down the avenue towards the road. Before the trees blocked his view, Michael stopped and turned side-on and looked back across his shoulder. The weeds and thistles waved gently as if roused to a half revelry or some blithe farewell and the house was dark over them and its chimneys were dark against the sky. He turned and walked on.

It'd take a silence any day, he thought.

2

I n the summers of his childhood his parents rented a caravan
up behind the dunes of Ventry Bay and every day the three
of them went down to the beach with a bag of sandwiches and
a flask of tea and some crisps and sat there on the sand and
when it was raining they stayed in the caravan and played cards
and his mother would read against the window for the light.
The other children in his class came back in September talking
about it sweltering down in Schull or Tramore or Ballybunion
and Michael would think them liars for he had never seen such
a sun and he'd go home and tell his mother that they should go
somewhere else the year following.

His father would sit on the sand in his anorak and look out
at the water and speak about his holidays in Youghal when he
was a child. "We'd spend five days in a hotel just off the beach.
It was like Spain down there in the thirties. All the merries and
arcades and donkey rides."

His mother was always quiet, raking the sand with her fingers,
winking up at the sun to track its place in the clouds. She'd
walk over a low mountain and wander around Dingle town in
the evening in an airy dress and wide brimmed straw hat and
sunglasses and peer into shop windows at woollen sweaters and
pipe-smoking leprechauns and stones with 'Ireland' painted on
them and other knickknacks she thought ridiculous and she'd
watch Americans buy them and shake her head. Sometimes she
wore red lipstick that was mis-applied and seemed clownish and
there'd be traces of it still in the corners of her mouth on the
drive back to Cork.

One late August heading home, her son watched her from the backseat. He could see the side of her face; she turned away to the hedges at her window now and again and then she'd gaze out to the road ahead and he could see her dimple shallow and vanish and her jaw begin to tremble like she was muttering or cajoling herself, and he knew that face, it was the one in the kitchen, the one cleaning the house and stoking the fire and it was returning as she returned, a two-week August face seeping away into the blurred hedges at her window and another coming mile by mile; the September to July face, the Cork face, the only mother he knew except for those two weeks of each summer. He watched her for a while, suddenly curious of her having a nature like that; a general, quiet, seriousness.

Their last holiday was in the early August of 1977. They got stuck in a tailback in Macroom and Ballyvourney and slow-rolled past the July cars coming the other way and the drivers exchanged nods and Michael felt sorry for their holidays being over.

"At least they had the weather," his father said. "July-ers always get the weather." He leaned forward and placed his chin on the wheel and flicked his eyes about the sky. "We'll be grand," he said. "The clouds don't know what month it is."

There had barely been a drop of rain the whole of July in Cork and Kerry. They'd take the same again for August.

The three of them walked along Ventry Strand and they stopped at intervals when his mother bent to something in the sand and picked it up and nudged it in her palm, and father and son would look down to it and ask, "Any good?" and she'd tuck it in her pocket or drop it in the sand and carry on without speaking.

A ball rolled across their path and carried on down to the water's edge. His father went down and picked it up and turned and walked back up the beach with it. A bald skinny man in his fifties came trotting down the beach with a cigarette in his lips and his trousers rolled to his shins and his undervest sliding off one shoulder. His father threw him the ball and the man caught it at his chest and cast his face askew from the flick of sand.

"Ta," he said.

"You're grand," his father said.

They walked on, husband, wife and son. His father began to talk about a rapacious landlord, a Lord Ventry who owned the whole area long ago, that he didn't give anyone a bite to eat in the famine, that his house was still standing only for the Kerrymen of the time not having the gumption to burn the bastard out, not like the Corkmen.

"It's around here somewhere," he said, and he'd pivot as he walked, taking off his sunglasses and shading his eyes with his hand to pause and squint at some faint hills. "They still use the stables apparently. Oh, they love their horses, that lot."

His mother was quiet, her steps short and slow. He watched her bare feet in the hard sand. They were stark white and shapely for her age, unveined, unused-seeming, implying that little life of hers and those little journeys between the walls of her home and no more.

His father paused again, then turned back down the beach, then faced the dunes. He cast out his left arm. "So if Slea Head is that way—" He cast out his right arm. "—and Dingle town is that way—"

They walked on, mother and son, and his father walked after them, animated and boisterous, not halfway gone on his two-week August stretch. When he caught up with them, he said, "It's back towards Dingle town. It has to be."

They walked on up the beach and cut across the beach grass and the dunes and onto the road and Michael's mother coughed her forty-a-day bronchial symphony; it was sonorous and rich and violent and put a wetness and timidity in her eyes that looked wrong with the cigarette wedged in one side of her mouth with the other arced up as though sneering.

They went back to the caravan park and Michael's parents went inside. He could hear their low voices as he played outside with a tennis ball and racket and then a football and then he chased butterflies in the beachgrass on the dunes. He went back to the caravan and the dinner was ready and they ate it together inside at the dinette. There was hardly a sound in the caravan park for it was early and the sun was still high behind the clouds and people had not returned off the beach and elsewhere.

His mother cleaned up and stayed in the caravan and Michael and his father went out and walked along the beach with a plastic bag for shells his mother could peruse on their return. They were gone over an hour and walked back into the caravan and gently lay the shells on the dinette table and spread them out and called her. She did not answer. His father walked over to the door of their bedroom and tapped it and poked in his head, then withdrew it slowly in the same motion as he pulled out the door.

"Sleeping."

"She's sleeping?" Michael whispered, and his father looked at his watch.

He shrugged his shoulders and nodded.

Michael looked out at people returning from the beach. "God. It's only early."

"Erra – sure – she'll see them tomorrow. She'll get a nice surprise in the morning."

His son looked down at the yellow shells she'd asked for, then he picked one up and rubbed it ethereally with his thumb and set it down again. His father found a paper that someone had left behind in a cupboard and he sat down and opened it on his knee and Michael went outside and stood alone by the door and saw that the park was empty again. Some dogs barked about the caravan doors; there were sounds of clanking crockery and laughter, parental admonishings flashed randomly in pockets of air and died like ephemeral worlds supplanting each other. He walked back up to the dunes for a while and came back down and went inside.

"I'm going to bed, Dad."

His father tugged at the band of lace drapery at the window and looked out. "No one around?"

"Nah."

"Okay, love. Goodnight and God bless."

"Night."

He walked to the door next to his mother's and opened it and stood taking off his clothes in the doorway and his father looked over his paper when he dropped his shoes for the thud they gave. He gathered up his clothes and shoes and swung them up onto the top bunk over his head then he turned back to close the door. He got into the lower bunk in his underpants and pulled the blankets under his armpits and lay there and listened to the dogs again and their owners returning out to them and children stepping off the cinderblock steps and asking each other what they'd eaten. He heard his father fold the newspaper and turn off the lights and his feet stick and unstick on the laminate plastic as he walked to his bedroom. He fell asleep sometime in the evening with the noises of people outside his window and the light on a strip of blanket under where the curtains met.

He woke in the morning and opened the door and saw his mother sitting at the edge of the dinette, smoking. He could hear his father outside muttering and cursing. He walked out and watched him fling a deckchair in the boot, then shove it with his foot.

"Five days in!" he said. "She barely leaves the house... and now... now she can't bear being away from the place."

They were packed and gone by 9 am. They pulled onto the Dingle road and his father said, "Jesus Christ – five days only." His mother squeezed her box of cigarettes and the paperboard gave a little squeal like it was alive.

No one spoke on the three-hour drive; trees, hedges and fields ran up and withdrew from the windows over and over and there was no sound except when his father murderously rolled down his window and the wind swirled around the car and a crisp bag crackled somewhere under a seat until he rolled it up again. Michael watched the back of his father's head for a while. There was something sad about the back of an older man's head, he thought. Something pitiful. The front had recourse, the front had focus, guardianship. The back was alone, unknown.

He looked at his mother; she had already acquired the post-holiday disquiet he had begun to notice in recent years. He thought of the look the man had given her the day before, on the beach, after they threw him the ball. Just a momentary widening of his eyes, then a narrowing, so the wrinkles fell from his forehead and seemed to re-appear about his temples. They had walked on and he thought no more of it. But he thought it strange now, and stranger still that as they'd crossed over the dunes some minutes later, he'd looked down the beach and noticed that, way back down the sand, miniscule as he was – the man hadn't moved, but was motionless, holding the ball on his hip, appearing to stare up the beach to them.

On the edge of Macroom town they could see the smoke from the gorse fires way off in Gougane Barra, rising like columns out of the land to prop up the sky. When they got home it was on the news. A farmer talked about campers in the woods with open fires and the cigarette butts of hillwalkers and bits of glass that could magnify the sun.

"Any one of them could get it going," he said. "And with all the dry weather – you got twenty square miles of tinder."

She never came down the stairs the next morning. Nor the next day, or the day after that. Her husband would walk up to their room in the afternoon and open the curtains and the light would rouse the smell of burn from the cigarette ash in saucers on her bedstand and the pockmark singeings on the carpet. The days drifted on and father and son sat in the evenings and watched television, throwing their eyes upward when they heard a noise. After three weeks her husband called the doctor.

The doctor sat with her a while and held her hand and when he'd gently ask her questions she'd turn away and stare out the window. After a while the doctor got up and stood with her husband by the wardrobe.

"Sure one would never get out of bed if they gave thought enough to the world, Elaine, and our place in it. Isn't that right, Martin?"

"'Tis, 'tis."

"Up! Up now, Elaine and be done with it."

The men stood there and watched her and their eyes fell to the folds in the sheets and the room was silent and when they looked back at her she had a mild smirk of derision and they walked out of the room.

His father wanted an answer, a fix, a timeframe most of all. He'd worked for the County Council since his early twenties, making out bus timetables and cross-departmental oversee of routes and schedules for the bins and sewer inspections and the Corpo worker rotations and the tree pruning and green cutting around the city; he'd make sure the potholing of a road lined up with a drainage pipe replacement so the encroachment on the footpath didn't need to happen twice for different jobs. All he wanted was an extrapolated sequence, an estimable time to fix on and ride out and carry on with their lives. When he'd hear her on the ceiling he'd flinch and turn down the television and his eyes would flit in his head like there was import in every footstep.

The doctor came back a week later and sat next to her again and held her hand again but this time he instructed her to stay in bed and think about why she was there. She stared into his face and then turned away again to the window as though there were another speaker there.

"Out of the blue," her husband said. "I don't understand it. On holidays, happy as Larry, normal, and then... snap." He clicked his fingers. "Out of the blue."

They came down the stairs and walked into the kitchen. Michael rolled a dinky car on the windowsill and made intermittent crash sounds so they wouldn't lower their voices.

"Bit of depression, Martin."

"Depression? You mean like... sadness?"

"Yes. Though not so much a sadness, as I understand it. A gloom, I've come to think it, in other patients."

"'Doom', she calls it. Just a day-on-day feeling of doom. That's the way she describes it to me."

"Y-es." The doctor nodded gently at his father and smiled with sorrow or reminiscence. "Back in the day they used call it 'melancholy' or 'melancholia'. That's probably where you got 'sadness' from."

His father nodded and shut his eyes. "Should it last this long?"

"Can do. Can last... a long time."

Michael could hear his father breathing through his nose. He watched him lean back in his seat and his head drop disconsolate into his neck flesh, which puffed at the edges like a sat-on cushion.

"I'm going to put her on a dose of hydroxyzine, Martin. Three times daily with food."

"Yes, yes. She won't like it, of course."

"No. There'll be resistance. There was a lady I used treat up in Waterford, I was only starting out. She used to say, 'Oh, here he is with his thermometer and his stethoscope. He's gonna wipe away me demons. Wipe, wipe away, child!' She'd pretend to pull off the top of her head and take out her brain, and she'd hold it out for me to wipe it. A riot of a woman. Next time you'd see her, she mightn't have a word for you, crying and... awful."

"So it's people with demons?"

"Pardon me?"

"It's the ones with demons end up with the... depression?"

"Not necessarily, no. It's often not experiential at all. It's not a *result* of..." He dotted out his fingers. "It's not about 'demons'."

"Okay."

"The other thing I want to do, Martin. I want her to try and talk."

"To talk?"

"Yes, to just sit and be able to say how she feels and what she thinks about things, perhaps her thoughts on why she of all people, why should she be beset with this 'gloom'. That's often a thought with depression: 'Why me?' It can help to just talk about what you're going through. Just to unpack things from the mind. It can be very, you know..." He swipes his hands down his flanks like he is brushing something away.

"By God."

"It does help, Martin. I've seen it. Just talking as cleansing, offloading."

"Yes, it makes a lot of sense."

"And you never know – it might throw up something."

"Like...?" his father said, and he poked his head slightly forward and askew.

"Well," the doctor said. "Sometimes – of course – sometimes – there *are* demons."

They walked out to the hall and his father opened the front door.

"Thank you, doctor," he said.

The doctor stepped out, then turned back in the porch. "Just a small thing, Martin. Sometimes, with depression, there can be a spark. Something, anything. A random happening. Some lingering antagonism of the past. So, when she's talking," his hand was up again, but rotating like he was gently whisking eggs, "get her to think: Did something set it off? As you say, she was fine on holiday, everything was fine, and then, snap." He clicked his fingers as his father had. "'Out of the blue', as you say. Sure. But get her to wonder if something set it off. That can be very helpful in the recovery – finding the spark. *Talking*, as we said," he touched his lips, "can be very helpful."

He walked up the driveway and his father gently pushed out the door and stood for a while picking his tooth with his nail and when he turned his son was standing in the kitchen watching him. Michael turned out his hands and then turned up his thumb and his father turned up his own thumb and walked into the kitchen and they sat at the table and faced each other. His father rubbed his face and delicately pinched his earlobe, then tickled his neck and he clamped on his father's hand with his chin and giggled.

"We'll stop this, Michael, sure we will?"

Michael sat there and nodded against his father's hand. He could hear his knuckle hair on his skin. "We will," he said.

A sound came from upstairs and both looked up and roamed their eyes about the ceiling. He dropped his eyes down and saw his father still looking upward and when he swallowed his Adam's apple rolled and his throat bulged and he thought it froggish.

"We will, Michael," he said.

The doctor came back two weeks later. Martin greeted him grimly at the door.

His father walked up the stairs and the doctor followed him and did not take off his coat. Michael stood in the hall and could hear his mother when they opened the door.

"I've been talking, doctor." She coughed and seemed to giggle and someone closed the door. He sat on the lowest step. He heard her low, wheezy tones at first and the doctor repeating, "Yes, yes," now and again. Then she began wailing.

"I saw them dying, doctor. Children starving to death. They'd look in your face with massive eyes then slump back down after you'd walked past and you'd hear them muttering to each other. God knows what. What do starving children talk about?"

When the door opened Michael ran to the kitchen and sat at the table with a toy car. His father entered and said nothing but got a glass and filled it with water and drank it back and set the glass on the counter and walked out, slow and slumped, and up the stairs again.

When the men came back down the stairs they stayed out in the hall and whispered frantically in bursts that overlapped and cut across each other like a couple arguing in a restaurant. His father walked the doctor to the door and patted him on the back as he walked out and the doctor looked back and raised a defiant finger and said, "We'll sort this, Martin. We will, we will," and Martin clenched his fist and said, "We will doctor, we will," and waved at the doctor walking out his gate and he watched the doctor drive away and he waved again at him then he closed the door and walked into the kitchen and saw his son sitting at the table.

"She getting better, Dad?"

"What?" he said blithely.

"Is she getting better?"

"She's talking, love. She's talking."

"Oh, that's good, isn't it?"

"What?"

"That's what he wanted wasn't it, Dad? The doctor?"

"What? Yes, yes, that's—"

"Did he find the spark?"

"Ha?" His father walked over and stood by his son and gazed tiredly out to the garden and placed a hand on his shoulder and tapped in rhythm on it like it was the pulse of his ruminations.

"Did he find the spark?"

His father was quiet a long time and after a while Michael turned on his chair and stared himself out to the garden like the answer might be out there. In the silence, his father said suddenly, as though dislodging it from his throat: "He did."

His son turned back and looked up at his father again. "Oh – that's good, isn't it?"

"It is, it is," he said and stared out to the garden and began tapping his son's shoulder again in the same rhythm as before and Michael turned back out to the garden again and they were silent for a long time and the garden seemed to darken as they looked out to it. His father's hand dropped flat on his shoulder; he could feel its slow heat through his clothes.

"Course..." he said and he paused and Michael turned back up to him and saw something of his mother in his father's face, as though it were a contagion he'd acquired in the weeks at her bedside and it was virulent all of a sudden. His father withdrew his eyes from the garden and cast his head upward to a space of ceiling. "...we didn't know about all the tinder."

3

Michael went to the door and opened it and three men stood there and looked at him.

"Is your father here?" one of them said.

"Yes," he said and just then his father caught the door over his head and pulled it wide.

"Hello, doctor – doctors," he said. "Please come in."

He took their coats and slung them over one arm then walked with them into the kitchen. The men stayed in the hallway, leaning into photos on the wall. His father came back out to the hall and lifted his arm towards the stairs.

"Okay, gents," he said jovially. "Shall we?"

"Yes indeed," said one of the doctors.

They walked up the stairs in silence and Michael walked back to the kitchen. He sat on a chair and watched their coats folded over the back of another chair on the far side of table: beige and brown and dark brown, impressive things, like their owners; length and grade, repose in the stripes of their corduroy. He heard his father's voice upstairs.

"Stop – Elaine – please." There was movement on the ceiling and he heard muffled voices and then more movement. Then his father spoke again. "No. No. Stop."

He could hear the prolonged murmurs of the doctors. At times they seemed to rise and hasten as though to pre-empt something, then slow and lower again. He didn't hear his father again. He did not hear his mother's voice but figured it was mixed in and drowned out by others. The door opened a short time later and he heard the men on the stairs.

Central Library, Henry Street,
An Lárleabharlann, Sráid Annraoi
Tel: 8734333

In the den off the kitchen was a chest-high bookshelf which had potted plants and framed pictures and some pieces of Aynsley relegated from the mantelpiece, and across the top shelf was a set of Collier's Encyclopaedias that his father had long ago received as a gift and along the bottom was a photo album and his father's old 7"s and his three or four LPs; there was a copy of O'Casey's *Dublin Trilogy*, and next to it some old books with battered spines and newer ones that held them upright.

His father walked into the kitchen and the men followed him and when his father saw Michael sitting there he shooed him gently with the back of his hand and Michael walked out to the den and left the door slightly open. The men pulled out chairs and their hard-soled shoes made declarative little taps on the vinyl and their pens clicked and they cleared their throats with their mouths closed.

His mother had never more fascinated him than in the past few days, since his father had come down the stairs and suggested to him over the dinner table that he stop listening to her or believing her at the least and in the days following he'd sat and watched her and felt the gravity of her words, for what could fascinate more than the dark mind and its incantations and lies and the knowledge that the badness of this world was not merely in the Ladybird books in his bedroom, but in the person and mind that bought them? He'd sit at the bottom of the stairs and listen to his parents talk and when he heard his father's feet on the floorboards he'd run into the kitchen. "We need help, Elaine," he'd heard his father say. "Proper help." And here it was, perhaps a week later. Dr Hanley, the man who'd found the spark, and two other doctors he'd brought with him as though to boast about his discovery.

Michael could hear one of the doctors suck on his pipe, the saliva squeaked faintly in the shaft and away in a back garden he could hear the metronomic squeals of a swing; they sounded like some tiny agony. He leaned out on the edge of the couch, he could see the man of the pipe turning up his pages for his father to see them and his father closing his eyes for a time and then opening them as though stuck in a slow-motion blink and Dr Hanley tapping supportively his hand on the other side.

The doctors stood up and shook his father's hand and chewed their lips and whispered into their shoulders as he showed them to the hall.

"She'll be grand, Martin," said Dr Hanley. "Out in no time."

Michael heard the front door close and his father return to the kitchen and sit back down. He got up and walked in to his father and saw him sitting holding his elbows. He could smell them in the room when he walked in and he felt the house was less theirs somehow, the soul of the house had changed for the added heat and interlope smells, as perhaps was the way with doctors; they conquered rooms and left sentry smells behind when they left. He sniffed demonstratively through his nose.

"Pipe," his father said. "The psychiatrist had a pipe."

Michael came and sat with his father. His father turned his head to the hall. "How do I tell her?"

"Is she going?"

"Well – we knew she was going. I just didn't know where."

"Where?"

His father turned back and put his elbows on the table and brought his fists together and pressed his lips against them.

"Our Lady's."

"What's that?"

"A mental hospital. Out the Lee Road."

"You said she needs it." Michael tapped his temples.

His father watched him and closed his eyes and shook his head. "Not there. Jesus."

"She won't like it?"

"No one likes it. You daren't look up at the place – it would send you into the very sadness that would put you there."

"God."

"And the thing is, if she'd only signed those VHI forms, she wouldn't be going public. She'd be going to some private place that didn't look the stuff of nightmares. She's going to find out now where O'Casey and Marx and Manifestos got her." His son looked at him blankly. "Y'know – those books of hers she'd be reading. You drive past there your whole life and wince and then one day you're making the turn for the place. And sure enough there'll be people wincing at me when they see my indicator. 'Up the Lee Road' they used to say in my time. And people knew what you meant. The Cork Lunatic Asylum it was, back in the day."

"What'll you say to Mammy?"

"She probably already has an idea. She looked at the doctors a minute ago and said, 'Ye're going to lock me up, aren't ye? Can't have anyone saying all that. Put her away so's no one hears her. Put her up with the lunatics. Isn't that right, lads?'"

Earlier, when it had fallen on his ears for the first time, the word had sounded like the doctors and his father were sitting around a table ludicrously addressing each other as 'best boy'; grown men, serious, sombre men, stroked their jaws and clicked pens and called each other 'best boy' as though infants placating each other or as though whispered to themselves in some bizarre professional self-aggrandizing that perhaps doctors did when they sat in groups, each of them the 'best boy' that their mothers had assured them they were from their earliest days and vindicated now in their doctor-ness; yes, they were indeed the 'best boys'. And then he discounted it, reasoning the word was another; that it was something else they were saying. He thought now of asking his father about the word, but preferring instead not to disclose his eavesdropping, he did not ask.

His father got up and walked over to the counter and turned and leaned on it and began tapping his teeth with his finger. Then he walked to the table and sat back down and nodded gently and threw his eyes around the room then slunk them back to the table and began tracing the grain with his finger.

"Out in no time, Michael. And we won't look back, sure we won't?" He picked some air off the table and tossed it over his shoulder, rubbed his son's cheek and smiled. "Gone." he said. And his son smiled.

They drove around the hills of Rochestown and Douglas just talking and listening to the radio and then they went on to Passage and Monkstown and stopped off at a shop to get ice-lolls then his father circled back around and drove the narrow road past Oldcourt Woods and Garryduff and he weaved in and out of the potholes and cow pats and his son's head rolled on his shoulders and his eyelids dropped and opened again. They came down the other side towards the Rochestown road. His father pulled off the road and stopped the car in a patch of grass that was littered and patched black from fires and the wiring from burnt tyres crunched under their wheels.

"What are we stopping for, Dad?"

"The view, of course. Look at the view."

His father stared off over the houses and trees to Lough Mahon a mile away. Michael held the stick of his ice-loll like it was a pen then he dropped it on the floor and looked out across the lake as his father did.

"Lovely, isn't it?"

"Yes."

"What's that water, Dad?"

"I think it might be an inlet, somewhere between the end of the river Lee and the sea. Lough Mahon."

His son looked out across the lake and over the land to rooftops running like armour belts into the haze miles away to the north. He dipped his eyes down to the mudflats of the lake. Behind them were some trees, then a lone building, a beige Palladian pile with a sunroom out along its left side and twentieth-century add-ons out the other with steel fire escapes clawing them like growths or parasites.

He sat up and shuffled up to the seat edge and pushed his finger against the windscreen.

"What's that, Dad?"

27

"Out there? That's Blackrock."

"That place there." He flicked his fingernail up against the glass. "Out there – close to the water."

His father glared out across the lake and when Michael turned to him his father seemed to have lessened, withered somehow, sitting there looking out across the water.

He did not speak for a time. When he did, it was low and throaty. "That's what we're here to see, I suppose."

"Are we?" The boy turned and the man nodded and stared out across the lake.

"Mammy stayed there once."

"When?"

"Long time ago."

"Before ye were married?"

"When Mammy was a child."

"What is it?"

"A convent."

They looked at it a long time and did not speak. His father took long slow breaths inward then blew them out through his pursed lips like a child attempting to whistle. Michael looked across to it in silence.

Eventually he spoke. "Why was she in there?" His father didn't answer. "For praying?"

"Y-es."

"God."

They stared down to it and Michael would drop his eyes down to the dashboard or aside to his father, then look back again across the water.

"Ya know," his father said. "I'm looking at that place now. And I'm thinking I'm looking at the explanation for so, so much. Things she said years ago, the way she said them, looks she'd give me, silences, every murmur in her sleep, every tremble in her hand when she was holding a teacup. Long before there was any damn depression. Seems now like it was always there, really, waiting for her – the sadness. Well, we're probably looking at the reason out there. And I heard about the place growing up. You'd just hear of such places and take no notice. One day – you're sitting with your wife. She stops talking for three weeks – not a damn word. One day, she starts up – doesn't stop. Can't seem to say anything else: 'Bessborough, Bessborough, Bessborough.'"

They looked out across to it and the lake began to ripple in the wind and some gulls flew up off it and away and clouds were coming in overhead throwing a purple across the sky like a great drifting bruise. His father started up the car and pulled out onto the road and they headed down the hill watching the convent dip out of view and they did not speak and they drove on towards Ballyredmond village.

When they got home Michael's father peeled some potatoes on a newspaper and threw them in a pot and put it on the stove to boil. Then he went and sat at the kitchen table and folded his arms low across his stomach. His son came in from the front room and saw him there and went and sat down in front of the television and turned it on and watched it for a few minutes then turned it off again and sat there in the silence. He could see his father's dark shape in the glass of the television.

"When's she going to hospital?"

His father sniffed loudly. "Next Tuesday."

Michael turned out from the chair to say something but said nothing, just leaned on the armrest looking back to his father. He seemed an old man and a scolded child, sitting there in slacks and cardigan brooding on his punishment.

"Back in the day, they used say half of Cork was up there. You never think it'll be you." The boy turned back into his chair and his father carried on. "There used be a saying – or a poem – a limerick maybe. You'd hear it the odd time, some reason or other. What was it again? *Up the Lee Road they go...*"

He watched his father in the dark of the glass of the television, patting his hair into a side crease the way he did when he was thinking, then he sat his chin into his palm and tapped his cheek with his fingers.

"Ah yes. I have it:
Up the Lee Road they go
Someone ya know
Up the Lee Road they hide'um
In the ol' asy-lum."

Michael watched his father's head shake faintly in the glass. He thought of the place across the water. He knew now what the doctors were saying. Indeed, it had not been 'best boy'. He knew it now and he would always know it. He sat there listening to his father breathe and he mouthed it over and over in the silence.

"Bessborough, Bessborough, Bessborough."

4

They couldn't visit her for the first week in hospital, not until she was 'orientated'. Seven days after she'd gone in, her son walked to her bedside and kissed her and caught the smell of the place on her skin, as though she'd been dabbing its bleachy air on her pulse points in the morning. Her eyes were fixed forward and to look at one of them she'd robotically edge her whole head in their direction and follow with her shoulders if the exchange lingered; she held her cigarette box out from her body as if to keep it in sight, or like it was a candlestick in the dark. His father said on the drive there, "Sure she's only a guest," and linked his hands over the steering wheel and stared off and the car behind beeped and he looked up to the green light and drove off slowly.

They parked the car and got out and walked past the asylum men sitting on benches overlooking the river Lee and its floodfields; they smoked and nudged each other for cigarettes and some turned side-on and watched the two strangers and made soggy-lipped incoherencies at them and a man went past whimpering something about his mother or father or brother or all three. He had a lurching, scraping walk like his shoulders were in a hurry and his feet were not and he wore a stained, bedraggled suit that looked like it was all he'd ever worn. The building seemed housed in him, in them all; domiciled in their eyes and pulling on their faces, they sat on the benches or walked around with it tugging on their clothes; when he walked to his mother's bedside she was the same as them, a length of silence under a blanket, propped up against the backrest. The

31Central Library, Henry Street,
An Lárleabharlann, Sráid Annraoi
Tel: 8734333

metal bedframe was painted white but chipped or worn to the chrome or to a grottier white of some other paint from some other time when some other woman lay on it and he thought there must be lives marked nowhere in this world but in the metal of an asylum bed and he felt a deep sadness for those lives and he tried to envision them in the space where his mother lay.

She didn't talk; she was sleepy. They were sitting on the side of her bed. His father held her hand. A patient sloped over and asked him for a cigarette. She might have been his mother's age, so perhaps mid-forties, but a purer specimen, a long-stay that drifted in from another ward for she held a pan without its brush in one hand, and before she approached them, had been roaming about the room randomly dropping down on one knee and dipping the pan to some phantom dirt pile and carrying on again, and she wore her day clothes, some cursory assemblage of blue and grey, for this was her home and always would be and she watched the women in the beds as if they were something anomalous, something immodest there in nightclothes in the daylight.

"Sorry, no," his father said over his shoulder.

She stayed behind him and Michael watched her bobbing and rubbing the pan up and down her leg, her eyes wide, her lips pinched to a cigarette butt circle which she broke to repeat every few seconds, "Cig-rette? Cig-rette?" His father looked over his shoulder to her then turned back to his wife, shaking his head; his wife's eyes had closed. He silently caressed the folds of her blanket. He smiled reassuringly at his son. Michael was reminded of his first day of school when his father walked him to the classroom door.

He watched the woman slowly stretch out her arm and then extend her fingers as if she'd learned to move from a manual. She touched his father's shoulder and he jumped with fright. "Christ," he said.

They watched her scuttle down the ward and out to the corridor; his father turned back to his mother and shook his head. Her eyes had opened and she stared at him blankly, then looked away. He sat with his hand on the bulge in her blanket, watching her face. His son studied him from the other side of the bed.

They stayed another half hour, then both rose and kissed her sleeping face. They walked out to the car. An old man stood away and watched them. He wore a brown cardigan and knee-length trousers and socks pulled high out of his tennis shoes. As the car drove off, he stepped in behind it giving slow, weary waves; they watched him through the back window. They drove down the Lee Road and over the bridge towards the Mardyke.

"I'd nearly take to the bed myself, Michael," his father said, chuckling and shaking his head. Michael laughed a little.

They were silent and drove across town and through Turners Cross and Douglas.

His father spoke after a while. "We had a teacher once, long ago, I was about six years of age. The poor man had an awful stutter. The children used to say the patriots in heaven took his voice for standing in British trenches. 'Jelly-jaw', we called him. 'Jelly' for short. His whole head jumping over every second word, his mouth open like he was trying to shake out the syllables. He was the only teacher that didn't beat us, and yet we hated him; I can't say why. You follow, I suppose. You go with the flow."

He drove on. "And it's funny. I had a dream about him the other night. I was walking along some leafy footpath somewhere and up ahead I saw a hatted man sitting at a bus stop. I walked up and stood right at his side, facing him. But he didn't move. He just stared serenely at the passing cars. 'Hello,' I said. And nothing. He didn't move. 'Hello,' I said again, louder this time. For a few seconds there was still nothing. Then, without ever speaking, he turned towards me, slowly took off his hat and looked up at me. There he was. Old Jelly, just sitting there looking up at me. I woke up, and that was it. Forty years after ever laying eyes or thought on him. Old Jelly, pulled from God knows where."

Michael said nothing. He hadn't really been listening. He had thoughts of his own these days that he took to his room and sat with for a time or sifted and skipped in his mind as he gazed out the car window. Like Mrs Kearney across the way; she was old and spent half the day washing her windows and hoovering her curtains. She was rough and scared the children and scared Michael and she appeared to hate the neighbours all about her. She went out in the mornings to meet the postman before he got off the saddle like she was taking the war to him. And yet she seemed to like his mother; she used give him bags of rhubarb or crab apples from her back garden, hand them to him over the gate like they were the bitter bearings of her own enmity or some détente offering between Norries under the alien skies of the southside, then watch him all the way to his front door, like he'd pitch them in the sewer if she didn't.

In the days since his mother went to hospital, he'd seen Mrs Kearney once or twice watching him from her window and he figured she knew something, gleaned something, if not from the doctors' comings and goings, then from his mother's absence at her own windows with cloth and brush and whatever else. She waved at him and he waved back, not wishing to peeve such a person any more than they already were, learned as he had that the ways of adults were not carved in the day-to-day but in other days that had marked themselves on their moods and voices and gave Mrs Kearney an anger and roughness that was irretrievable.

Before his mother ever went in, they were readying themselves to forget everything after she came out, a focused return and restoration of all they ever knew. But some things he knew would remain. They'd washed too far up on the memory's shoreline for a retreating madness to pull away into the tide. The day before her admission he'd come down from his bedroom and walked in the kitchen and saw her standing there before his father, holding out her breast.

"You weren't allowed to breastfeed," she said. She turned to her son and said the same thing. She circled the outer edge of her nipple with her finger where a scar ran down and across her flesh like a malignant smile.

"Jesus, Elaine, please," his father said.

"What?" she said. "You think I'm lying? They did – they burnt my breast with a poker from the fire. That's what I got for breastfeeding." He didn't know what on earth she was talking about. He looked at his father and his father looked back at him and rolled his eyes and tapped his temple with his finger.

He remembered the days of his father sitting in the kitchen, talking, telling his stories about getting a peach and an orange for Christmas when he was a child and being damn happy about it, or the mackerel breaking in Ballycotton when he sat on the side of the little boat and watched his own father cast out his line and draw it back almost instantly with five or six of those beggars jumping on it and his father would pull them off the hooks and stick his big fingers in their gills and the crack as he pulled their heads back. Michael and his mother would sit there, enthralled. She might rise from her chair and walk to the kettle with that abiding drabness that, to him, was statement enough of a prosaic past.

He never heard what she got for Christmas or where she went or what her parents' names were. Nothing. His mother's life seemed to begin when she met his father, and there must've been a contentment on his part about that, but even more, an indifference; an indifference to her past that they shared, that he supposed he'd learned from his father. Perhaps all Northsiders are like that, he mused; for what really is there worth knowing? They scared him when he'd see them in town, standing around on the courthouse steps spitting and cursing with a pram and a scowl and pulling on a cigarette with a squint set to one eye as though in grim appraisal of the civil world. Perhaps the ones that came across the river – they seethed on like Mrs Kearney or went quiet like his mother.

He only came to notice her silence, *really* notice her throbbing self-disinterest, when of course it was gone. She started talking one day, and the whole thing turned on its head; the heretofore silent woman now poured out every last thing and the once-cheery chronicler sat silent with his palms burrowing in his forehead and now and then he'd sit up and give conclusive slaps of his thighs to quieten her. But the subject hadn't changed, it was still about the past, only now it was his mother's and seemed to be nothing but tears and screams and scarred nipples and basis enough to have never been mentioned.

His father said, "You told me that scar was from falling in the fire when you were small." She laughed derisively at him. Then she walked up to him and held it up to his face in testimony.

"Don't, Elaine, don't. Please – can't we be normal?"

The car laboured on the hill near home and when his father changed gear it revved and halted, then they drove on up the hill. Michael took his face from the window. He looked down at his father's hand on the gearstick; the skin seemed fibrous and woollen and veins ran from his wrist through his knuckles to the wrinkles between his fingers. He thought of the scar on his mother's breast and shuddered that his mouth was ever there.

"Are we normal, Dad?"

His father looked at him and said, "We are. Of course we are."

5

He walked up and down the Western Road under the big trees and the college railings looking for the 'egg-blue Victorian'. The footpath was wide and ran up towards the County Hall a mile away; the houses seemed wary and withdrawn from the road and coach house arches at terrace ends were ivied or were freshly painted in fidelity to other days; there were no numbers on the house doors but rather names on the gate pillars or the letterboxes. An old woman stood at her door just watching the road and he stopped at her gate and called out to her.

"Hello, can you tell me if John Howard lives along here?"

She was stout and short and had grey hair with a centre parting and a floral day dress that was faded and balling at the hips from her resting hands and she seemed to him to belong there standing under her house, that she'd most probably taken her first breath within it and would one day take her last there, for such places tended not to pass out of families and why would they? She looked at him with a slight smile and flicked up her head.

"Are you his friend?"

"I am."

She looked some more at him and the smile grew and she began to nod somewhat, then seemed surprised like she had suddenly remembered to answer. "Oh yes," she said, and she came off the step and advanced towards him, stopping to point over the hedge.

"Three up," she said. She counted out the houses with her finger and said "Yes," on an inhale. "Three up."

"Thanks," he said. "Egg-blue – isn't it?"

She looked over the hedge. "'Twas. She had it painted. 'Tis maroon now."

"Thanks."

"So you're his friend," she called.

"Yes," he called back.

She reversed back under her doorway, nodding with her arms folded. He thought how bereft the aged must be to linger over such banalities. His mother used say, *A fella would give his eyes to hear your problems and a spit for their looking after.*

He walked on and opened the gate and walked up the pathway to the front door. The doorbell had an ivory button set in forged brass. No one answered for a while and he stepped back from the door and looked about the house, and at the ones further down, these houses of backstairs and basement kitchens, the houses of the Cork rich in the last century and century before who were neither gentry nor the landed Anglo-Irish but had carved a reasonable wealth in a profession near the city and settled their families and perhaps a housemaid on the outskirts along the Western Road or Blackrock or Montenotte and lived there in a line overlooking the river with their fellow comfortable.

She eventually came down the stairs and put her face to the frosted glass.

"Yes?" she said.

"Is John there?"

"John? He is – just a sec."

She opened the door; she was wearing a silk lemon dressing gown that rose and parted on her right thigh and her hair was wet and long and brown and her fingers sifted unseen under a towel until she started raking them down her hair. He thought she was his sister; she extended her hand to him and dipped her head for drying and her hair fell away from her neck.

"Kay," she said.

"Michael."

"Hello, Michael," she said and she stood there running the towel down her hair, seeming a conglomerate of browns; her skin, her hair, her eyes, for sure, he thought, the nipples under the lemon dressing gown, her calves and ankles and toes. This was no Garretstown tan or Ventry tan; this was the all-over continental brand of the 1980s classy. "I'm John's mum."

Of course she was a Mum, he thought, for the *Mums* of Cork looked and spoke differently to the *Mams*. They had their drinks served by Mams and their hotel beds made by them and the Mams attended to the Mums' nails in Cash's before weddings, each sneering at the other over the hand rest and holiday talk; it meant something to be a Mum. It seemed to him that all the trifling insignificances and temporalities of his childhood only grew and gathered meaning somewhere out of sight and began presenting themselves in his teens so that nothing meant nothing anymore and what you called your mother could have social and cultural and financial entanglements from which you may never escape.

"Oh," he said.

She turned and walked down the chequered tiles of the hallway and beckoned him over her shoulder with a curled-up finger, still dragging the towel down her hair. She turned into the kitchen and walked past John who was at the table dipping bread into beans. She turned on the kettle and came and sat next to him. Then she pointed at Michael pleasantly.

"You're the fella that keeps himself out all night, drinking in an old mansion." She reached for something in John's hair, inspected it, then flicked it away. They sat at each other's shoulder and seemed not even mother and son but the same person or that no third party had been needed, that nature had conjured a way to conserve and continue her. They looked beautiful to Michael.

"Yeah. I like it up there. He complains mostly."

"You're his only friend since he was expelled. Oh – I probably shouldn't have – did he tell you he was expelled, Michael?"

"Yeah. You could tell by him anyway, by the face. We'd get the odd expulsion coming in from another school. It's all here." Michael waved his hand over his face.

"Did he tell you *why*?" she said. She nudged John with her shoulder and he smiled.

"Yes, he did, I think, yes. Didn't you?"

John nodded. "He knows, Mum. He knows." He lifted his hands from his lap and opened them and cast them either side. "My struggles with my... beginning."

The phone rang and John's mother rose and slid back her chair. She squeezed gently her son's neck and tapped it. "*Their* struggles with it," she said, pointing her chin out towards the front door. Then she walked out to the phone in the hall.

John looked after her, nodding reflectively. Michael gestured with two fingers to his lips and they rose and went out through the hall and John got his coat and they went out the gate and walked up the Western Road. An asylum man would pass by now and then, floppy-jawed in a frayed jumper, staring at his feet, looking up for a dog or a lady with a pram that had crossed the road. Michael had an urge to stop them; to reach out and grab their arm as they went by: *Did you know Elaine Connolly? Pale blue eyes, black hair? Elaine Connolly? Missing tooth and scarred ti–* No. He would not ask. For she had been a short-stay in the women's ward. He'd look back to them after they'd passed, seeking some kindred correlation with his mother, then he'd turn and walk on. He was probably a short-stay too once, he'd think. Let him out to walk the roads when he stopped wanting to leave. They never let the short-stays out to walk the roads. He knew that. He knew that.

On the boys went.

"So – your mother is – nice," Michael said.

"Yeah."

"And pretty."

"Fuck you. I knew that was coming."

"I don't mean it like that. But she is. And young for a mother."

"Ya. I've seen a few fellas in my time. Wrinkled suits in the kitchen in the morning with their coffee, red eyes. I'd be staring at them like I was committing their face to memory. They'd be gone by the time she was out of the shower. She'd be odd a bit. Head out to the bench out front and watch the students go by on the road. I ended all that for her. College, husband, another baby. The bastard destroys all." He tapped his chest with fake bravado. "All from a drunken night in there on a park bench."

He gestured with his thumb at the railings of Fitzgerald Park, then they walked in through its gates.

"How ya mean, John?"

"The supernova that is John Howard was started one night on a bench in here." He flung his arm out to the path in front of him. They walked on through the park and Michael would eye the benches as he passed them, wondering was it there that that beautiful woman had opened her legs and spawned the life next to him; and wonder too as John's mother shuffled her feet in the leaves and cigarette butts about a bench seventeen years before, if his own mother's cigarette butts didn't figure among them for it was one afternoon in late October of 1967 that his father had got down on one knee and proposed.

She'd told him so one day as he sat on the side of her hospital bed, that it had been "on a bench with the leaves at our feet, and fag butts. Your father picked me up on the Sunday and suggested we go for a walk along the Mardyke. We parked by the cricket club and walked through the park and out to a bench by the water's edge. We talked for a while. Youngfellas were blaggarding behind us in one of them rundown pavilions, their curses echoing; a woman pushed a pram, a man walked a dog and bate him with his cane when he barked.

"I remember your father, he was quiet – which was rare – and jerky a bit. He looked up at the clouds and said 'Rain – maybe' and I looked up. I remember a patch of bright blue in the west seeming to be from some other day. He put his elbow on the backrest and looked back at the youngfellas; I knew he

41

was buying time; I knew he was going to ask. Then he got down on one knee.

"'Would you marry me, Elaine?' he says.

"'I will,' I said. 'I will.' The teenagers in the old pavilion nudged and pointed. A marriage is a sacred thing."

Michael and John walked out of the park and headed up to stand under the County Hall and look up at it. They then walked into the Lee-fields and walked out along the river and sat in the grass. Our Lady's mental hospital was there, just across the river up on the hill perhaps a quarter-mile away, stretched out along its implausible length, a thousand gothic eyes upon the jaded drivers on the Straight Road and walkers of the Lee-fields and swimmers in the baths.

He searched for her window up there and figured he had placed it, third floor and the eighth last window from the right. But she was not there now. He dropped his head down and stretched out his legs on the grass and ran his hands over his thighs, then he stared up at it. It had the blotched greys of a burnt-out car.

"The river breaks in two down there," she'd said once. "You can hear it sometimes, when the water is high and they open the windows." She had risen from her bed and walked over and stood at the window and stared down to the river and he and his father had come and stood with her.

He looked up there now. He took out two cigarettes and flung one at his friend and lit his own and leaned back on one hand.

"A trailblazer, my mother," John said. "When you think about it."

Michael looked aside to him and said nothing. He blew smoke rings in the crisp calm and pensively watched them break.

"It took a lot."

"What did?" Michael said.

"Not giving me up."

"Yeah."

"In those days. It took a lot."

Michael looked at the river and blew more rings. He pushed the cigarette into the earth by his leg and the leather of his jacket gave a low whine.

"You ever hear of Bessborough Home for mothers and babies?" John asked. Michael said nothing. "That's where we were going. If it wasn't for her." John looked at his friend. "You ever hear of that place?"

Michael turned up his face to the sky and closed his eyes and inhaled in bursts through his nose, like he was more smelling the air than breathing it.

"Michael?"

"Hmm?"

"Have you?"

"What?"

"You ever hear of Bessborough?"

He dug in the grass with his heel, then he stopped and pulled up his legs and fastened them with his arms and stared out to the river. His jacket creaked like a tree in the wind.

"No," he said. "I have not."

II

1

M ost of the Ballyredmond boys his age went to St Joseph's College on the south-eastern fringe of the city and a few went to school in Douglas or Carrigaline and the girls went to South Presentation Convent over in South Parish or The Sacred Heart on the South Douglas Road. Some people sent their kids back out to country schools having drifted towards Cork for a job or spouse or distance from the land they'd lost to an elder brother; they'd send their kids to country schools like it was some sort of going home, like living six miles from the city was too close as it was, they'd deserted enough their arcadian roots without the final treachery of sending their kids to city schools if they didn't have to. Some parents went all out for their kids and went private, shelled out for better schooling to pave their path to better wives and careers and grandchildren.

Michael's father had gone to St Joseph's as many of the boys' fathers had. They stopped off in the hallways in the course of any day and pointed at graduation classes, or some Dr Harty Cup hurling panel, or cross-country runners vested and muck-dappled, breaking the 6500m tape. They were stopped at the pictures one day, mocking each other's fathers and punching each other's shoulders. He looked at his own father, smiling out at him with freckles and crooked teeth. He had big, baggy white shorts that looked like pillowcases on each leg and a baggy white vest with a black stripe diagonal across his torso. Michael felt he was cheating his father, standing there, knowing what was coming. That looking at old photos was a smug hindsight betrayal of the vitality and youth and mirth staring out in black and white.

"Where's your old man, Connolly?"

"There, in the front."

He heard them laugh. They did not punch his arm as they did others. There was a quiet when he approached them most days, a scurrilous calm that exhausted him and left him whispering in bed at night of the things he'd do to them and he woke in the morning and went into school wishful of a punch in the arm, its integrity at least; anything other than faint sniggers. He'd spend a few days in Somerville House and then go back to school, and he'd hear them again. He could see that John Howard unnerved them. It took a lot to be expelled from a private school, throwing off money and tradition and opportunity. That he had befriended Michael Connolly unnerved them all the more.

Someone said, "Hey, Howard – your old man around here?"

"No," John said, glancing to the side where two rows of black and white team photographs ran the length of the corridor. "I doubt he came to this school – whoever he was. I never knew him. He fucked my mother and was never seen again." He shrugged and chuckled. "I suppose he *could* be up here somewhere for all I know."

He leaned keenly into a photo of an Under-15 Football Championship Winners Panel from 1965 and gave the faces a once-over then moved onto the All-Ireland Runners-Up Senior Basketball team, then withdrew his face from the picture and drew up his tongue onto his upper lip.

"I'd like to meet him, though."

Michael watched them watch John, side-eyed or from under their eyebrows.

John looked momentarily again at the faces on the basketball team, then walked with Michael to assembly and the other boys turned and watched them walk away.

In the days that Michael came to school he spent most of the time looking at his hands. He'd shrug if the teacher asked him a question, he counted down the minutes and the hours till the day's end then he walked out the school gates in the afternoon and felt revived for a while. After he finished his last Leaving Cert exams, he looked back at the building a last time like it was a disease he'd been cured of. Then he walked away.

He came back five years later looking to be a teacher, back to the very classrooms for which he always had a mute loathing, thinking they were the very things that held him back, that loathing them was. For his teacher training he took two classes each morning in which he had to stand up in front of the kids and learn how to teach by doing that very thing: 'Teaching Practice', they called it.

He went into school in the morning and taught his classes and headed off to UCC in the afternoon for lectures and tutorials and subject methodology meetings with expert educationalists and vanguard child scientists. He thought he was going back to walk the very halls, stand in the very rooms of his youth to pick up the conflict where he'd long ago set it down for a stoical silence, armed now with adulthood and authority and a diploma; he thought he'd claim a victory and carry on. But he loved teaching, and began to think he'd always suspected it; that he'd gone back out of some vague self-awareness, back to the very furniture of a traumatised youth and cast it all away in the betterment of children, to help and renew and purge whatever was left to purge.

He re-lived those early classes in the evenings in the pub with John. The 'student-centred' approaches he was learning about up in the college and trying out in the classroom in the mornings, 'teaching for understanding' and 'engagement through interest – not fear' and the evils of rote learning; he'd be bouncing in his seat in the evening over pints with his friend.

"You're the last person on Earth I thought would teach, Michael. And not St Joseph's of all places."

"Why not St Joseph's?"

"Ah, I don't know. It always seemed to me like it was the people in there that bothered you. The ethos, the students. The *aspirant middle*."

"Was I not *aspirant*? Am I not?"

"The only question I ever heard you ask a teacher was, 'Why do we learn Latin and not Woodwork?'"

"A fair question."

"If you cared."

"I wanted to know."

"You wanted *them* to know. You wanted them to hear it. Or admit it."

"Admit what?"

"Their climbing, soles-on-knuckles, scaling bourgeoisity."

Michael chuckled and thought about it. "I remember that."

"You're glad to be teaching in that school. You're right to be."

"The school's nothing to do with it."

"Straight-A kids getting dropped off in Volvos. I see them around the southern villages. Fuckers in boat shoes at the farmers market and hot mothers with eating disorders. I know a clawing ambition, I went to a private school for five years. You get with the programme or you get turfed out. That'll keep their heads in the books. I was probably looking for a way out. And I suppose I found it."

"Nothing wrong with a zeal for achievement."

"I wish I had it."

"Yeah, well, you've other things."

"But you wanted to make that teacher uncomfortable."

"I wanted him to think about it."

"About what?"

"About decisions to teach one thing and eschew another. That behind that is the design to gather in one student type, parent type – and push another way. That some jugs miss the glass on purpose."

"And the water wanders about the flat of the table," John said, and he pointed into his chest with his thumb and he laughed.

"And some people buy a funnel."

They spoke about their school days a lot when Michael went back, remembering and resolving. They were hard days for them both and they wished to re-live them or find the good and the wrong in them and allocate blame though they blamed only themselves and the good they found was only in the other; the answers and judgements of youth right there every night on two stools. And so they talked on.

He was given the first-year history class. They looked at him like he was conceived right there in the school, among the desks and blackboards and wooden floors and copybooks, some classroom creation to stand and judge and impart and frown at the sight of anything unlearned. He practiced in the mirror for days before he went in; the teacher voice he thought he needed. It didn't sound right when he had his first pubescent audience. They seemed not to believe him. His eyes roamed, tethered only to his wrangled nerves and his voice trailed off after second syllables and he spent the entire class grappling his way towards someone normal, knowledgeable, unnerving the kids who'd already been terrified for the teachers themselves seemed unsettled here and the would-be troublemakers eyed him steadily.

When he was afraid as a child, he'd say *the bird is in my belly*, perceiving a singular presence in the pit of his stomach stamping the poo watery and stealing his breath and flying out to his fingertips to play an invisible piano. The bird hadn't left when he started teaching; remaining as it remained for other processes and procedures of life: passing himself off as a teacher, playing sport, driving with someone in the passenger seat, going to the self-checkout at the supermarket. He'd cast the bird out for a few weeks with a course of Xanax or Inderal or Lexapro, but he always came back, fresh and fat from his hiatus. As a child he'd perceived him a robin bouncing about his insides, spirited and pugnacious and alive. Now, he imagined a lumbering gluttonous pigeon, peevish with its own living.

The first kid he addressed was named Anthony. "What's your name, please?" The child stuttered his name, then hunkered down and twitched a look either side of himself.

"Hmm?" Michael said.

"A-Anthony," the boy said again. They watched each other. Michael wondered were the child's nights as his were, staring into the dark, listening to the noises in his father's house: the wood and the drywall cooling, the pipes knocking and the cistern in the attic and the dishwasher's little clicks every half hour. When the wind blew, the metal bins beneath his window nudged each other and he'd lie there waiting for them. He'd watch the tiny sway of the lightbulb. He hated the night, he always had.

"Start reading for me, Anthony, please. Page one of your textbook – Historical Sources."

He did not smile until Christmas, as he was advised. He had a centre crease down his pants and he discussed Primo Levi over his sandwich in the staff room and he loved everything about those early months, teaching at his Alma Mater, where the children were untroubled and eyed the cars of their classmates' parents in the mornings and gauged each other's backgrounds by their lunches and PE gear.

When he got his diploma, the principal told him they weren't taking on new teachers; they were over quota as it was and there was no place for him. Michael didn't believe him. He saw the principal more than once through the glass panel on the door, standing in the hall measuring the noise within his classroom; he came in and frowned at the kids then looked up to Michael and raised his eyebrows.

The kids got more and more rowdy as the weeks wore on, the greater learning in their class being that their teacher was a walk-over, that he was a quiet, soft spoken man who had no control and grew more and more nervous with the passing weeks. He saw the principal watch him from the window of his office as he exited his car; he lingered over some notes he'd dropped, then emerged with haste and dread in his step, eager for the road back to the early days before the kids had his measure. There's no road back, he thought.

He looked up and smiled stiffly at the principal, and the principal nodded.

For five years he drew the dole. The first time he went into the social welfare office he took a ticket and sat down. Three little kids with filthy faces and stained clothes ran around the chairs while their teen mother screamed and pointed her finger at a lady behind the glass partition who shrugged and held out her hands and said something that enraged her further. He watched people watch the children as if feral dogs, then look away when they came near. He pondered the great lottery of birth and watched the children at some game in their north-Cork bawl and he shook his head at the injustice of it and dared not lift his head to the mother who walked out in a storm of cursing which the children began to imitate and get wrong in some dismal blend of crime and comedy. He wished her dead for her children's sakes. And then he re-thought it, reasoning that a mother is all they had in the world and all they'd ever have. They moved gradually towards the door, slapping each other's hands in that game of theirs. Michael watched them; he watched their smiles and their cheap shoes squeak on the sheet-vinyl flooring; he looked down at his own shoes and felt a great sadness. The birth lottery.

The mother came back in and roared at the children and they walked out after her. Some people have no chance in this world, he thought. Wings or weights. You get handed either one at birth and you keep them for the rest of your life. Poor kids. They couldn't rise if they tried.

His number was called and he walked to the lady behind the glass.

He got a job eventually at St Kieran's, a co-ed on the north bank of the river. The school sat at the bottom of one those north Cork bluffs that stretched from Montenotte westward, to St Luke's Cross and to Shandon, then Fairhill and Guarranebraher and

Knocknaheeny, slung like Falstaff's arm over the city's shoulder. It was on the North Mall and faced across the river to the south bank of the Lee, to the Opera House and a Laura Ashley and a row of wine and tapas bars, and the large east-facing redbricked wall of The Crawford Art Gallery.

He loved the first-years; the child still there in them and a general nervousness not unlike his own and in second year he watched them change like a nascent malady that was awoken the first day of the summer holidays and they came back with it effusive in their mouths, telling tales of their sex lives and Michael carried on with the Middle Ages, islanded up there at the top of the class; the virgin amidst non-virgin children, intrigued and jealous of them.

In his car in the morning he listened to Belinda Carlisle, The Bangles, Kim Wilde, Pat Benatar, and Abba for the frivolity of an eighties pop chorus. He did not listen to music on the way home for he enjoyed the silence and he'd muse on the classes that went well and the ones that didn't and he'd worry for a while on a number of children and plan for them in his mind for the weeks coming. They seemed, to him, another people north of the river, the width of the water enough to reset look and language and he felt a foreigner up there and wondered was that how his mother felt, his opposite, tucked away in those southern undulations. He heard her in the voices of the children and he watched them sometimes at their writing for some vague trace of her. Perhaps these were his cousins, perhaps nieces and nephews, perhaps she'd left herself up there, another child he hadn't known of.

There was a photo he saw somewhere once. He thought of it sometimes, driving home from school. Two little girls playing hide-and-seek in Bergen-Belsen. In the foreground was a pile of bodies, skin pulled like clingfilm over bone, some mouths open, as though gasping or aghast and glazed half-lid horror in their eyes, some mouths closed with eyes closed, as if death had been a tranquil thing. The girl's hand, for leverage, reached blithely into this amalgam of feet and faces, hair and skin and lengths of limb. She peered out from behind it, smiling.

In the background, spread around like infernal haystacks, were other piles. Behind one of these, another girl peeked out. She wore a pair of men's boots and a woman's Sunday hat and something vest-like that caught on her hip bones and would not cover her genitalia. She looked not long for the pile herself. And yet, deep-dimpled, she too smiled mischievously. He wondered had those girls survived. He tried to picture them as adults. What a betrayal they surely found adulthood to be; its rabid flimsiness. The child endures, he thought. It's the adult who crumbles. Sometimes he dreamt that his mother was there, peeping past the bodies with the two little girls.

In the staffroom he'd sit among the teachers and listen to them complain about the children and their parents. They'd laugh and share anecdotes and when the bell went one would say, "Once more into the breach" and they'd laugh again.

One day at lunch, as a teacher complained of a student, the erudite senior history teacher piped up over his sandwich – "The lumpenproletariat, according to Mr Marx." The other teachers turned to him; he read books in crowded pubs and said sapient things: on the 12th of September 2001, he had mused "This was coming."

"Humanity's sag," he continued. "His degenerate, vagabond brother. The unworkable working class."

Michael braced himself and blurted a response. "Marx didn't believe in class," he said. "It was counter to—"

"Yes, but he believed a certain group was an impediment to a classless society." The teacher tilted his head towards the door. "The lumpenproletariat," he said. The others laughed. Michael said nothing; he drove home in the evening affronted by his own silence. He allowed the thought that perhaps it was not the silence that shamed him, but the shame the silence.

"You should hear him," Michael said to John in the pub. "Postulating prick if ever there was one."

"Sounds like it." There was a stretched-out silence and they sipped from their pints and sipped again.

"My father was a Norrie," John said. "According to my mother. She didn't know much else. But she knew that."

Michael shrugged and pursed his lips. He would've said his mother was a Norrie but that would've brought a question, so he said nothing. Since the early days of their friendship when they were sixteen, John talked about his mother and shook his head at her strength and if he'd drink on him his voice would crack and his eyes would wetten and his friend would search out ways to change the subject lest it fall at his own feet. At forty-five he was still doing it.

"Maybe I'm tired of teaching," he said.

"Maybe," John said. "What else would you do though? Become a layabout like myself? Just a word of warning – you need a lot of energy to sit around doing nothing all day. A surprising amount of mental fortitude. It'll get you down otherwise."

"I don't know what I'd do besides teach history. Studied it, taught it to kids. It always seemed right, comfortable to me, history; the big *before*. I loved Somerville House years ago, sitting there in its dusts and moulds. Its rooms. There was a story there, we mightn't know it, but there was. The gone-ness. That's fascinating to me – the end of things."

"Maybe Norries are the problem."

They sat for a while in silence.

"I kicked a student out of class once. He wasn't paying attention, talking, messing. I called him back in when the bell went. I told him he was a problem, his attitude, his work, the usual ol' spiel you'd give a kid. He says to me calmly, into my eyes: 'Sir – you've been saying that to someone since the day you came in here.' He pointed up to the staffroom. 'The same as the rest of them. The problem is ye think *we're* a problem full stop. And it isn't from the talking or messing.' I'll never forget him."

"Give me a Norrie any day. Instead of compost-Nazis and their solar-panelled summerhouses."

John flicked a look down the bar and Michael looked after him. A man at the other end glanced up at them.

"Lads."

"Gavin," John said.

The man rose, picked up his fishbowl gin and tonic and began walking over to them, peeling a charity leaflet from his elbow; he pointed it out from his body as he went, as if a sword. He handed it to John and Michael.

"Can I interest you gentleman in sponsoring a child?"

"A child?" John said.

"In Africa."

"Are you serious, Gavin?"

"Oh, deadly serious."

John looked back at Michael who was staring into his glass.

"You are?"

"Yes."

"Serious enough not to know that I already sponsor a child out there. Michael too. We can't have a birthday or Christmas without buying half a farm off you."

"And how great you must feel about yourselves."

Michael turned and leaned out past John and looked at Gavin to see if he was smiling, then he turned back straight again.

John said, "I'm forty-five and on the dole. My mother got me a job in a bank once. I held it for six months before I walked away. I call myself a writer and I can't string two sentences together. I live with my mother in the same house I was born in. I've no wife and no children. Yes, I am happy with myself actually. And that's the saddest thing of all."

Michael smiled into his glass.

"How about you, Michael?"

"No thank you, Gavin. I'm good for now. I got two direct debits from you."

"Okay, gents. Okay."

"I'll take a sail-club application form though," John said.

"A what?"

"You were telling us the last day you were joining the yachting place below in Crosshaven."

"Y-yes."

"You have any of those forms? I'd love to go sailing. Not really to go sailing, of course. To be a member, though."

Gavin looked at them both to see if John was joking but Michael had turned away and John stared blankly at him with his hand out.

"I don't—"

"Well, can you bring the forms the next time you're here?"

"You can't just—"

John jumped off his seat and tapped the back of Gavin's head, then began pulling at his ear lobes and Gavin was fighting him off with his charity brochure.

"Get out ya chancer. A donation docket in one hand and a sailing club application form in the other."

"You're a wanker, John Howard. Bona fide wanker."

"I know sure. The lady in the dole office tells me the same thing. 'I'm an artist,' I tell her. 'Feckin' bullshit artist,' she says. Same thing every month."

"Pull up a seat, Gavin," Michael said.

"Thanks, Michael," he said.

The three of them talked for a while until the golf came on, then Gavin turned around and spoke no longer. His phone went sometime before closing and he walked down to where his leaflets were still fanned out. He collected them in one hand and walked out. They watched him leave.

"Gangster," John said.

"He's alright," Michael said.

"Alright? He tells his wife he's doing charity work and he walks down to the pub."

"He does both."

"He's a bullshitter, Michael."

"I don't know anyone who isn't. And the living lie – that's tiresome."

They were drunk and Michael knew his friend watched him. He could feel his stare as he often could. He turned in his seat and faced him.

"It's time to watch me again?"

"I'm not."

"You've been watching me for thirty years."

John's head slouched and when he blinked Michael was sure his eyes wouldn't re-open, but they did and his glasses slid down his nose and he suddenly cast his head upward and sat there, squinting down his face at Michael like he was a book in a foreign language, knowing there was a story there, but it was beyond his deciphering. Michael knew he would not ask what he wanted to ask. It would've come before then, somewhere down the years.

"You studying me, Howard?"

"No."

"What then?"

"I wonder sometimes—"

"Oh God – go on."

"If you were under house arrest for the rest of your life... I don't think you'd be bothered much."

"You don't think I like being outside?"

"The world keeps calling you onto the dancefloor, and all you're doing is trying not to make eye-contact. But you go – in the end. I think, sometimes... you wonder about leaving the disco altogether."

Michael looked over his friend's shoulder and swung his gaze around the bar then returned to stare at him mockingly. "From your latest novel?"

"No," he scoffed.

They left shortly after that. Michael sat on the wall while John tried to hail a taxi. Then he walked home to his father's house. His father was watching television and he came and sat on the couch next to him and his father looked at him, then looked back at the television with a glaze in his eyes that hadn't been there seconds before.

"How many pints d'ya have?" he said, his lips hardly moving.

"A few," Michael said.

"A fair few I'd say," and he looked at his son and looked away again. He was watching an old episode of *Who Wants to Be a Millionaire* and his eyes had set into the casual malevolence with which he watched all English game shows, as if they'd been conceived to ruin lives; that having lost the world, the Brits had set out as entertainment gaudy humiliations of their own citizens, one by one and week by week.

They watched it for a while, slagging each other gently over wrong answers.

When it was over his father turned off the TV and rose and took his cup to the dishwasher. Michael remained on the couch, rubbing his palms on his hips.

His father closed the dishwasher and began walking to the hall. "Night, Michael."

"Dad—"

"Yes?"

"You'd be my *Phone a Friend* if the question was about regret."

"What?"

"I see it. I see it growing on you with the years. And I thought it would fade."

"Night, Michael."

"You could ask me about it sometime – if you liked."

"What?"

"Regret. I know a bit about it."

"You've been drinking." His father stood at the door, holding the handle with his back to the room and his head bowed. He got such talks from his son maybe twice a year and his son would ache watching him.

"I don't think she'd have liked this," Michael said. "The great nothing after she'd gone."

His father hunched his shoulders like a sullen child, then dropped them down and his arms swung faintly off his shoulders.

"Why'd she do it then?" His father's head quivered slightly.

"Well, we know why. All she said."

"All I have after thirty-two years is the wedding ring she held in her hand and a thought that there's a number on all of us the day we come into the world. You hit that number, goodbye. Some of us go early, and we don't like it. Some of us carry on and on and may not like that."

"I think you think you'll see her again. And that's what amazes me. What'll you say to her when you do? That we just stopped talking about her when she was gone?"

"She was never gone."

"You know what I mean."

"She said to me once when she was unwell, 'Your child is never gone from you.' She pulled her flesh out from her arm. 'It is you. When they're gone, you're gone.'" Michael watched his father, pictured his face which he could not see.

His father continued, "Course, that's why she clasped her wedding ring. Not for me. But for what she'd had inscribed on the inside. I never knew it was even there until the doctor handed it to me. I knew then she was going, that she'd gone to him."

Michael watched his father, who turned around to him and said, "Goodnight."

"You should do this more often, Dad. That's all I'm saying. It'd be good for you."

"I've heard that once upon a time! Don't get me started. *Talk. Talk. Cleanse the mind!* And we know where that got us!"

"You know what I mean. Just us."

"I come from a time when I didn't need to know your every thought and you didn't need to know mine. People say the old Ireland didn't know a damn what was going on, with the church and everything, but I think we were right about that. If a man had a thought in his head, he went down the pub, he could say it or not say it. Listen to people saying theirs. You and me talking about your mother, I know the old Elaine wouldn't have liked it."

"And the one that came later?"

His father lifted his head in some meagre amusement, then he looked at the floor and his son watched him at another silent thinking where his face dropped away into his jowls and his eyebrows bounced up and down as though in constant surprise or wild offspring cut loose of the hairline. "We know what she was for."

His father stood there nodding towards the floor for a while and his son watched him. "Right," his father said. "Goodnight."

"Night, Dad."

His father closed out the door and Michael sat on the couch thinking about the coming days. His father would avoid him for a while like he'd transgressed his son somehow and then he'd catch him in the kitchen and Michael would shoot the breeze with him about anything at all just to make him comfortable. He remembered his mother saying that to them once, many years ago now, propped up on a hospital bed with her eyes half closed: "They only get away with it because we all ignore it. There wouldn't be women behind convent walls if we'd only talk about it. But we won't. Any other ol' shite will do. Anything at all will do us."

She lifted her arm up and pointed for a moment to the beds in a row on the other side of the ward then her arm fell down into her lap and her eyes closed and the women across the ward sat on their beds or sat on the seats next to them and some looked across at the visitors and some knitted and some were putting lollipops and plastic cars in children's luckybags and way off in that place some other woman was screaming.

2

I n the 1930s, the boys of Ballyredmond would walk about the village picking up cigarette-ends and studying the teenagers by the low wall and they'd stick bottle caps to the heels of their shoes to mimic the metal click of their fathers' quarter-ironed Sunday brogues. They'd head over to the GAA pitch or go up to the woods to slog apples or get chestnuts in September. They'd poke around in the leaves for the ones that had fallen then hurl sticks up into the branches to get the big ones. They'd post someone to watch the mansion away across the grass for their parents had told them of a wax-moustached, top-hatted man and a lady with eyeglasses in their own youths who'd open the big door and walk down the steps and the man would shout into the trees that he knew their names and was going straight to the police barracks with them. The teenagers had said they saw no man at all but an old woman with glasses who used to open the door and walk carefully down the steps and stop there and stare into the trees for a while and look at the land about her then turn back up the steps and close out the door. The last they saw her they said she was sitting on the top step in a fold-out chair, reading with a blanket over her lap and another over her shoulders and her hair not so far from the coin-ish grey of the house behind.

But the young boys never saw her. They never saw anyone. They walked home with their pockets bulging year after year and supposed themselves better skilled than those who had come before, supposed their sticks more exact in the trees and quieter and that they were better hiders and better whisperers for no old woman ever bothered them. Even when the chestnuts no longer held their interest, they wandered up there in other autumns as some seasonal or sentimental impulse and they talked freely and drifted in and out of the trees in front of the windows and looked up to the house occasionally and carried on with their games.

One October, they walked up the steps and rapped on the door and ran away into the trees and watched and waited for the door to open. And there was nothing. They did it again. Nothing. They kicked about the leaves for sizeable chestnuts and went back and hurled them at a downstairs window and when it was finally put through, the sound of smashed glass sent them again to the trees. But the house was still. The boys went back, walked up and cupped their hands against the glass. They went home and told people, "There's no old lady up in Somerville House. The house is empty."

Martin Connolly was one of those boys.

The men and women walked with their children along the road to the church and the tips of headstones rose above the wall and the adults would eye them with reverence and vague dread and some turned back to hurry children who'd fallen behind, the bored and less practiced and the less eager in their petitions to Paradise.

This Sunday in 1942, they sat in the church and the priest did not appear. They waited fifteen minutes or more, the altar boys began to look at each other and the children in the pews fidgeted with their fingers and their parents nodded and dropped puzzled faces at others across the aisle and looked up to the priest's door and looked back at each other and jumped their shoulders.

When the door finally opened, the priest came out and the people stood up into their aggregate heat and talc and mothball musk and stared keenly at the man for signs of illness and finding none they returned to the solemn calm of every Sunday, for here – whole and hearty – was the messenger, the saved man endeavouring to save who else he could. He did not speak. He looked about as though in grave thought and he shook his head and looked about some more. He walked down from the altar and stood centrally before the people on the last step.

"Somerville House has been raided," he said. "The whole place robbed of every last book, every ornament, every door handle. Probably over a few weeks. The front door pushed wide – oil-paintings, furniture, rugs, plates, cutlery. Wallpaper! Wallpaper expertly peeled down and taken away. The bolt on the front door unscrewed and taken. Mattresses! Taken. Mirrors! Taken. The size of some houses! Gone. Silver serving sets. Gone. Every glass, every cup, every saucer. The wine cellar empty. The dinner gong in the hall. The pots and pans and dried fruit in the kitchen. Great saucepans the likes of which no family would need.

"Some of you – I can see it in your faces – *Itinerants! Yes, it was the itinerants!* But don't you dare in God's house think such a thing, for well you know that is a lie. Sergeant Furlong was not even the first to inform me. A number of you came to me already – watching as ye described it – night after night – tables and great high-backed leather chairs and huge rolls of rug walking down the village in the dark. 'Twas I disabused Sergeant Furlong! 'No, no, Sergeant – this was no one off divestment, an itinerant band one or two nights, never to be seen again. For some parishioners with Jesus in their hearts have told me what they saw, night on night.'

"Let me say this to every one of you who crossed the threshold of Somerville: Jesus knows. You may sit with fine china this evening when the curtains are closed. You may butter your bread with a great silver knife and tap your mouths with embroidered napkins, and you may straighten your shirt in a gilt bordered mirror. But Jesus knows.

"And so – let me say this. Sergeant Furlong is not going to go kicking in the doors of the village. He wanted to, mind! He wanted to. The house and contents were signed over to the state. 'Twas state property ye stole. I said, 'Sergeant, let it to God. Let it to God. For some sins are less for the state and more for the soul. Less the judge than the High Judge. The village will do it. They will bring back what they took. They will return the sin. They will give up their sin to the church, to Jesus, for they know he watches, for they cannot sit amidst their fraud and sin. They will cast it out for it is a stain on their home and on their souls.'

"And so I say to you all this one time: Return what was taken. For the next week only, you can bring whatever items you have taken and bring them around to the back of the church and leave them there on the grass. Ye can do so during the day if you choose or at night if you prefer. Hide your faces if you must. This has been arranged by Sergeant Furlong and myself. We will, between us, deal with this great transgression against God and his Son. The only path to undoing this is to give it up to the Sergeant and to myself. It will go no further and no one will know. And we will go on. A week. No more. And may God forgive ye."

From there the Mass proceeded in the vein of all others before it, as if nothing had ever occurred and nothing had ever been said. People did not linger outside the church that day and those who did made no mention of all the priest had said. There was never another word about it; not in Mass nor outside, not in the butcher's among the women nor the men in the pub. No one knew what was taken or returned and the name of a single thief was never uttered. No one had ever heard an un-Latin word in Mass until that day and wouldn't again for another decade and of this too no one spoke. The village moved on, knowing and unspeaking, a ministry of memory, the unsaid burrowing down all the more to where the mind was rich and zealous. No one ever went near Somerville House again, child nor adult. The rooms remained empty and the paths in the woods dwindled and disappeared and the house and the land fell into the rhythms of wind and rain and silence.

One day, forty years later, a teenager would turn in the gate and walk up the avenue and sit on the steps of the house. He'd remember a time he came off his bike and his mother had spat into a tissue and wiped his scraped knee. She'd held him for a while, then dabbed his eyes as he walked away. He'd stare out across the old lawn to where the pines were tilted and black against the distant sky and he'd cry like he never cried, sitting there on the steps, thinking of his mother, thinking of the smoky bouquet of her spittle.

Sometimes Michael's father went down the village to buy a paper or some milk and he'd return and slam the front door and throw the paper on the counter and begin clanking cups and plates and cutlery, and Michael would know then, he'd met someone. He was the same when he'd come home early from a local wedding he couldn't get out of, but at least he was prepared for them. An impromptu street catch-up he hated most of all. Michael had seen him; his father would stand side-on with his legs apart, half walking away before the conversation started. For the village remembered. It remembered his mother. How could it not? There in broad daylight she had been with the whole place watching. His father would devote the evening to such a conversation, surmising and calculating what his interlocutor could know and what they could've seen – what they'd been re-playing behind his eyes as they nodded calmly at him. And then it would come as they ate dinner.

"We should've left, Michael," he'd say. "Should've fecked off to England or Canada years ago." Then he'd get rueful and go quiet and minutes later he'd say, "We can't. Can't leave this house. Or her grave."

He was eighty-two. To his son he seemed unsure of the world, like he was new to it. He sniffed uncomfortably when Obama came on the news in the same way he sniffed at a condom commercial. And yet he wouldn't go back if he could. Michael watched him and wondered if that was the way it ended for everyone – the past, present and future – all equally repellent, a going with gusto to the grave.

His father cheered new housing estates going up around the village, for he believed time and outsiders would wash the village clean of all memory of her and she would lodge solely in his mind and the mind of his son. But the blow-outs were a problem. The move-aways who returned on Sundays to take their mothers out for a drive or take fathers up the village for a pint and a chaser. Christmas, Easter, August, funerals – the far-flung indigenous come home. The old native he met on a footpath in the village: his mind was not cleansed. He knew the past. He remembered the plundering of a big house; he remembered the madwoman and what she did. *Elaine Connolly* was probably the first thing he thought of when their umbrellas collided outside the newsagents.

After one such stop-and-chat, Michael took his father to a pub in the village that he and John frequented, assuring him the older people eschewed the place for the proprietor was not local, if even legit Irish, and it being a Tuesday evening they'd have the place to themselves. They sat at a lowdown table and his father turned his back to the door and left his coat on. When John came in, he shook his hand and threw his notebook and pen on the table and went to the bar and called a pint. Then he came and sat with them and used his notepad as a beermat and began to speak immediately, touching his father's shoulder as he spoke and calling him 'Marty'. His father barely spoke, but Michael knew he was not bored. He'd leave his beer on the table and sit back and listen to John, then lurch forward now and again like he'd remembered it was there.

Later, when Gavin came in, John flicked his head out towards him, inviting Michael and his father to watch him and when Gavin sprayed charity brochures on the counter and pointed people towards them, he looked back at the barman and pointed up at the television and John went, "See, Marty, see," and Michael's father said, "See what? What does he mean, Michael?"

On Michael's birthday, he brought his father again. They clinked glasses with John, and Gavin came down to the table and pulled up a chair, stared solemnly into his eyes and said, "Happy birthday, Michael. But we must remember as well – not everyone has the luxury of celebration. Not everyone makes it to forty-five."

John rolled his eyes and Martin smiled at him.

"Have you thought of being a priest, Gavin?" John said.

"A priest? Are you joking?"

"Ah now – I think you'd be an excellent priest."

"I can think of nothing more absurd than a priest."

Michael looked at his father.

"Presumably you have a problem with sanctimony and shameless moralising?" John said. Michael shook his head and took a drink.

Gavin flicked his eyes between the men. "Yes, I do. Oh, I see – I'm priest material because I'm a hypocrite – is that it? You're the hypocrite, John. With your writing pad and—"

"Sure I've been telling you that for years. You seem to have a problem accepting it."

"Asshole."

"Well – I'm not sure I disagree with that either," John said.

Michael raised his hand. "I'd certainly agree," and he laughed.

"Don't mind me, Gavin. I'm only jealous. I still live with my mother. I still ask her for money for cigarettes, for Christ's sake." He stuck his tongue in his cheek and paused for a moment. "A great woman," he said.

"Where do you live, John, with your mother?" Martin asked.

Now Michael moved in his seat and stared into his glass as he drank from it. He put the glass down.

"I live out there on the Western Road."

"Lovely," Martin said.

Central Library, Henry Street,
An Lárleabharlann, Sráid Annraoi
Tel: 8734333

They watched the television for a while. A news bulletin came on. A drug dealer had been killed in Dublin after dropping his child to school. The driver window was shattered and in the middle was a tennis ball-sized hole.

"*Blood will have blood,*" Michael said.

The others nodded.

"We may need to accept – there are *levels* of humanity," John said.

Gavin said, "There was once a political group, they used to think that. It led to gas-chambers and crematoriums."

John said, "I know. I know. But..." He threw his hand towards the TV. "I saw a documentary a while back. It was about meth in America. This homeless brother and sister, in Missouri, they get into the meth and start fucking each other. Sorry, Marty. But anyway, doesn't this fella... doesn't he get his sister pregnant. They crawl home to their mother's one night a few weeks before the baby comes, looking for money. Mother sees the doorknob turning and takes it for a burglar – blows off the daughter's head before the door opens. You see the mother and son screaming at each other on the lawn and the cops trying to separate them and the daughter headless on the porch with the bump under her t-shirt still moving, the material bulging out and falling like an ocean swell. You see the cop putting him in the back of the cruiser and getting in the front seat and the cruiser pulling away and the cop just shaking his head like he was wondering how in the hell he could be the same species as whatever the hell was wailing in the backseat behind him. Like he was thinking, *It's for the best that kid don't see the light of day... and you, pal... you shouldn't ever have seen a light either!* Is that Nazism? I'm not sure."

"So the phasing out of poverty by the phasing out of poor people!" Gavin said, aghast.

John sat back in his seat; he held his palm up and pointed it at Gavin as though displaying him to the others. "Behold – the lovely middle-class. All for helping the disadvantaged with his bargepole and binoculars. Fighting poverty so it doesn't move next door."

"You don't know what you're talking about."

John ran his tongue along his molars. "There's Grace Kelly and there's that wino that came into the public library and emptied her bowels in a potted plant. We're all somewhere in between. I'm not high-end humanity – but I accept there is a range."

"But there are reasons why they're not the same: socio-economic forces that—"

"Oh, there are reasons alright," John said, and he winked at Michael and his father and they looked away.

Gavin stood up and walked out.

Michael and John and Martin looked at each other, then Michael went over to the bar and gathered up his charity leaflets and brought them back to the table.

"It was only a wind-up. Did I go too far?"

"A bit," Martin said.

"He's a poser though. One of those poverty-posers."

"Know something without saying it," Michael said.

"I'm a writer. I deal in truth." Michael reached across the table and picked up John's notepad and placed it on top of the charity leaflets and they stared at each other. Then Martin took it off the pile and handed it back to him.

"Thanks Martin," he said, and they picked up their glasses and drank from them.

They watched the bartender at his work and they watched people approach the counter to order food.

Martin asked then, "How long are you writing, John?"

John sat back in his seat and puffed his cheeks and shot his eyes to Michael.

"My mother got me a job in the bank, years ago. I hated every minute of it. Spent the whole day just counting money. All fucking day! Sorry, Marty. I probably should've stayed on though. Some people – some people walk away. Some people grit their teeth and carry on through the shit. I'm a walker away-er. My mother – she's a carry-er on. She probably looks at me coming down the stairs at noon and wonders why she bothered. That last day in the bank, I dropped down my pen and rolled back my chair from the counter, went and got my coat and walked past the Thursday queue and walked out the door. I stood outside for a moment, staring at the traffic. I moved off into the people of Patrick's Street. Never went back. Did a creative writing course some months later, drew the dole and bought some writing pads. Started calling myself a short story writer, then a poet, then a novelist. I was young when I walked out of the bank. And I've not a thing to show for it. Telling stories, taking the piss out of lads in the pub is all."

"I don't mean to pry, John," Martin said. "But you've mentioned your mother."

"Ya."

"Is your father ali—"

John laughed and sat forward and set his glass down on the table. "My father was a walker away-er, Marty. Just like his son."

"Oh," Martin said. He dropped his head and spoke down at his shoes. "Sorry, John. I shouldn't have..."

"You're grand, Marty. I've no problem talking about it. Michael will tell ya – talk too much about it if anything."

"You should let us read some of your writing," Michael said.

"Nah," he said.

"Why not?"

"Shakespeare. What'd he say? *Bastards are inveterate cowards.*"

Martin looked at his son. "Shakespeare say that, Michael? I wouldn't have thought—"

"It was in a play, Dad. A character in his play was... cowardly."

Martin nodded and now he eyed John dubiously and he did not speak for the rest of the night.

Later, Michael walked home with his father. They made tea and sat for a while. His father went up to bed and Michael went over and sat at the old PC they shared that sat atop one end of the kitchen table with a grey upholstered office chair tucked underneath. He watched porn and masturbated and heard his father overhead roll across the springs of his mattress.

When he was done he wiped his hand and his stomach and walked out to the back toilet, flushed the tissues away and washed his hands. He sat on the couch and stared at their wedding photo over the television. He stayed there a long time and now and then he heard his father cough or turn again in his bed. He thought of him lying up there alone. He thought of himself sitting there in the silence; a thirty-year silence.

"You walked away, Mammy," he said.

3

He saw her comforting her friend outside the exam hall when they were in college. Her friend's chin rested on her shoulder and she made a circle with her thumb and forefinger and ran it a few times down the distraught girl's ponytail. Her friend said something about island-hopping around Greece, then sobbed between sentences.

"I've failed. I know it. I've failed. Just go without me, Jill. I'll have to study for the repeats."

"No. We won't go," she said. "We'll wait."

"No, no. Just go without me. And I'll only ever get a pass. A pass degree! A pass degree!"

Michael thought of the graffiti on the wall above the toilet roll in half the cubicles in the college – it said, *Pull here for Hons Arts Degree.*

"I should have studied. Why didn't I attend lectures? I barely wrote a thing in there. My paper was half blank!"

Her friend put her chin back on her shoulder and wept aloud. She stroked the back of her head and resolutely tapped her back.

He'd seen her on a Monday morning walking hurriedly through campus with a white hairband and a folder at her chest and clicking a biro at her side and he thought she was made for Monday mornings, for college, for anything.

She saw him watching them. She cast out her chin to him then widened her eyes and wobbled her head which he took to mean a breeziness or an overreaction on the part of the weeper.

"How did you get on?" she whispered.

Her friend broke off to look at her, then realised she was asking another.

"Grand," he said.

In the three years of college, they had never spoken. He knew this. He supposed that she did not know, that she could not know, given all the fleeting words she must have spoken, all the men that put time and planning into positioning themselves for just such fleeting words, and so he was calmer than he thought he'd be, knowing that for her, such fleeting contacts probably happened ten times a day.

"Michael, is it?" Her friend started to wipe her eyes, the better to view him.

"Yes."

"How's your twentieth-century lit? That's after lunch."

"Not for me. I'm only minoring in English. History is my major."

She shook her head and rolled her eyes. "Not looking forward to that. Are we, Kar?"

"No – we aren't," her friend said, and another whimper fell out.

She took her friend's hand and turned and said, "See you, Michael," and she led them away up towards the library, holding her folder in her palm like a waiter with a tray of drinks.

He stood there smoking, watching what he could through and over other people, amazed and delighted that she knew his name. That was the last time he saw her.

Seven years later, he walked into the staffroom of St Kieran's for his first day. She was sitting at a big table facing the door, dashing copybooks in great outward strokes of her pen and flicking the pages of a magazine with her other hand and she looked up to the door when he came in. She smiled, then dropped her head down slowly and retreated her eyes across the carpet and across the table edge and back again to her copies.

Jill Roche.

He sat on one of the low, soft chairs near the kettle and microwave and when she finished her corrections she walked up behind and came around and held her hand out to him.

"I'm Jill," she said.

"Michael," he said, shaking her hand. It was soft and warm and he felt her nails in the heel of his hand.

"I could be wrong here, Michael but..." She peered at him with one eye closed and leaned back as though to take him fully in. "UCC. Arts?"

"Yes."

"Knew it," she said.

"Yes, I remember you," he said. "That seems years ago now. Which it was, I suppose. It was years ago."

"God, ya," she said. "What was it – seven, eight years? I came out in '91 after the Dip."

"Me too."

She looked at him. "You did the Dip in '91?"

"Ya, ya," he said.

"Where else have you been teaching before here?"

"Nowhere," he said. He pointed at the floor with both hands. "First job," he said.

She stood there nodding. "Well, you'll love it here, Michael. The kids are lovely."

"Brilliant," he said.

She put out her hand again. "Best of luck."

"I must ask you," he said.

"Sure."

"Back in college, you were consoling a girl outside the exam hall."

Her eyes darted from side to side. Then she turned her head slightly aside, like she was surprised he remembered and surprised he mentioned it.

"Yes?"

"She was quite distraught."

"Yes."

"Just seeing you now – I got a flashback of that."

"Oh."

"I hope she was okay."

"She was. No problems there. Some people need a little..." She flapped her hands in the air. "I'll see you soon, Michael," she said, and she turned and walked back to her table.

They would not have as lengthy a conversation again until she came and sat next to him at the summer party five months later, with hot dog mustard dripping in her fingers which she licked then dabbed with a napkin. She had a tiny peaked nose and ex-braces teeth that slightly protruded and gave bulge to her lips when she closed them. When she walked around the corridors of the school, he'd watch and marvel at her motion and he would walk away and watch other males, staff and student, watch her and he would smile at the meagreness of men, so enthralled by a simple pencil skirt and heels, jealous of the book under her arm, the apple she was chewing, the bottle of water she carried.

When she finished her barbecued hot dog, she wiped her hands and took up her glass of white wine that she'd set down.

"Awful," she said. "Not the wine. That." She pointed at the paper plate and the used napkin on top of it, folded and perched upright like a tent. "So – how's Michael?"

They spoke for over an hour that night. Other teachers came in and out with plates of food and desserts that had been laid out on the veranda overlooking the city and the smoke would sometimes take a turn and drift in and the two of them would spin and pivot on their seats and carry on talking. Her father was a maths professor up in the college and her mother had been a sociology lecturer until she left to be editor of a left-wing magazine that hated, in equal measure, Israel, America and Christianity. She seemed disappointed when he said he had not heard of it. It seemed to him that she was living proof of something he'd long believed: that academics made great parents, the three pillars of good parenting being insight and logic and one's own childhood; those very things that produce the intellectual from the outset. For one looking to marry, he supposed there could surely be no better than the daughter of academics. All her effortless charm and confidence that only years bathed in a languid daily culture of direction and affection can bring; and she had more. She had the quasi-innocence, the ancillary sugar-sprinkling upon all that marriage-material 'substance', that made him want to hug her, kiss her, lay her down underneath some warm covers and make love to her gently.

But he could not have her. He deemed a woman such as her to be unhaveable anyway, least of all by such a man as him. She seemed to him a third strand of mankind, prodigal in some way, untouched, undestroyed by it; content with what she liked and disliked, but without the passion to hate or adore, nor a wish for it, and so he gleaned from her words that she was childless and husbandless and content with that too and content with her friends and colleagues who yearned for those things, choosing for herself nothing more than to applaud them for it, and to go her own way, in pursuit of apparently nothing other than her students' happiness, and in achieving theirs, she achieved her own.

"So you're not married?"

"No," she said. "Nearly – but no. Thank God."

He held his pint on his knee and when he took it up he saw the ring of wet on his pants. He put his hand over it.

"Are you married?"

"No," he said. "Not 'nearly' either. Just no."

She watched him speak and though he ached to drop his eyes to the dark line of her cleavage he would not for she would surely see it and so he stared back at her and then looked away and came back and looked away again and every time he looked up to her, the same self-certain eyes smiled back at him.

"Kids?" she said.

"Jesus, no. One comes before the other, anyway."

"Does it?" she said, nodding demonstratively like she'd learned something.

"I suppose. Usually – doesn't it? Ideally?"

"Usually, maybe. Ideally? I don't know if I'd agree with that. Or if my daughter would agree."

"You have a daughter?"

"I do. She's two."

"Oh. God," he said. He regretted it immediately and she watched him the same way she'd been doing all evening. "I don't mean, 'Oh God – that's awful.' I meant, 'God. Brilliant for you.'"

"Why would it be awful?"

"It's not. That's what I'm saying. It's the nineties."

"Calm down, Michael. It's fine. You're a lovely fella. And I've gotten the same roamy eyes from the others when I mention her." She flashed her eyes towards a group of teachers by the bar. "If your face looked any different – that would be the surprise. And it wouldn't matter either way to me. You'll fit right in over there."

She got up and rubbed his shoulder and walked over to the teachers by the bar. He watched the women crawl their eyes down her body and the men do the same when she turned to the women.

If she had been out of his range before, she was permanently out of it now. Now that she'd had a child. For whatever chance he had of her soiling herself with him, the child was a hundred levels up again. And the marriage material that he supposed she was looking for was so surely not him, so surely far from father material was he, that he spoke to few others that night and left when the others went out to the dancefloor. He hailed a cab on Washington Street and went home.

He had assumed she was married since the first day he'd walked into the staffroom. Then they'd spoken again and his hope grew with every minute she remained next to him that he didn't at least appal her. And then she had no husband. Those few minutes were the greatest in his life, he thought. Until she said she had a child. For Michael Connolly was many things, but he was assured in this more than anything in the world: He lived with his father. He'd spent three years of his childhood going in and out of an insane asylum to visit his mother before she started parading herself around outside Mass with a sign. He could never get away from that. The whole village saw it. They'd been living in disgrace ever since. The two of them holed up in that house like flood victims, like thieves after the theft. She was gone a month after his twelfth birthday. He was twenty-seven now. He felt he was almost raised by the sentient silence of Ballyredmond. She probably knew already; the cursed closeness of Cork, its heinous smallness. Anyone could've told her.

"Oh, you teach at St Kieran's, Jill?"

"Yes, I do indeed."

"Do you know a Michael Connolly?"

"Yes, I know Michael well."

"Mmm. Did you not know about his mother?"

"No, I did not," she'd say.

"Oh, a troubled woman. A troubled woman indeed. She used picket Sunday Mass with a sign."

Yes, yes, that's how it would've gone, he mused, staring out at the Cork night from the taxi. If there was only one thing he was less catered for in this world than marriage, it was fatherhood. And she surely saw that. Saw it a mile away. If there had been any doubts, he'd given his thoughts on single-parenting and she'd stood up and walked off. He tried to picture the man that could have a baby with her and walk away and he would not come to him. Of course he won't, he thought. He does not exist. It was she who walked away. And from the father of her child. What strength, what courage.

As the car drove on, he could think only of a multitude of reasons why she was beyond him. He turned his head and looked out the other window and thought he caught the faint scent of mustard. He pulled the shoulder of his jacket up to his nose and held it there, then let it go and turned back out the near window. He watched the people in Turner's Cross and Douglas coming out of the pubs and wandering around outside and drifting onto the roads and throwing out their arms. Then they drove on and the streetlights turned to black hedges and the cab driver rolled down his window and sent a breeze into the backseat.

When he got out he walked to the front door and fumbled with his key. He opened the door and walked inside and closed it. He could hear the TV and saw the light from the kitchen under the door. He stood in the dark in the hall and pulled the material up to his nose. He turned away to exhale, then turned back to the jacket and inhaled deep and slow, then turned away again. He took his coat off and slung it over the bannister and began to walk towards the kitchen.

"That's where you're at, Mr Connolly," he said, laughing. "The mustard in her fingers."

And he laughed.

4

He descended the road from Ballyredmond in the morning and the moon was faded and deficient in the sky and he tried to make out the bright beige of the school building out across the miles and the river, the land looming up behind in some Lego-like swell, a quadrate kingdom of slate and chimney. He sat on the dual carriageway for a half hour, slow rolling at walking pace in his silver 02C Ford Focus.

A few payslips into his first job, his father had brought him down to the Ford garage by Páirc Uí Chaoimh. A sprightly suited man walked over to them and cast his face upward and aslant.

"Are ye looking for anything in particular?"

"Hello," his father said, holding the knot of his tie. "Is Kevin here?"

"Kevin?"

"Ya know, Kevin…" His father pointed up and down the rows of cars. "He was the salesman – the head salesman."

The man looked past him to the new and newish Fords that edged towards the chipped hubcaps of his father's green Sierra saloon. Michael could smell his aftershave when he looked over.

"Do you mean Kevin Prendergast?"

"Yes, yes," his father said, and ran his tie through his hands repeatedly.

"He's gone years, sir."

"Is he?" his father said. "God now, that's something."

The man looked at their car again and nodded.

"He is, he is. Did ye buy that off him?"

"We did."

"Lovely fella, Kevin."

"Ya, ya. Salt of the earth. Every car I owned, I bought off Kevin. Would you believe that?"

The man nodded and watched his father under his eyebrows. It seemed the only way people talked to his father, their eyes and voice in lockstep on some road between pity and irritation.

"Well, have a look around – get a sense of what you might be looking for. I'll be walking around anyway, give me a shout. Or else I'll be in the office."

"And your own name is?"

"Shane." He pointed at his badge. "Shane," he said again, and turned towards the office.

"Thanks, Shane," his father said.

They went home with a two-year-old silver Orion hatchback that day. He drove it for twelve years before he went back and bought a two-year-old Ford Focus.

He'd sit in his car in the teachers' carpark and wait for Jill to drive in and he'd get out of his new car and wave at her and she'd wave back. She called out to him.

"New car, Michael?"

"About time, Jill. The other thing was falling apart."

She pointed with her thumb over her shoulder. "Sure, don't talk to me. Look at me, with this."

"Nothing wrong with it."

"And that's what I said to my father. He was trying to drag me to a garage with him. I said, 'Dad – don't be silly. I have a car.'"

"You're right, you're right. I just couldn't be looking at my thing any longer."

"And I'd be only buying a car for it to sit on my driveway for a year." He looked at her and tilted his head. "Didn't I tell you? I'm taking a career break and myself and Char are going away for a while. Going to see the world. She's in transition so – a long school tour for her." She put her finger to her lip and giggled.

"Oh," he said and he smiled with his mouth closed.

"I went from school to college to teaching. I just need to – I don't know – do something else for a while. I don't know what I want to do. So many things. I'm going to give the obituary man a few more lines to write than: *Jill Roche. Teacher.*"

"That's good," Michael said. "Honestly, that's good. It takes courage to just walk away for a while. Do what you want." He pulled up the handle of his door and threw some copies and pens on the passenger seat. "When are you leaving?"

"Finishing up in the summer. Back in a year."

He bobbed his head and cast his eyes diagonally into the sky like he was measuring out the days. Then he was embarrassed, for one who didn't care would not do such a thing.

"Well, I'll see you then," he said, snappily.

"Yes, you will. And every day for the next three months," she said.

He nodded dramatically and smacked the top of his head. "Of course, of course," he said.

She had always been his when she sat in the staffroom with a book or crossword or student copybooks. She had been his when she passed him by in the corridors and smiled at him. She had been his when she sat next to him at a few staff meetings. She had been his when she sat next to others, when she smiled at others. He'd watch her out his window walking her students out the school gate heading over Patrick's Bridge and on towards the City Library for the Library Card for Life Programme she'd initiated for her students and which was duly followed by every other English teacher soon after. The principal said at a staff meeting that it was a good idea but thought it reflected somewhat negatively on the school library. She sat with her legs crossed, tapping her notepad with her pen.

"Yes, Mr Nolan," she said. "I agree. It does not reflect well on our own library."

They stared at each other and the other teachers flitted their eyes between them both. She did not look down until Mr Nolan turned his head aside and rubbed his neck.

She had a Lipstick and Literature Programme for senior girls. The kids called it Lip and Lit. Once a week she paid for a couple of beauticians to come into her class after school; the girls would sit listening to poetry or prose while getting their nails and faces done and then they'd take a turn reciting something themselves; some stood at the top of the class with the lacquer not yet dry on their nails and read aloud something of their own, and those readings she loved most of all. A few boys went in the first weeks and she made them read but they stopped coming when the novelty faded.

She was his then. Forced though she was by the forces of the world to appear every day under the same roof as him. She was his even when she came in some Mondays telling stories to the other women of some fella she'd met over the weekend or some date she'd been on that was excellent or terrible. But he was alive because such tortures never lasted. Within a month there would be nobody. He'd ask her in the carpark, or at the kettle in the staffroom, "Any plans this weekend?" She'd say, "Nothing, Michael. Taking Charlotte to Waterford," and he would assure himself that there was no one. She was his because she was no one else's. And that sustained him for years, stuck and straddling fear and hope.

But abroad – she was gone. A mitigation too far. She was the world's then.

He sat on the dual carriageway each morning for that year, slow rolling towards the city and its myriad bridges. He'd give furtive glances at other cars and ascribe lives to the drivers that they never had. Some had kiddie stickers on the back windows and some had yoghurt spray and other little vandalisms and some had tennis balls or toys rolling around behind the headrests.

He thought of her often in his car. In the mornings and in the evenings. He wondered what great notions must have been conceived in traffic. In all those little capsules of thought, outer minds for the inner ones to wander and fixate as they chose.

Central Library, Henry Street,
An Lárleabharlann, Sráid Annraoi
Tel: 8734333

He saw her there with other teachers in the staffroom. He walked up to her as she hugged people and touched their arms as she spoke to them and he stood there waiting for her to finish, then she turned to him and hugged him tightly and he hugged her back. He walked over to the kettle and flicked the switch and got a cup and threw a tea bag into it and stood there waiting. If it weren't for the wetness in his eyes he would have been surer, but he thought he'd seen her own eyes glistening as she broke away from him. He stood there and heard over his shoulder the places she'd been and who she'd met. The experiences she had with her wonderful Charlotte. And he heard no mention of any man. "I love men," she'd said to him once. "I love patting their arses as they're walking away," and she'd winked at him.

He heard her tell the others, who were gathering around her and falling away as the bells went, that she'd started writing in some sweat-box hotel somewhere in Florida after visiting Hemingway's house. She'd been 'inspired'.

Another writer, he thought. He looked over his shoulder at her and turned back and smiled, looking down into his tea.

As he walked past with his tea she caught his arm and broke off from a conversation.

"Call up to me, Michael. I've so much to tell you. The places. The history. You'd have loved it. Call over at 3.30 – I must tell you."

At the end of the day he went up to the second floor to her old classroom as the students were leaving. He'd never been there before. When they'd spoken it had always been in the staffroom or in the corridors at break time and the occasional time she'd stop by his class at the end of the day. She'd walk right in and stand over him at his desk or perch her behind on the edge of his desk and he would go home and try to relive it, failing for he hadn't fully taken her in, prone as he was to look away somewhat as they spoke, affecting an airiness that was a lie.

He stood in the doorway looking at the posters on her wall. She had her elbows on her desk and her fingers were interlocked under her chin. She looked up at him, then followed his eyes around the walls.

"Michael Collins and Stalin right next to each other," he said. "How odd."

"I know what you mean. I thought about having one Irish section and an international section and one for the wars. Then I thought, is there any one section without the other? Just mix them up, I feel. We'll join the dots ourselves. The same with the English. That's why Donne is next to Heaney."

"I see."

"Sequence is important. But illustrating a connection – that was my thinking. Throw them all into the air, I say. You'll see there's nothing not related. I'm glad she left them up while I was gone. I asked her to, of course. But I hoped she would."

"Who?"

"The sub."

"Oh, right."

When she looked over to him in the doorway, he was still looking around the walls with a vague smile.

"What are those ones?"

She turned to the wall on her right, close to the corner. "Those? Those are photos of residential institutions." She rose from her seat and walked over to them. She put her finger on them individually. "Artane. Daingean. Goldenbridge. This one is Magdalene 'penitents' at a Corpus Christi procession."

He stood at the doorway for a while watching her and watching the pictures. He walked in past her desk and went over and stood behind her to the side. He leaned past her and crouched down with his hands on his knees. He did not take his eyes from the picture of the Magdalene women. They walked in twos with their hands pressed together and pointed skyward at their chests. They were all in white with white veils that semi-curtained their faces and older women walked with very young ones as though brides with communion girls and a few aged faces were amidst them like the denouement of womankind.

"Incredible," he said, studying them.

She looked at the girls. "I know. If those women could talk. I mean these ones – in this picture. They're all gone. There are stories that will never be told. Not when people spent their lives working to not tell it."

Members of the Gardaí walked alongside the women and in front of them were a number of priests and behind them in rows of five, an order of nuns; a black ring about the train of white like there was something glorious or deadly about it.

She pointed at one of the Gardaí. "I'd like to talk to that prick," she said. Then she circled the group of priests with her finger. "And those fuckers. Parading them like that – parading their dominion."

She straightened up and rubbed his shoulder. She waved her hand about the pictures. "It's important the kids see what we did to women. It wasn't all Markiewicz and Elizabeth Bowen."

"Yes, I agree," he said.

They stood there looking at the pictures.

"We must go for coffee," she said suddenly, and excitedly. "It's been so long, it feels."

"Yes, definitely," he said. "Let me know when you can."

"Grand," she said.

He turned and walked to the door and turned back and walked away.

He went down the stairs and smacked his hip with his hand then shot a look back up the stairs lest she be standing there. But she was not. He squeezed his fist at his side.

"Coffee," he whispered.

5

He loved teaching the Holocaust. He loved that the kids loved it; stunned and disturbed into a silence he saw with no other topic in history. He would teach double classes and they'd barely move in eighty minutes. At the end, when the bell went, they'd jostle for position at his desk and throw questions at him and ask him for books and films and documentaries and tell him about their own growing literature on the subject. He'd watch the concentration on the faces of some of the toughest kids in the school, leaning forward, necks extended; they'd watch Hitler speaking at Nuremberg and prop their heads in strange positions and stare at him almost obliquely, like they might the sun or some ethereal thing that could disappear in a full frontal gaze; they'd cast an ear elevated and squint at the subtitles. He loved those Nazi classes. He was known for them. He'd be talking about Sean Lemass or the Industrial Revolution and some kid would put up his hand and ask about the Einsatzgruppen unit in the Ukraine and Latvia or show him pictures of a street child in the Warsaw Ghetto and he'd sit at his desk and stare at it for a while, hand it back and say he'd talk about it at break time for those who wanted it.

"Sir, you're an easy sell," they'd say.

"I am, I suppose," he'd say. He'd look down at the picture. "We must remember how close this was. This happened in your grandparents' time. In my father's time. Not on some other planet. Not a thousand years ago. Here. In Europe. Seventy years ago. That's what boggles most of all. Its closeness."

They started doing flights from Cork to Kraków. He heard it advertised on the radio one morning on his way to school. And it occurred to him: he could take them. He could take his fifth years to Kraków. He walked into the principal's office that morning and pitched a school-tour to him.

"And why Kraków, Mr Connolly?" he asked.

"Auschwitz, Mr Nolan. I think it would be a great experience for the kids. Lifelong. An experiential learning."

"I see." He adjusted the blinds with the string and weaved his head slightly, weighing it. "Might be tough on them. No parents there. A place like that."

"Tough is fine. Should we avoid things if they're hard to look at? Hard to live with?"

"It's not that. It's... you'd be dealing with them over there."

"They'd be fine, Mr Nolan. They'd love it. As in... their interest – it would be immense."

"Your fifth years?"

"Yes."

He looked at Michael and he tapped the edge of his desk with his pen. "How many?"

"Twenty students."

He sat back in his seat and lifted a foot and rested it on his thigh. Then he scratched his ankle under his sock. "You'd need another teacher."

"Of course, yes."

"Did you talk to anyone else?"

"No, no. Just an idea, since hearing about the flights on the radio. I don't think there'll be a problem. I'm sure another teacher would be interested."

"Mr Connolly, I'm not certain there will be a whole load of teachers looking to spend their mid-term breaks in Auschwitz away from their kids. Remember – their kids will be on mid-term as well. They'll need someone at home. But if you find another member of staff, I'll certainly think about it."

"It'll be good for the school. Good for the prospectus."

"Yes, yes. We'll see."

He put his foot down and sat into the desk and rubbed the face of his watch and he did not look up.

He said, "How many of the twenty do you think can afford it, Mr Connolly?"

"I'm not sure about that."

Mr Nolan looked up with a slight smirk, like he'd conferred an insight. "These are things one needs to consider. As we know – there aren't reserves of money at home for these students."

"Another reason for them to go. Why should only rich kids get to see the world?"

"Well – because they've the money."

"Well, I know. It's just... not right."

"It's not, I know."

"Anyone who can't pay, Mr Nolan, I'll cover them. Hotel and flights. How's that?"

He looked at Michael and leaned forward onto his elbows and lay out his hands like they were levers or scales. "Leave it with me," he said.

Michael got up and walked out and walked up the hallway towards his classroom. He stopped suddenly in mid-stride and turned and went back down the hall and turned in at the double doors to the stairs. He walked slowly up the stairs and then down the hall and stood there looking through the strip of glass. Jill was rubbing her lip with her finger and touching her knuckle off her nose, then she picked up her pen and began writing on a page. He knocked on the door and she waved him in.

"Just a quick question, Jill. Did you get to Poland on your year off?"

"No," she said.

"I'm trying to put a tour together. To Kraków with twenty kids. Visit Auschwitz. Back in three days. I need another teacher. Any interest?"

He waved his head in the way she had years before outside the exam hall. He watched her narrow her eyes and roll it over in her mind. "Sure," she said. "My mum could take Char for a few days. I'd love it."

He drove home in the evening and stopped off in the pub in the village to celebrate. Now that he'd found another teacher, he was confident Mr Nolan would not turn it down. And Miss Roche, the loved, the respected, the feared-if-you-crossed-her Miss Roche – she would be perfect to partner him as far as Mr Nolan was concerned. And as far as Michael was concerned, there was no one better in the world.

John looked up from his laptop when Michael walked in. Michael bought him a drink and walked down to the table where he sat.

"You're happy," John said.

"I am," he said.

He left the pub an hour later and left his car in the carpark and walked home. He hadn't known that John was so interested in the Holocaust. When John expressed an interest in piggy-backing on the tour, Michael asked him how long he'd wanted to visit Auschwitz.

"Oh, a long, long time," he said. "All artists do. What bigger window on mankind?"

So three adults went, in the end. Michael, the artist and the love of his life.

Michael sat on a bench outside the museum and watched the students come down the steps, quiet and ashen-faced. They turned onto the path and headed up into another barracks. John came after them, alone. He took the steps like an old man and seemed close to fainting. He was brushing something from his clothes. Michael supposed it was the smell of the place.

He himself felt close to fainting in there, standing looking at little girls' ponytails lit up in lights and the shoes, the shoes and the suitcases with family names, and the spectacles and the dentures, the fucking dentures. He started to take shallow breaths to take as little as possible of its air into his lungs, then he walked outside and found, ludicrously, a lovely varnished teak bench. John came and sat with him, his knees swaying irreverently like he was at the fair, and Michael knew he was trying to affect calm but was too addled and had overplayed it.

They sat on the bench and said nothing.

Some students came down the steps of another barrack and saw Michael sitting there and they turned on the path and came back to him.

"You alright, sir?"

"I'm fine. How're ye doing?"

"Fine," they said, and they looked at their shoes. They looked back up the path and started walking and some looked back to him.

"Where ye off to now?" Michael asked.

They pointed weakly. "Block 11 – up there. That's where they tortured them. That's where the first gassing happened."

They looked back at him and walked on again, five or six of them. He wondered would they thank him for this, sometime in their futures. Laying bare the depths of their species.

He looked up to them entering Block 11. They were silent and circumspect and nudged each other up the steps with the backs of their wrists.

"Good kids," John said.

Michael turned back in his seat. "Death," he said after a while. "Teenagers love it. They love it in their music. In their movies. Dealing it out on their PlayStations. They come to a place like this – there's a lot of rethinking to be done. For all of us."

"It's insane. This place."

"It's absurd is what it is."

He shook his head and flicked a stone with his foot. "An orchestra," he said. "An orchestra in Auschwitz. Playing Mozart as the inmates filed by on their way to fourteen hours of labour. And again as they returned, the dead and the dying and the wishing for death, a kapo's stick beating Bach on their shoulders."

"Words are..."

"Pointless."

"It's beyond the reach of words. Or beneath them, maybe."

John rose slowly and walked after the kids towards Block 11; he looked back at Michael and beckoned him and Michael held up his hand and shook his head.

A wind blew and some dried leaves under his bench scraped across the cement base. The clouds were high in the Polish October and they were a puffed and brilliant white and did not belong overhead and seemed derisive. He'd heard that birds did not come to Auschwitz. He listened for a while and heard none.

He thought of his mother. One of her 'cleansings'. She told him once of a young woman who'd refused to hand her baby over to the nun and the nun pulled the child one way and the woman pulled the child the other until a few more nuns came in and prised the child from her. *I only want my baby, Sister*, she wailed, over and over, clawing at her own face and tearing clumps from her hair. She took a picture of the Sacred Heart from the wall and pounded the glass and ripped the picture into pieces. The woman was carried off and her screams faded down the corridors and the nuns got down on their knees and plucked the pieces of paper from the broken glass, cradling them, weeping with a grief as sharp as the mother who'd just lost her child.

He sat and listened for the birds some more and there were none. He rose and walked after his students thinking that this world, this whole world was absurd.

He'd introduced them at the airport the first morning. Jill stood there ticking off the names of bleary-eyed kids and he walked up to her with John by his side.

"Jill, this is my friend, John Howard. John, this is Jill Roche."

"Hello."

"Hello."

She turned back to the students and John stayed looking at her as Michael knew he would. He caught his arm and guided him towards a seat. John sat down and called out to her.

"I appreciate being allowed tag along, Jill. You know us doleys – we don't get abroad much." She looked back at him and smiled warmly.

They did not speak again until the following afternoon when Michael and Jill walked up behind him along the train tracks of Birkenau.

"God, this is brutal," she said to him.

He looked back. "Yeah. It certainly was that," he said.

"I'm finding it all a bit overwhelming, to be honest."

"Well, you're right. It is overwhelming," he said.

He looked back at Michael and Michael said nothing and they carried on up the tracks. She looked away to the women's camp on their left, and Michael looked away to the right down through the rows of chimney shafts. She brought her head straight again and addressed John.

"John, Michael tells me you're something of a novelist."

She nudged Michael and John shot his head back in faux grievance. She hastened her step to better hear his answer and they walked on side by side. Michael watched them both.

"Well, that presupposes a novel," he said. "What I have – I don't know what I have. Five half-novels, fifty unfinished short stories. So no. Not a novelist. An abandoner of novels, maybe."

"Can I read something?"

"No."

She looked back at Michael, then to John again. "Go on," she said.

"I've never shown my writing."

"Go oonnn." She looked back at Michael and chuckled a bit.

"I haven't even shown my mother. She's been asking for years. Or Michael."

They walked along the tracks and said nothing for a while, just stared, the three of them, up to where the tracks ended.

"Michael said you go around in rags because you want to look like a poor artist."

"Did he?"

95

They looked back at him and she giggled a bit. "The rich man in rags," she said. "Bent on his writing. Bent on *the look* of being bent on his writing."

"Did he?"

"He did," she said playfully.

"Well – maybe he's right. I have to commit to the fraud at least."

"Ah, you're no fun," she said. "I wanted to cause some trouble."

They walked on towards the ruins of Gas Chamber II and saw the students passing across the tracks up ahead and heading over to Gas Chamber III.

When they came to Gas Chamber II, Michael walked around it. He stood at the steps and looked down them and across the floor on which the Jews of Europe undressed and hung their clothes and tied their shoelaces together. He looked up and saw Jill across on the other side, her eyes glistened over her fists; they tapped some meditative rhythm on her lips or perhaps they trembled. She looked up and saw him watching her. She raised her hand from her mouth and held it up, then she dropped it again. He did the same but she had already turned away.

They stepped off the bus and the students all disappeared to their rooms and Michael and Jill were left fighting each other to tip the bus driver. When they came into the hotel foyer, they saw John in the hotel bar, up at the counter, with his back to them.

"The artist – pondering and drinking," she said, coming up behind him and setting her handbag on the counter.

"Oh, artists do love a drink, madame. For instance, I'm here all of five minutes and about to order my third brandy, as this man here will attest." He gestured towards the bartender and she smiled uncomfortably at him. Then she ordered a white wine and the bartender poured her a large glass.

Michael went up to his room and came back shortly after. Their elbows were on the bar and their shoulders were hunched and John's right elbow would slip out from under him and his whole frame would follow until he drew it up again. And she'd laugh.

"To our novels," she said.

John clinked her glass and swayed on his seat.

"How could you get plastered in twenty minutes, John?" he asked.

"Purge that fucking place from my mind."

He turned to Michael and fell off his stool and hit his head off the counter on the way down. Michael got him up to bed and gave him the bag of ice the bartender had given him and he took off his clothes and stood at the bathroom door when he ran there to vomit. He helped him back to bed and set the bathroom bin to the side and turned on the bedside lamp and walked out and closed the door.

When he went back down to the bar, Jill was gone.

He ordered a pint of lager and sat with it, scrolling old messages on his phone. He took a brochure for the salt mines from the carousel rack at the corner of the bar. He read it through and ordered another pint. When he finished it he stood up and looked around, put on his coat and walked out of the bar and stood for a moment in the lobby. Then he walked out into the Kraków evening.

The streetlamps were a muted orange that gave the movements of his fellow pedestrians a dark and grainy jilt like they were shadows or walkers of another realm or moment in time. A grim-faced man with a large moustache and a long black coat went by across the cobblestones on a white Segway, as though gliding acerbically from the pages of Dickens. Michael laughed and waited for others to laugh, but nobody did. He walked on around the large square, he watched people eat and drink under canvas canopies and he looked down medieval lanes that were half-lit or had no light at all and seemed to owe their existing to having been overlooked by man and his history. He stopped at the top of one alleyway. Halfway down, speakers were stacked on either side of a doorway and they blared The

Doors and men and women were shouting and laughing and dancing and they'd fall into each other as they spoke, holding their drinks over each other's shoulders, then pitch away across the lane and come back again and waiters stood waiting to take empty glasses and some people mocked them and flicked at their name tags and then hugged them vigorously. They'd break off and scream, *Break on through to the other side, break on through to the other side.* He stayed for a while watching. Then he walked down into it.

The woman showed him to a narrow room where a row of black-cushioned wooden chairs faced a great stark wall and some men looked up to him when he entered, then he sat there with them and felt himself at a museum or art gallery, at the Guggenheim to witness a Pollock or a Rauschenberg. A few men leaned out with their elbows on their knees, they tapped their fingers on their lips and looked up and down the room; others leaned back in their seats and had their jackets open and were grinning at their phones.

The girls came out in a line wearing underwear and heels; they did not smile but looked at the men making their selections and seemed to have selections of their own; Michael looked away. Some men rose immediately and walked to a girl and the girl took them by the hand and walked up through a door of beads and disappeared; two men stood by one girl and she took one by the hand and they walked away and the other man shoved his hands in his pockets and gave an outward nod to the next girl and they followed on behind. The girls and men that remained eyed each other discontentedly and one man muttered as though locked in some internal conference, then got up and walked off.

She was the closest girl to where he sat. She was pale and shapely and her limbs had a post-shower sheen that he supposed was the scrubbing of men from her ten times a day. Her hair was dark and long and her eyebrows were large and dark and her breasts were not large and did not adequately fill her black lace bra. She watched him as he rose, then stood before her with his head bowed. She took his hand and they walked towards the beads. He felt like a horse being led by a stable hand. Jill was right, he thought. She was right to leave the bar when she knew John would not return. She was right to walk away years ago at the summer party. If she could see him now; a gas chamber and brothel in the same day.

"I didn't plan this," he said to the woman, but she said nothing and walked him through the beads.

III

1

He sat on the couch and ate a sourdough sandwich from the new deli in the village. It had poppy seeds on top. There was ham and lettuce and coleslaw in it. He'd been eating the same sandwich since his mother sent him off to school at age four, but the new deli had its own bakery attached next door and there were queues outside in the morning before offices opened and again at 11am; people walked around with their nostrils flared and skyward.

He sat in front of the television with a plate on his lap and the sandwich in his hand. The news came on. They were talking about children being buried in a septic pit in Tuam, County Galway. A local historian had wanted to put up a simple memorial to the children and went looking for their death certificates. Eight hundred little bodies were buried in a pit of shit.

A man came on and said they used play there when they were kids in the 1970s. It was to the rear of their housing estate. Just gravel and grass and weeds, the odd rat and stray dog. There was a slab of concrete alien amidst the weeds and grass and earth, less a covering than construction detritus from the building of their parents' houses. He said they'd pulled it up one day to burn the insects underneath with a magnifying glass and they'd found a gaping darkness. They'd stepped back to let in the sunlight. At first they'd thought them large hatched eggs or abandoned beehives down there. They'd looked at each other, then lowered onto their haunches then dropped down onto their stomachs and elbows and squinted into the gloom and did not speak.

Eventually one of them had asked, "Are they – are they – ribcages?" The other had looked across to him then returned his gaze to the hole. Then they'd made out tiny skulls with huge eyes and myriad little bones bedding bigger ones and some bones were lined up "like shell arrangements on the beach". They'd lit a crisp bag and thrown it down and more tiny skulls came shaping out of the dark, as children to a bonfire. The boys had run home and told their parents.

On the news the man was middle-aged and he pointed to where he'd seen the bones as a child and people close by held teddy bears to the camera and a mile away behind them a steeple cut the sky like a black blade.

Michael's sandwich remained in his hand, hovering over the plate. He did not take a bite. A woman came into the studio and sat with the newsreader. She was young and scholarly; she had a languid, even tone that both assuaged and precluded quarrel. She said 'contextualise' a lot. And 'babies'. And 'death'. He predicted that she would say it. He waited and waited for her. She mentioned 'chains' and 'systems of institutions', then began naming them out on her fingers; and there it was on her baby finger: "the mother and baby home in Blackrock, Cork". She said its name over and over. "Go dig there, see what you find. If it's the bones of babies we're looking for."

He stared at the screen with his mouth half open, then he dropped his head down and stared at the grill lines on the bread that he now held between his legs. His mother had said, sitting up in her bed, the cigarette smoke flowing up in a line and breaking up in her ragged fringe, "Go dig up that place. See what you find." She said it whispered and sleepy in Our Lady's in 1978. She said it in the Regional Hospital in 1980. In 2014, there was a woman on the news saying that very thing. They seemed to say it in unison; a confluent utterance of past and present. "A lot of babies died there." She kept on: 'infant mortality' and 'babies' and 'burial practices'. The national average rate of infant mortality in state hospitals at the time was seven per cent, she said. Seventy-five per cent in Blackrock, she said. There was a silence. She dipped her head. The newsreader didn't seem to know what to say.

"No," Michael whispered. "Please."

She said, "So one can draw their own conclusions there."

Michael pictured a concrete slab turning over and a burning crisp bag drifting down in darkness. There was a likeness of him at the bottom amidst the skulls. They were flipping over his childhood with the tips of their shoes, crouching in.

She carried on: "...neglect to the point of... point of murder..."

"They said she was unwell," he whispered.

With his shoulder he wiped a tear that had travelled under his chin.

He looked down to his sandwich. There was a line of coleslaw juice running from his wrist down his arm and dripping off his elbow. The woman on the news sounded like those doctors all those years ago; she seemed to be saying 'best boy', as he once thought they were. But he knew what she was saying. He dropped his sandwich on the plate. The place across the lake where his mother stayed once. She sounded so much like his mother, for she wouldn't – she wouldn't stop saying it: *Bessborough, Bessborough, Bessborough.*

2

He was twelve when his mother committed suicide. It was 1981.

He'd walk into her room and see her propped up against the headboard or lying down and staring up at the ceiling, silent but for the wheezing. She'd sometimes have a book and sometimes a cigarette but most often nothing at all and she'd sit there slowly, gently rubbing her hand like it was some autonomous life form, or comically, like she had the thought to punch something. She'd be up and about some days, then she'd slowly retreat to her bed and the medications and cold cups of tea and thronged ashtrays and dinners uneaten and re-heated and uneaten again; her bedside table became an open catalogue of her hours and days. He'd go up with his father to visit her in Our Lady's and pass the rows of metal beds and pyjama-people moping silently around in the mingled smells of cooking and chemicals, as if someone were stirring pine disinfectant into a gravy.

His father spoke a lot on those drives to and from Our Lady's, probably as a distraction from where they were going or as some amnesiac measure after they'd been there; tie up the mind with the humdrum and by the time you got to thinking about where you'd been, there was already a distance, a fading. But not always. Sometimes it wasn't just some banality to fill the air. He told his son one time on a drive home about people back in his day, someone who'd 'take to the bed', and they wouldn't be seen for ages, "and then one day – there'd be a funeral. 'Died suddenly', they'd say."

He spoke about Our Lady's and he'd shake his head like he was appalled at his own thorough acquaintance with it, outraged at the fate that cast his family so regularly through its doors. There was a derision to the building, Michael had always thought. A taunting *Welcome* that your soul read loud and clear.

His father told him about the day he wandered off around the labyrinth of corridors and wards looking for a vase for the flowers he brought his mother, only to hear someone calling him from a cluster of beds at the end of one of those long grim wards.

"I just turned and walked away," he said. "'Martin,' the voice called after me. 'Martin Connolly. Is it yourself?' I just kept walking."

He shook his head again and went quiet and squinted a bit like he was bringing back the voice for another listen.

"I don't know who called me. And I've never gone wandering again."

But he couldn't walk away from his wife. He had to walk with her, wherever that was. "She needs us, Michael," he'd said. "We'll bring her round." He didn't speak again for a while. And then suddenly, "She's going to get better. Isn't she?"

"Yes, Daddy. She is," Michael said.

He remembered his father standing over her to watch her take her tablets. He remembered what happened when she didn't take them. The whole village remembered. Much better her sitting in bed staring at the door than picketing midday Mass with a sign. That was no small thing in the late-1970s. It's a rare terror that puts a crowd silent. He could feel the rancour in their body heat out on the church steps.

In the decades after she'd gone, on the rare occasions they'd speak of her, they'd remember things differently and quibble over who remembered correctly, then withdraw and go quiet and brood on the other's imprecision.

"Maybe she was over-medicated, Dad."

His father would look across to him. "No. And of course – when the drink started..." he turned down his thumb and let it fall to his side. "On top of medication? I remember she came out of hospital that first time and came in that very door and turned and walked to where the Christmas whiskey was kept and she got a glass and sat down there on that seat. We were on the clock from then on with her. Dr Hanley would say, 'Talk Elaine, talk. It'll help.' Well – she talked. And the drink, once it started, only fuelled it. Fires the thoughts, whatever they may be, as it always does. I remember the first time she told me all that happened her. Her jaw shook as she spoke – and her eyes – they'd changed."

Michael thought of her drinking; he thought of his own. When he'd pass by her sometimes in the house he'd hear the swish of fluid in her handbag. It sounded like his bicycle wheel through a puddle and it seemed to grow and become daily and unchangeable and when his father came in from work in the evenings he'd see her at the seat with the bottle and glass and he'd stand there rubbing the sides of his mouth. Then she'd be gone for a week to her bed, or back to hospital. Her movements seeming rehearsed and symbolic and gentle. Then she'd be out again and it would start all over. There's a story here, he thought. A thread. And somewhere it ends.

He walked in once when they were fighting.

"Now, Elaine. Please. Michael is here. Stop with this."

"I was there. I was there."

"Can we stop now – with Michael here."

"They were killing them, Martin. Oh, sweet Christ – I saw it."

"We've heard you. We've read your letters to the newspaper. What do you want us to do now?"

"You never posted my letters to the papers."

"Of course I did."

"They would've appeared in them."

His father looked down and shook his head. "They'd have to believe them." He looked up to her again. He said tenderly, "But I did send them."

She cried then, and his father wept a little and canopied his eyes with his hand.

"I can't go on, Martin. I can't store this here in my heart, in my mind and sit in my bedroom and run through it day after day... have you come up and hand me my tea and smile at me like I'm a lunatic. It happened. They killed my child, Martin. They killed children. I saw it."

She cried and left the room and they heard her slow traipse upstairs. It had been 1977 when Dr Hanley arrived and preached 'catharsis'. In 1980 nothing had changed. A doctor in Our Lady's said that some patients found that with the changing of the year or decade, the mind sought to shed baggage, like a 'changing of the guard'. The future overriding the past. They clung to that for six months, father and son. They kept reminding her of the year and the change of decade as though beckoning her into the present and she'd bob against the headboard and grip the blankets, seeming to brace for the journey. But there was no change. His father helped her with her pyjamas, fixed her pillows. He handed her a glass of water and a strong coffee and a pill. The quietness. The quietness. They'd wait three weeks for her to come downstairs and say something, and when she did, they prayed she'd stop and return to her stupor.

His father descended the stairs after a while.

"Sorry, Michael. Your mother sometimes, she doesn't know what she's..."

He bobbed his head and rolled his eyes. And his son nodded back and said nothing. He had wondered why he had been sent to the shop so often for the *Irish Times* and *The Cork Examiner*. Every day for a month he was sent. He'd bring them home and she'd rush out to meet him at the front door and take them into the kitchen, spread open the first one and scan the Letters to the Editor, her finger jumping about the page as though in spasm, then it would slow as though exhausted from the effort and collapse on the page or slip off the page and onto her thigh. She'd breathe hard for a while, tap the next paper like she was building or bracing for something, then flip it open and her finger would go again, her eyes frantic, her lips mouthing exhaustive frenzied whispers, and the finger would slow again and drop off the page with her eyes to her lap; she'd leave the papers as they were on the table and go upstairs to her bedroom and close the door. Sometimes she went out to sit in the backroom. His father would come in and see the papers and mutter to himself and fold them up and put them in the wicker basket by the fireplace and go and put on the kettle.

That's how Michael learned things, sitting there as his parents argued. He hadn't known that she had sent letters off to newspapers. But after a month or so, she stopped sending him to the shop. A calm descended again, the hope of a normalcy, all that father and son ever asked for. Perhaps it was the new television his father bought. There were no papers to greet his father in the evening, the way he liked it, the way it had always been. Even his mother seemed a bit better; quiet but upbeat, she sat out in the back garden one evening with his father, the two of them sipping tea and looking pleasantly up to the sky and chatting, laughing even, like any husband and wife.

The following Sunday, father and son came out of Mass and saw her standing at the church gates with big black letters scrawled across the cut-off cardboard from the box of their new television set.

Sometimes they'd hear her footsteps on the ceiling and his father would go up with porridge and tea and Michael would stand at the door and listen to them talk. After she got out of hospital the second time, she was fine for a few days, then she went down to the village and bought a bottle of whiskey. Her husband went up to her in the morning. Michael stood at the door. She sniffled and gave low whimpers and some words rode a heavy breath and became louder.

"You were up yesterday, love."

"I know."

"You had a few."

"Aren't I entitled to a drink?"

"Do you remember what the doctors said? 'You cannot drink alcohol with your medication.' It destabilises your... mood. It removes all the good that the tablets do. It destabilises the stabilisers."

"Can't have anyone *unstable*."

"It's not good for Michael."

"Michael knowing isn't so bad."

"It's very destructive."

"Do you block his eyes when the Nazis come on telly?"

"Elaine, please."

"Why shouldn't he know what happened to his mother?"

"He's too young, Elaine. Wait till he's older. Don't you care about him?"

"How dare you."

There was a silence for a while. Five minutes of total silence. He lifted her tea and handed it to her. "No," she said. "Leave it down."

"Okay, love."

"I want to tell him."

"About what?"

"You know."

"I don't want that. You agreed with me. We agreed that he didn't need to be hearing all those things."

"I changed my mind."

"Yes, Elaine. You change your mind every time you... 'Michael should know, the whole parish should know, newspapers, neighbours.'"

"What did I say in front of Michael?"

"Ah, the usual."

"The baby?"

"No. Not the baby."

She cried and stopped every few seconds, like it was a language or other mode of breathing.

"Ellie, it's okay. It's the alcohol mixed with the drugs. You go high. You talk about bringing society down. The whole church. Everything. Everyone."

"Maybe ye need it."

"Need what?"

"To be brought down." There was a laugh then, a chortle of hers that didn't leave her mouth but began and ended somewhere at the back of her throat and sounded more like an attempt to clear it.

"One day I'm going to sit down with Michael. And I'm going to tell him about his mother and her baby. I'm going to tell him about Bess-bor-ough."

She said it low and slow, as though to herself, just to hear it, string out the syllables like the word itself was a saga. He came in from school a few days later and she came down the stairs in her dressing gown and slippers with a cigarette dangling between her fingers and the ash arcing and ready to fall, only not falling for there wasn't bounce enough in the leaden shuffles of her feet. She sat at the table and pulled out a seat for him and called him to sit with her. She held his hands and turned them upward and rubbed his pudgy palms with her thumbs as if to tell his future.

"Beyond the grotto, down a dirt path," she said. "Past the ruin in unconsecrated ground. With all the other babies. The handicapped ones – they're further down, with the incest babies and babies of daughters blaggarded by fathers. The unadoptable. Some poor girl in from the lanes – baby born with palsy hands – you knew it wouldn't last. She'd go down to the day nursery one morning and find her child with pneumonia. 'Jesus is calling him,' Sister would say. Most babies were dying of hunger anyway. You weren't to give them the breast. Sister said the illegitimate couldn't take the purity of breastmilk. So the nuns fed them.

"If you could've seen these things, Michael. Miserable, tiny, shrivelled things. Some mothers would try and give their child the breast when the nuns weren't looking, but it was never enough. The child would die a few days later. The mother wouldn't get out of bed. She'd be up in Our Lady's before the year was out. She's probably still there. That's what happened to my baby. I said to Sister, 'Sister – he's starving.' She said, 'He's just weak.' My milk was gone after they burned my breast, so I went down to the kitchen and stole some. I brought it up to the day nursery and Sister took it off me. She called some nuns and they locked me in a bathroom for two days and nights. When I got out, he had pneumonia.

"'He hasn't long,' Sister said that morning. 'It happens, Marjorie,' she said. Marjorie was the name they gave me on the first day. 'Christ's will.' She walked around the room with that long white habit swishing, peering into cots. That's the sound of Bessborough – the swish-swish of a habit in the hunger.

"'He wasn't a strong baby, Marjorie,' she said. 'If they get sick at all...'

"I remember his last breath in the cot. His shoulders jumped a bit like a last knowing of life – then he died. Sister came in after five minutes – took him away. I watched them out a window... carrying his little body wrapped in a sheet, past the grotto and through the little gate and down the path. I stayed at the window and cried and cried and cried, I stared down at the Madonna, spotless white and blue and hands praying and her face sad, mock mourning for all the dead babies.

"'Why, Mary? Why Mary? What did he ever do?'

"I watched them return a while later – the burial girls. They looked up to me at the window then dropped their heads again. They knew where the mothers stood. They wouldn't look at you for weeks after. They'd be farmer's daughters, hardy, and landed a bit, and their child wouldn't be in a sheet in the earth.

"They were killing babies in there, Michael. I saw it often. Wizened, scabbed creatures in cots, beyond crying. Older ones, two- and three-year-olds, their mothers released to England, they'd be wandering around the toddler ward, woeful things with big baffled eyes. They'd stare up at you – then point at

113

their mouths. You walk on and hear them slump back down on the floor and start up that awful whimper-talk of theirs, a day-long muttering amidst themselves that you couldn't make out. It might have been 'Jesus is coming, Jesus is coming.' They'd sit there holding hands, like they were waiting for Him.

"Some survived, the wealthier girls' ones. They were allowed to use the breast. You knew the bumps that had a chance. You knew the ones He was coming for before they were even born. The incest ones – they never got a drop of milk. Poor mother might as well have squatted over the grave.

"Oh, my child... my child... my lovely baby. They killed him. They killed him. Michael – believe your poor mother – the starving children – I saw it – I saw it. I swear to Jesus. I saw it."

When his father came home from work in the evening, Michael looked at him from the armchair in front of the television and his father stared back at him and Michael started bawling. His father rushed to him and knelt and pulled him to his chest and they cried together.

"Is it true, Dad?"

"It doesn't matter."

"But is it true?"

"Nothing we can do. Let's just get on with our lives."

His certified, sectioned, Norrie mother. He sat in the front pew on his Confirmation day and he looked across the aisle. There were nuns from the girls' school there.

Why, God? he thought. Why would you give my mother the mind to say those things about those holy old women? The deepest parts of him asked, Why, God? Why would you give me that mother?

She did not attend his Confirmation. He supposed they wouldn't have let her in the church door anyway. Six months later, she took her own life with sleeping tablets and thirty-odd years after that they dug up a mass grave of little skeletons on the grounds of a Mother and Baby Home in Tuam. The news wouldn't stop with it. Nine days in and they were still going. They had a new expert. He was talking about 'fallen women' and 'fallen children' and a 'fundamentalist, puritanical strain of Catholicism' that existed in Ireland and how everyone must take a slice of the blame. He was posh and perhaps foreign-schooled and mentioned Bessborough amidst his analysis, pronouncing it *Biz-bro* as though it were a clown or a business park, and Michael pondered what it must have been for a girl to first hear that word, disorientated as she surely was, to be standing there within it.

He went up to the attic every year to get the box of Christmas decorations. The same baubles and dusty tinsel of his mother's time. She seemed to live more at Christmas, stretched across the mantlepiece *MERRY CHRISTMAS* and the sluggish Santas about the place. She had sometimes a bison hunch against the cold, as the fairy atop the tree seemed to acquire. So she became Christmas, as he supposed the dead often did, becoming boxes of decorations across the bereft houses of the world, taken down and dusted off and snow-sprayed and returned in a few weeks to the attic. And Bessborough did, it became a little dangling red ball in the attic of his mind, that he thought about perhaps once a year, and returned.

He looked at the chair where she sat that day, holding his hands, whispering, crying, rubbing his face, her voice tremored with rage and the pale blueness of her eyes twinkled with it, then she'd stop and look into the air and draw breath. She told him she had a son. He was unnamed for she would not use the name the nun had given him. He died one cold morning in the autumn of 1944 and they buried him in a mass grave that was unmarked down in a grove of trees behind a grotto. He remembered the quietness when she got up and left him there in the kitchen with his trauma.

It felt different now, with the August sun at the window and the faint whiff of barbecue. It seemed that the past had not passed and what had come down from the attic would not return but would sit there about them for the rest of their lives.

"There'll be a time," she'd said, "when I'll be gone and the nuns will be gone. But the new righteous will be there, walking in circles with taut fingers, horrified and looking for someone to blame. And beaming the next day at their child's Communion."

3

He feared his father's death a great deal; he feared the solitude; he feared the eulogy, for there would be only him to give it. The bird in his stomach would surely return for it, always there to watch as others watched, then depart as they departed; and Michael would pick over those trembling words when he was alone at home in the silence, staring at the remnant dip and breadsticks and sandwiches going stale on a tin-foiled tray and some woman's hat on a chair that she'd surely return for the day after, or the day after that, though perhaps not: her husband would probably tell her to leave it, buy a new one, the hat hardly being worth the unpleasantness of the return.

His father was old now, and seemed to have always been that way, like youth was uncertain and accidental and passed some people by. Michael would look at photos of old birthdays and appear an anomaly there between his parents, under their arms as if he'd wandered off from his real family and into the shot of some ageing couple who thought it delightful, smiling and looking down to him, his father with black-rimmed glasses and grey hair combed to a side crease, a dreary brown tie and elongated rhombuses on his cardigan and pouches of flesh on his jawline and a woman he can't but think witch-like with the darkness about her eyes and her missing tooth and where the man's smile was warm and full hers was stiff and pinned and seemed to be waiting for the camera-click so it could fall away.

They sat at the dinner table and ate quietly and his father would cast a look up at him occasionally and wink and point down at his plate and look up and wink again. His eyes were red, like they used to get on his 'swimming pool' days after his wife died. He'd come in the door with rusty eyes and say he'd been down the pool in Douglas. Here they were again.

He watched his father eat. He could hear him coughing in the night and turning over his pillow and slapping it. He thought of some hellish nights when his mother was alive, he thought of his father's patience, his dignity. He loved his mother. Michael was assured of that. He saw it every day.

He watched the food dwindle on his father's plate. He had half a spud left, some cabbage.

"They found tiny bones in a convent in Galway."

"Yes – I-I heard that," he said. His father didn't finish his meal. He gently placed his cutlery down and rose.

"She wasn't lying."

He stood there for an age. Then he sat down again. He propped his elbows on the table and pinched and pulled at the skin on his forehead like he was rousing his mind for action. He breathed in deep, then out. He glanced towards the television.

"No one said *lie*. They said *delusion*."

"Well, they weren't delusions."

His father shook his head and shrugged his shoulders.

"What'll we do, Dad?"

"Nothing. Live."

Michael nodded. "'Take what she says with a fair quantity of salt.' That's what you used say. And you'd touch your nose."

"That's what they told me. It was all so sudden. Her behaviour. Her words. I couldn't believe her. I was *told* not to."

"She told us. She told us years ago what happened to children in there."

Michael held his head in his hands and he could not feel it. Like his hands were touching someone else's head. Like he could've taken that head and bashed it against the wall and felt nothing. The corrupted head that his father had given him, coming down the stairs and rolling his eyes. He did not raise his voice. The perpetrators all dead, they'd probably go looking for the likes of his father; the colluder, the collaborator. He helped, he ignored, he signed committal forms. Michael thought of the childhood nights in his bed with the blankets pulled up to the bridge of his nose, listening to the voices down the hall; his father, his poor father.

"I did listen. I never did anything but listen. I just thought some of what she was saying – doing sometimes – was beneath her." Michael looked out from behind his fingers; his father waited for him to say something. He said nothing. His father carried on.

"Picketing Mass with signs saying... things. Three doctors told me she had manic depression. They said it puts these... thoughts... in the mind. Experiences that aren't real. The mind flares up like a box of matches – then... nothing. Dead for days. Can barely speak. Wouldn't blame a woman for not knowing what's real... and what... isn't. Part of the condition they said. Dead children, mass graves. That's why the medications were so vital. Why I was so meticulous about that. Combat the... thoughts."

He touched his head.

"What if they weren't 'thoughts'?"

"We'll see," he said. "Hopefully—"

"Dad, listen. There's eight hundred children in a septic pit in Galway."

"I know – awful. Holy nuns." He looked up at his son grimly.

"Mammy said that about Bessborough. She said there were children in there that were just left to die."

"Right."

"*Right*? Ye sectioned her for it."

"We sectioned her for her manic depression."

He looked at his father and rubbed his tongue on his upper lip, then combed it dry with his lower teeth.

"What will we do, Dad? What are you thinking?"

His father replied calmly, quietly, "I'm not thinking these days. One foot in the grave and I get hauled back half a lifetime and made to explain myself. I sit around hoping the news is wrong the way I sat around hoping the doctors were right. That my wife was just unwell. And that holy nuns didn't let children starve to death."

"What will we do?"

He stopped and looked straight at his son and gave a faint, inquisitive shimmy of his head and the flesh fluttered off his jawbone. He rose and stood in the middle of the floor, dropped his head down and put his hands on his hips, he slid a foot slowly forward on a tile, and leaned tiredly on the other. Michael watched him in the throes of his guilt, for what his father must have felt he could not imagine. "Believe me," she'd said to him and he'd wrapped his arms around her and rubbed her back and cried with her and caressed her neck and kissed her cracked lips and put her in an asylum.

"Today is always cleverer than yesterday," he said. "Everyone's clever now. On the news, everywhere. I think I'm dreaming sometimes. That the past is real. That holy Ireland was true. That my wife had delusions. And that I'm still a nice man. My people were nice people, my past was a nice past. 'I was a nice man,' I say. And that's what turns me inside out – I was a nice Irish man from the mid-twentieth century. How did I get here?"

He took his plate to the sink but his cutlery slid off onto the floor before he got there. He reached down and gathered them. His shirt rose on his back and Michael saw the band of a pair of underpants he'd once bought him. He stood up and walked with the cutlery and plate to the sink. He ran them under the tap and placed them in the dishwasher. He closed the dishwasher and stood staring for a while out the backdoor to the garden. He moved his jaw from side to side, like he was distracting himself by giving his face something to do; then he rubbed it frenziedly.

His son watched him with a great sadness. He wished then that he had left him alone, said nothing. He missed the getaway car; he outlived it, the last langer caught at the crime scene. And what did he do anyway? He married a tainted woman, for

Christ's sake. He loved her. He still loved her. This Ireland of shifting sands and wagging fingers. How dare they.

"Grass could do with another cutting, Michael."

"Ya."

"Maybe last one this year."

"Okay."

"Tomorrow so. Grand. Tea?"

"Okay."

He put some water in the kettle and put it down and flicked the switch and stood leaning on one leg, scouting out some crumbs on the counter and pressing his finger on them and rubbing them off into the sink. He made the tea and came and sat back down and slid the cup to Michael. Michael wrapped his arms around the edges of the table as far they would go.

"This is our waterhole in the Kalahari, Dad. There's life and death here. There always is at a kitchen table."

His father said nothing. He was speaking less by the day. His son watched him stuck there between the oldness and newness of his shame and felt he could do nothing, for he was there with him, bonded both in blood and guilt. He may as well ask the question.

"Did you send her letters?"

His father set his cup down but kept hold of the handle which he began to tap softly with the nail of his thumb. He stared into the tea, still rotating from the spoon. He breathed out and his head eased forward.

"What letters?"

"Her letters."

"What difference does it make?"

"So you didn't?"

"I said, what difference does it make?"

"It could've – if they'd printed them."

His father shook his head.

"There was a girl, in the village, long ago; maybe late '40s, in and around 1950 we'll say. She was a bit younger than us, maybe fifteen she was. And she was always going to be a beauty. I remember her wearing her Confirmation dress to Mass for months after. This lovely white frilly thing, her hair curled in service to it. I suppose we must've been looking at her even then, and she not yet a teenager. Her hair was long and blonde and her teeth were large and straight in a big mouth, her eyes were that bright blue and huge and pleasant. I'd heard she was doing a line with someone, some fella in towards town. He wasn't from Ballyredmond. You'd hear from the other girls that she'd be writing his name on her copybook in school and doing love hearts and all the rest of it. Things like that – we were all jealous. She was as close to Hollywood as we'd ever get.

"And then – without warning – she was gone. Just disappeared. Vanished. And no one knew exactly when or how. You'd have the odd few whispering about it, but no one really knowing anything. Nothing is said. People just carried on. You'd see her parents mouthing the *Our Father* in Mass and their hands trembling, their heads poking out of their clothes like fugitives. You just carry on and not know you're carrying on. The normal just comes back. She was never seen again. I think her name was Marie – or Mary."

"Wasn't anyone concerned?"

"How do you mean?"

"Didn't anyone care that a young girl had just disappeared?"

"You don't give the village a reason. Don't give it something to watch. You make sure it isn't you."

"But they did nothing?"

"They did. I told you. They went and made sure it wasn't them."

"So everyone was complicit."

"Speaking up would've done nothing. Except maybe bring the Guards to your door." He raised the cup and pointed at his son with it. "And the same with those letters. Would've done nothing but bring someone to our door." His son nodded. He continued. "We were happier in my day, I think. People didn't run to the papers or the radio with everything. First I saw of it was the way no one ever mentioned when Somerville was robbed of every last thing. You'd talk to someone down the village and ye'd both know and say nothing. Bringing it up was almost to repeat it, like you knew something more than he did. Like it was rude. That girl disappearing, same thing. To bring it up is to know too much about it. A woman outside Mass with a sign. There was community in my day. And sometimes that meant silence. You'd get a tap on the shoulder in the funeral home – that's what the village can manage. You don't want anything more. You don't even want that if you can manage it."

"Jesus, how we've changed."

"Your mother knew all about silence. Until she didn't."

"Yeah," Michael nodded.

"And I don't know have we changed."

"No?"

"One time – we were walking in town. Christmas it was. Your mother had her hat down and scarf up about her chin. There was a homeless woman sitting on a rug with her cup outstretched. People were walking past her, flicking their eyes to the contents of her cup or looking away entirely. We walk on, I say to your mother, ''Tis sad, at Christmas'. She doesn't respond. I glance to my side and see her not there. I look back and there she is, at the edge of the woman's rug, foraging in her bag for something. The woman is looking up at her and offering some blessing on your mother. Your mother lifts her hand momentarily out of her bag and flicks it backhandedly in the air as though swatting a fly, then returns it to the bag. She drops something in the cup and walks away. She walks back to me and I turn and we walk on up the footpath. I say, 'That was nice of you, Ellie.'

"She just shakes her head. 'Nothing changes. Disappearing women yesterday. Homeless ones today.' She tosses a hand out from her pocket like she is addressing the entire footpath: 'Ye

123

just don't care. It doesn't start mattering till it's you.' And she was right about that."

"Yeah," Michael said.

"People don't care till it's on their doorstep."

Michael rubbed the sides of the table again, then smiled at his father.

"Till it's here, Dad."

"But it was funny, y'know. I remember looking at her curiously as we moved through the crowds; her mentioning the disappearing women. I knew I never told her about the beautiful girl from Ballyredmond who vanished long ago. I supposed they must've had their own Marie or Mary disappear in Blackpool when she was growing up. Of course, I didn't know then they had. And there she was walking right alongside me."

4

She was in his mind as it straddled the conscious and unconscious in the seconds before his eyes opened, there in his shaving mirror and on his dashboard and TV and there at the newspaper stand and kitchen table. All the talk of 'investigations' and 'committees' and 'marches for the mothers' and a far-reaching 'government report'. He read in the paper that the Chief Medical Officer in Ireland had shut Bessborough down sometime in the '40s because of the infant mortality rate and the bishop had told the government to mind its own business and opened the place up again. He read that the nuns wouldn't let the women breastfeed for a variety of dubious reasons. *The illegitimate can't take the breast. Too weak from the mother's nine-month trauma.* That's what the nuns told the inspectors.

He thought of the mark on his mother's breast; a bowed purple swelling of flesh sweeping under the nipple that seemed wormish the more he caught sight of it and he'd wince as a child when he thought of it or eyed the little bulge of breast through her clothes. It became her essence after she was gone, as did the tales of her trauma, sewn into the silence that followed down the decades. He did not think of his mother without thinking of her scarred breast, it perhaps being more her than her face or voice, for they were mandates of gene and biochemistry. The breast bore the very scars of her life, was the very lure, the path to all that happened to her; the ugliness of her life and theirs was seared in a scabrous chronicling under her nipple.

She said once, "For every child dancing at a crossroads, there's two down a hole in a convent," and he looked away and his father began winding his watch. They'd come from nowhere, these nightmare non-sequiturs, bursts in the quiet as she peeled the potatoes. "If they'd only dig – they'd see. I'm not lying."

But it was thirty years after she was gone and a hundred miles away in a septic pit in County Galway where they found, as the world did, that she hadn't been lying. And he knew and his father knew one unearthing would surely lead to another and another and the shovels would one day be at the gates of Bessborough.

He ached for his father; he wished for a cleansing senility to sweep it all away; he pondered whether he'd trade his father's life for his father's release, a tucking away in the cosy August earth. He had known for years, this was not a secret to his father, this was not the 'unknown Ireland' they mentioned on the news; this was in his kitchen every day for three years, this was screaming in his bedroom, this was walking the grounds of an asylum with him.

His son found him one day sitting in the back room where his mother once lived, he saw him through the glass. He was sipping on a whiskey or brandy, his head was dipped and he was circling the rim with his finger like he was taking counsel from someone unseen. He spent his days watching the news bulletins with his knuckles bucking over his mouth as he gnawed his nails away to nothing.

A contributor on the RTE News said, "If one child dies of malnutrition and neglect – it can only be called one thing. But we could be talking hundreds. Bessborough could be a place of mass... manslaughter." Father and son sat there and wanted so much to change the channel. But they did not.

He turned to his father. "We had this coming."

"We did."

His father reached across and held his son's hand and they sat there like the condemned.

Porn and suicide wisdom, the internet might have been created for those two, he thought. Death was not death. There was a difference between the dead and the self-dead, the dying and the killing. For to wield the dagger against thine own flesh was to declare a reason, a rationality, a causality to the act of self-ending; one did not search out such things walking out of a cancer ward. The doctor gave you the reason; he told you she was dying, and why. You went home, sorrowful indeed, but knowledgeable too.

There was no ward for suicide, or perhaps there was, and you stayed in it forever, wandering around the placatory, incessant seating and machine-tea and looking up and aslant at new entrants and feeling better or worse about yourself, depending on their shoes and coat and smell; everyone possessed with the knowledge that suicide ran in families, like eye-colour or athlete's foot, and the never knowing, the eternally absent, the effervescent, unanswerable *WHY?* You spend a while with the great *Why?* and it wasn't long before he introduced you to the other great character on the ward. He was quiet at first, intermittent and one of many, but he grew loud and laughing and perspicacious, the irrepressible *ME?* And there you sit with the two of them until, until, who knows when. Until you learn to live in the vacillations of *Why?* and *How?* and *If only* and *Me?* and *Him?* and *Who else?* and the whole lot becomes an endless drone that lowers and rises depending on the day.

Some days it disappears. Some days you forget that you haven't heard it. You could go weeks, perhaps months without hearing it. But it doesn't leave. It's there – always – like your elbow, not in view, not thought about, unless you choose to look at it, unless something collides with it.

He remembered, in school, kids talking about her. Their parents told them something, they weren't quick enough with a hand up to their eyes outside Mass. *What's that lady doing, Mummy? What's on her sign?* The woman who wouldn't get out of bed.

She only got out of bed to picket Mass and tell priests to go fuck themselves when they called to the door. Father Dan came down the stairs, white as a ghost, blessing himself, shaking his head; each calling the other a liar. She followed him to the front door and slammed it behind him. "Liar," they said together. She got down on her knees and repeated it out the letterbox as he got into his car.

Rage and regret. That's what suicide did. He wished and he wished for her to go away, to give him an unbroken night's sleep, to let his father have a moment of peace, to give him one day where he didn't see a pointed finger in the school yard or receive a teacher's knowing nod, a gentle patting on the shoulder, a look the other way when his homework wasn't done. Just go away, Mammy, he thought. Go back to Our Lady's or that lovely new place, The Regional. Go.

He looked into her coffin, the rosary beads wrapped about her hands. *They were killing them, Michael, they were killing the children. They wouldn't feed them. They killed my baby. They killed me.* The words seemed to rise from her, out of the death-stiffened sneer at the edges of her mouth. He returned and sat with his father.

"She won't like the rosary beads, Dad," he said. His father squeezed his thigh gently.

"She's with Jesus now," his father said.

"Yes, Daddy." His son wept. "She must be with the baby."

"She is, she is."

"She told me once: 'That's what the nuns said when he died.'"

"What?"

"'He's with Jesus.'"

The priest stepped to the microphone and father and son looked up to him.

He read the paper a lot, waiting for the Terms of Reference for the Commission of Investigation into the Mother and Baby Homes. It was taking forever for them to decide just how far and wide and deep the whole thing should go. His mother used to say sometimes, before or during or after the tears came, "I'm the top of the pyramid poking out of the dirt. They just keep kicking the dirt back over."

His father went around the place now with hunched shoulders and drooped head, with the elongated ears that seemed genetically exclusive to his generation and navy slacks that were pulled too high on his waist. Our Lady's was no longer a hospital. The nuns were long gone from Bessborough. She was gone. The church was all but gone. He remained, to hear the shrill outrage of his country.

On a Sunday they'd drive past the church and he'd watch his father watch a few elderly people scraping towards the steps and he'd see his father's desire to get out and walk there with them; the die-hards, the devotees of another land to which they returned each week to hear and wearily chant of and see in the wet of each other's eyes.

"Would you like to pop in, Dad?"

"No."

"Might be good for you."

"I go in there – I'd never come out."

"Maybe you should think about going back there."

"I can't get it back. I'm not asking God for anything. Who I owe, I don't need to be in a church to see. She wouldn't be in there anyway. If anything, I owe it to her to *not* go."

They drove on to Fountainstown beach and they walked along the water's edge and Michael would pick up flat stones and skim them on the water and his father would watch them blithely. They saw a crab in a rock pool. When they leaned in it scurried to the side under some seaweed.

"I know how you feel," his father said.

He laughed and his son tapped him between the shoulder blades. They turned around and walked back up the beach. They drove home and Michael stopped off in the shop in the village to buy the Sunday newspapers.

He sat in the front room and Michael handed him his tea and sat down and the two of them sat reading the Sunday papers with the television on low and their slippered feet outstretched and nearly touching. They read and the only noise would come from one of them folding over a page and tapping it down and twisting it out of the glare from the window. They did not speak for a long time.

The room was getting dark when Michael put down the paper on the floor by his feet.

"What'll you say if they ring?"

"Who?"

"Government people. Whoever's doing this investigation."

His father's eyes remained on the page but Michael knew he wasn't reading it. He gave slow blinks and his whole face twitched like there was effort in it.

He said after a while, "I'll tell them."

"Everything?"

"I'll say what she said."

There was silence again and his father did not look down to his newspaper but gazed over the edge of it to where his feet rolled gently on their heels. They both seemed to be waiting for the phone to ring.

"It came to me last night," his father said. "Lying in bed. These things float in from the abyss – I don't know how. The time we were sitting at breakfast, you reading the cornflakes box, me slurping my tea, which irritated her. Maybe that was why she decided to throw it out there – out of the blue. Knowing I wouldn't like it. She said just then: 'The further the girl was from poverty, the closer her child was to living. Death wasn't random. The child's living or dying was written in the registry book with the mother's address.'

"You live with things like that at breakfast. They just become normal. You forget them. If they ring up and ask me what I know – those are the things I'll tell them. They're sure to ask: 'How could you forget something like that –

the death of children – at breakfast? You weren't ready to remember, I suppose.'

"'Maybe,' I'll say. 'And where were you, Mister Journalist or Garda or Magistrate? Where have you been these past thirty years? I wasn't ready to remember – well, you weren't ready to listen.'"

Michael chopped mushrooms and onions and left them thick so they'd have a bite to them and wouldn't shrivel in the pan and his father came over and watched him for a moment and walked away and Michael smiled a bit for he knew they were too chunky to his father's mind. When he'd finished chopping he took out a separate pan for his father and he dropped some olive oil in the two pans side by side on the stove and scraped half the board clear into one pan and the other half into the other and began nudging them with the spatula and they'd hiss lowly. He waited a few minutes, then sprinkled some soy sauce and cayenne pepper into his own mushrooms.

His father came up behind him with a small pot of water with two eggs in it and he put it on a third ring and turned it on and went and sat down at the table and watched it until it came to the boil, then he rose from his seat and turned the heat down to simmer and went and sat down again, holding his watch to his face, nodding minutely like there was meaning and magnitude to the seconds.

They sat at the kitchen table and ate their dinner. His father made little childlike *umms* as he chewed and his head and shoulders bobbed somewhat as though to an internal music or simply that, there and then, all was right with the world and Michael looked up and smiled at him with love and pity and a prescient mourning. His father pushed some mushroom slices across his plate with his fork, then swept them the other way with his knife in the same way he once did when Michael was a child, sitting at that very table, he instructing with leftover beans, how the shopkeeper back in his own childhood used to

131

measure out the sugar into paper pouches and how the women with prams would lick the ball of a finger and dab it in and drop their finger into the baby's mouth walking out the door, maybe take one themselves; his child watching incredulously, his wife nodding shallowly.

His father held the cutlery at the ends, between thumb and forefinger, as though puppeteer rods or drumsticks.

"I went down to the pub yesterday," he said.

"Oh ya?"

"You said you'd be late getting home from school. I just thought I'd head down."

"Oh ya?"

"Never in all my years in Ballyredmond did I go to a pub in the village. Suppose I had my reasons. Went down a few times with you a while back but – I was sitting here yesterday – got myself a notion."

"It's good for you. Get out of here for a while."

"Yes, a few pints. Never did—"

"Meet anyone?"

"Your man was there. Your fella."

"John?"

"John, yes."

"Did ye just say hello, or...?"

"No, no. I sat down at that table, he was at the bar. He came over, sat down. 'Hey, Marty, how are ya?'"

"Ya?"

"Ya. He'll talk for ya – that fella."

"Ya."

"A writer."

"Ya. Sure you knew that."

"Sure you'd be forgetting things."

"What did ye talk about?"

"Erra, sure, things, things. You have a few pints – ye'd talk away."

"Like what things?"

"Any ol'—"

"No, but what *things*?"

"What's wrong?"

"I'm just interested in what you and my friend – who you hardly know – would've talked about – that's all."

"What's wrong, Michael?"

"Nothing's wrong."

"Nothing?"

"I'll just let you know – I've known John thirty years. I've never spoken to him about my mother. Let me just say that right off."

He watched his father, watched him pinch the collar of his shirt and run it along to the knot of his tie and he could tell by his face he told John, told him something. Fucking private school bastard. His father alone in the pub. *Let me buy ya a pint, Marty. Ah go on, go on... So, that's my mother's story. Now you were saying something about your wife?*

"What a man wants to tell a man is his own business."

"Christ."

Michael dropped his cutlery on his plate and propped an elbow on the table and leaned his face against his hand. His father began sweeping the mushrooms across his plate again, then gathering them into a pile.

"I didn't tell him everything, Michael. I wouldn't – the way he'd be. But a nice fella, when ya get talking to him. Talk the hind legs off a donkey, he would."

"I'd like to know what you told him about her, about my mother."

"That's my choice. My business."

"*Your* business? What about honouring her memory, honouring our privacy, *her* privacy?"

His father leaned back and put his knife down and began rubbing the side of his face.

"I didn't think—"

"What's the value in John Howard knowing anything?"

Central Library, Henry Street,
An Lárleabharlann, Sráid Annraoi
Tel: 8734333

"You're probably right, Michael."

"So what did ye talk about? I'm imagining he was a great listener for once."

"Not a whole lot. I had a wife. She was quiet, as long as I knew her. For a few years, she wasn't quiet. Far from it. That she died. At her own hand."

He seemed to grow more rueful with every word he spoke. Michael watched him and suddenly felt a great pity.

"Never mind, Dad. It's out now. The toothpaste can't be put back in, as they say."

"Ya. I didn't think..."

"I suppose it's not that big a deal. John's not a gossip. Who'd he tell, anyway?"

"Ya."

Michael watched his father. "But you enjoyed being out anyway – the chat and craic?"

"I did." His father nodded reflectively and looked down at his plate. "He reminds me a bit of me – in a strange way. When I was that age, your age. Yappin', telling stories. Happy with the little I had. It was all I wanted. It was easy to talk. I don't know what that was down to, maybe it was him. He fatherless, me wifeless. Maybe I went down there to talk. In my day, the only talking was done in the pub. What you let out, you let out, what you didn't – you took back home with you."

"You can always talk to me, Dad."

"Of course I can. But you're always with me." He thumped his chest gently. "You're a fellow traveller. Sufferer. Your childhood was gone so fast. I'd look in your face and see my own. A small little me staring back. Big eyes that saw too much for their years. I wept sometimes for your childhood, your serious little face."

"No need, Dad."

"There was, there was."

Michael reached across and took his father's arm.

"In John's face," his father said, "and you'll probably laugh at this – there's a strange kind of – I don't know what."

"What?"

"I don't know. A kind of... child. A peace."

He watched his father, he nodded faintly. "You mention Bessborough to him?"

"I did. He knows all about the place. He would've been born there, if his mother hadn't outright refused."

"I know all about his mother."

"Well, a man needs to say what he needs to say."

"What was he like after you told him?"

"Quiet."

"That's new."

"Well, maybe he's a talker 'cause you won't. Maybe he was waiting for you. Filling the void."

They finished their meals and Michael took their plates and walked to the kettle and flicked the switch and watched it boil. He filled their cups and returned to the table and sat down and stabbed his spoon into the sugar bowl and pulled it out and tipped it into his cup and began stirring, slow at first, then quickly, clinking the spoon repeatedly off the side like someone wishing to say a few words somewhere, at a wedding perhaps, or a christening, the kind of functions they both avoided. He withdrew his spoon from the cup and leaned in and stared blankly into the little tea-vortex until it fell away and a lone spec of something rotated around and around. He stared on until it stopped. He picked up the cup and took a sip.

"I mentioned her Nazi fixation," his father said. He smiled out one corner of his mouth, like he remembered it fondly.

"Oh ya?"

"I did. Remember – she was often reading something or other about the Nazis."

Michael sipped his tea. "I remember."

"That's what I put it down to when she started going on about it. That it was something she read had put her thinking it."

"Thinking what?"

"All the children dying in that convent. That it was..."

His father's eyes wettened and he dipped his head to swallow.

"That it was what, Dad?"

"That there was... something intentional about it."

5

He sat at the end of a low wooden table and stared out at the cliffs a mile away and the great rocks lying out before them like their kin cut loose and when the water would draw back and return to lash the cliff face the spray would rise up and roll across the headland like a phantom rain vanishing in the earth over and over. Behind him on the table, sea shells were in a bowl on the kitchen table, the walls had framed photos of the very waves and cliffs out his window and there were ceramic sheep and seagulls on the mantlepiece; in the kitchen area on either side of the sink was a little fridge-freezer and a microwave, in the top drawer were a few knives and forks and spoons, a spatula. There was a dehumidifier humming in the hallway and there were little instruction notes by most switches and stuck on the washer-dryer in the closet. A summerhouse. A middle-class incursion back to the land from which they'd been drifting since the Great Famine and returned for bank holidays and non-foreign holidays in summer, the beaming bungalows about the coasts of Ireland that outdid each other and bred and became the very suburbs left behind in Cork and Limerick and Dublin.

He'd rise in the morning and walk out to the living area and sit on the table and watch the sea from the sliding door. He'd sit there for an hour or more sipping tea. Then he'd rise and pour some cornflakes and return to the edge of the table and sit there eating. In the afternoon he'd head out on the road towards the village of Ballyferriter and he'd turn now and again and look up to Sybil Head rising up and ragged against the sky like it was torn off something by a wanton god and he'd look across the fields to where they slid to their end and the Three Sisters cliffs flicked up like some pulse of the land. Then he'd turn and walk on.

He'd buy groceries in the village and walk them back along the road and stare up at the edges of the land and he'd smell the Atlantic air and pull his scarf up to his face and breathe deep against it to feel its heat. He'd been there a month already and was planning to stay at least one more. He'd booked and paid for the place from October to Christmas but told the landlord he could be gone by November and he wouldn't come looking for some refund but that it was just as likely he'd come looking for January in the new year and maybe even February after that if they were available.

In the afternoons he'd walk along the sand of Ferriter's Cove and he'd walk up to the golf club to drink and watch a few people teeing off, the violence of a golf swing, its circular savagery. When he'd return in the evening the house would be cold and he'd microwave some soup and butter some bread and carry it to the couch and sit and dip the bread in his soup, listening to the wind. It did not sound like the wind at home. It sounded coarse and unknowing of land and living things and the seagulls seemed angrier and would fly overhead or hover there over the cottage, howling. He'd walk back into the village and drink in one of the bars and talk to a few of the locals if they spoke to him first.

He was walking along the road one evening when it was near dark and he heard something behind him and he turned over his shoulder and a man was there only a few feet away. He said something to him from under his hat which Michael did not understand. His face was fat and apple-red and Michael thought him in his sixties.

"Nil aon gaeilge agam," Michael said.

"Corcaigh?"

"Tá."

"'Tis a fine drive."

"It is. It is. Used to be a lot longer."

"Oh, gan dabht, gan dabht."

"We used to come here in the seventies. That long drive. The old stone cottages, roofless things just off the road. They're gone now."

"Gone. Knocked. Whether a fella wanted 'em knocked or not. 'We're knocking your shed to widen the road and that's that,' as the man said." He puffed his cheeks and made a sucking sound, like he was tasting its probity. "The seventies," he said. "Jaysus Chrisht. That's a fair while ago. I was bare a man meself then."

"Yes. I was a child."

"Where'd ye stay – back then – Granvilles was it? Dún an Oir?"

"We didn't come to Ballyferriter then. We were over on the other side." He threw his head sideways towards the sea. "We always went to Ventry. Stayed in the caravan park by the beach. We didn't go too far from there, as far as I can remember. My father might say different if he was here. We'd go into Dingle alright. And out the other side along Slea Head. But I don't remember Ballyferriter or Smerwick or anything out this far." They walked on.

"Maybe that's why I'm here," he said after a while.

"I seen ya the past few weeks – on the road here. Goin' and comin'. I've been behind ya sometimes." He rotated the flat of his hand on his chest. "I had a bit of a heart attack twelve month ago. Doctor says get out on that road for yourself and start walking every day. So I do a bit, I do a bit in fairness."

"That's good," Michael said.

The man seemed deflated, tired suddenly. He pushed out his lower lip and it was fat and shiny. He walked with his hands in his pockets and his shoulders cocked and his elbows out and his head low like he was pouting. There was mud on his otherwise white runners.

"Erra, I still help himself out, but I don't do much now. I wouldn't be going mad now at all. I do a bit. A bit, says you."

"In the farm, is it?"

"The farm – ya."

"Who does the farm?"

"The son, the son, ya. You haven't a fag, have ya?"

"I don't. I don't. I gave up years ago."

"You're grand. No fault, no fault, says you."

They walked on.

"Did you come down with your family?"

"No," Michael said. "I came down on my own. My father's still at home." The man was silent and when the wind fell away Michael could hear him wheeze slightly. "Am I going too fast? Will I slow down?"

"No, no. You're grand out. This is my shpeed, says you."

"Sure?"

"Have ya a wife at all?"

"I don't. Unfortunately."

"Well now," the man said. "Some fellas would say you're as well off. I might say it meself."

He flicked Michael with his elbow and Michael sniggered. "I don't know," he said.

"So you walk into the village every night? Where ya staying?"

"A cottage there by the old Ostán. Right on the road. Great view in fairness. Lovely. Wild it is – the wind at night. You'd think there'd be nothing left of the slates in the morning."

"Erra, they'd be well on or they'd be no good to no one. The builders around – they'd know the shtate of it out here."

"I suppose."

"Did you like Ventry?"

"I did."

"D'ya get back there?"

"Since I've been down? No."

"No."

"No. I don't know if I will either. Might just stay here."

"Erra, get around anyway lad, Jaysus Chrisht."

Michael smiled at the man and looked away to the fields on his left. "Maybe," he said.

"Do. Do. It'd be good to get back there again. If that's where ye used go. See the place again. You been into Dingle?"

"I have, yes. Once or twice. Driving. I didn't stop off."

"But not Ventry."

"No."

"Hidin'."

"How do you mean?" Michael said. He chuckled just so the man could hear it, but the man made no sound. They walked on for a while and all around was slipping deeper into darkness, the road and the hedges and the sky and the air in front of them.

"Ya here walking, every night for weeks. And ya haven't gone out yet where ya used to go every summer long ago? Some reason he don't want to, I say."

"I'm not hiding," Michael said. "I will. I'll probably go."

"Ah, don't mind me, lad. I'm only talkin' to talk."

The lights of a car came from behind them and lit the hedges and the road like a travesty against the night and nature and the car passed them by and carried up the road. The road was wet from an earlier rain and the tyres sounded like the water breaking and vanishing in the sand of Ferriter's Cove. Everything, everything here falls in line, he thought. They start sounding somehow like the wind or sea or rain and smelling like one or all of them.

"I'm within touching distance," Michael said. "And that'll do me."

"G'man."

A bit further on up the road the man stopped and tapped Michael's shoulder. "Well – 'twas nice talkin' to ya. This is my shpot. A mile and a half up and a mile and a half back down. Three miles a day, says you." He walked away into the black with his hand raised up.

"Nice talking to ya," Michael said.

He went into the village and had five pints up at the counter of Tigh Ui Catháin's and spoke to no one. He rose from his stool and walked out the door of the bar and walked in the drizzle towards home. A length of footpath was bright from the street-lights and he could see ahead of him the pitch black where it ended and away to the right the lights of houses shimmered in the drizzle like shards of the sun.

Tomorrow, he thought. Yes, tomorrow he would do it. He'd drive over there and sit in the sand. He walked home in the dark and the drizzle fell and tickled his face and he could hear the ocean away and faint somewhere out in the black like the quiet trespass of another order.

He did not go the next day. He stayed in bed until the afternoon, then read for a while on the couch and looked up now and again to stare out at the waves hitting the rocks. And he did not go the next day. He bought a few bottles of wine in a tiny shop on the road and he stayed in and got drunk and did the same the next two days, walking only to the old burial ground off the road and trying to read the years of burial on some of the headstones. He walked back again and opened a bottle of wine and drank the wine out of a teacup.

Talking just to talk was right, he thought. That's all he was doing when he told his father he'd been thinking of coming down here. And then his father said he should. But that he wouldn't be joining him. And it sounded better then, that he'd be alone. And the more he thought of it the better the idea became. Get away from that house of misery and regret. Go down, go down and walk on the same sand, smell, breathe the same air, see the same mountains and hedges and fields. But at a remove, for he did not want to immerse himself straight away. He'd stay out along the Peninsula somewhere and when he wanted to, when he chose to, he'd go over there to Ventry.

He went to the doctor and told him he wanted to take some stress leave from school. He didn't want to go back until the following September. He rang the principal and told him and put the doctor's cert in the post and went home and flipped open his laptop and looked at cottages to rent on the Dingle peninsula. He packed a bag and hugged his father and drove out along the same roads he had with his mother and father forty odd years before and after three hours he took the right turn to Ballyferriter after the bridge, instead of going straight on to Ventry as his father used to do.

He woke the next day and walked up to the golf club for a sandwich and coffee. He walked down to the cottage and sat at the end of the table again swirling wine in the teacup. He stared out at the water and the rocks and he looked out over the headlands to a crop of rocks arched out of the land like some Jurassic vertebrae excavated by the wind alone and he saw a tiny strip of road passing alongside it the width and colour of a needle and he knew that the road he had to travel for Ventry beach was out there ten miles or more along the coast road. He promised himself there and then that he'd go the next day. He'd wake in the morning and he'd go there and walk on Ventry Strand the way he had for the last time with his mother in 1977, before she went mad and started telling them the truth, before they all went mad from it. He'd walk across the sand where his father had tossed a man a ball. He'd go there and he'd walk and he'd cry and no one would know it wasn't the Atlantic gales in his face that did it. He'd walk there, and if he didn't, if he didn't, he'd pack up his bags and get in the car and drive back to Cork and throw it on the pile with all the other things passed by and undone.

The colour of the red wine where it touched against the white insides of the teacup reminded him of the worm he'd stood on once as a child. He'd kneeled over it and watched it coil in its own guts. That was the first time he recalled a sadness for something else in this world beyond himself. He'd thought of that worm sometimes growing up. That first stroke on a great canvas of regret.

He stared out at the sea. It swelled and dipped like it was breathing.

He woke in the morning and he dressed and he walked out to the living area and he sat on the couch and did not eat. Cows went by on the road. He could see their backs loping along. The farmer slow-rolled behind them in a four-wheel drive and he heard a dog barking that he could not see. The hills and headlands were misted over but closer in he could make out the single triangular rock at which the sea had been hurling itself for a month. It looked like a spearhead or a black diamond and when the waves hit it the water flashed up and disappeared into the mist.

He could not eat but he did not want to. He needed the alcohol in his blood to get him out there on the road. Food would mitigate the whole thing, soak up the dull in his brain and by the time he was done with breakfast he'd have called the thing off. He went to the bedroom and opened the cupboard and came back with his jacket on and sat back down on the couch. He made some tea and sat on the low wooden table and sipped. He went back again and made another cup, then he did it again. He remembered his father doing that for his mother. All those cold cups of tea. There were no microwaves then, he thought. When the tea was gone, it was gone. No resurrection. They didn't have the science. He sat there and watched the mist fade and the land come shaping through in its beauty and indifference and adamancy and infinity and he looked away after a while and turned back towards the kitchen fearing he was losing his nerve just by looking out, that that vastness had some alchemic calibre that sped the mind to wherever it was going, whatever thoughts were gathering, good or bad.

He rose and got his car keys and walked out to the hall. He stood at the front door and tapped it with the ignition key in the manner of throwing a dart. Then he opened the door and walked out and got in his car.

The sun came out as he drove. Inishtooskert Island lay way out ahead and the ocean sparkled all about it like grave goods at a

Bronze Age burial and he carried on up over the hill and passed by the rocks he'd thought dinosaur-like these past weeks and he saw tourists stopping there on bikes and in mini-vans and taking photos and hardy couples setting off in short pants up through the rocks to look out over the Atlantic.

He swept left and came over the rise and when the road flattened and went on straight he looked out to his right to the Great Blasket Island lying black between the ocean's glint and the blue and white sky and Inishtooskert reappeared again and Tearaght Island was between them miles away in the haze and he felt a sadness in that beauty for there was nothing at all of man in it but a thing independent of eye or mind and the lives and literature it stole and made, a beauty that set a mind edgy for its elemental indifference to time and god and man.

He drove out along the road and he looked out over the Atlantic and across on the cliff road. He could see the odd roof of a car behind the low stone wall. He drove along Slea Head and at intervals cars would be pulled into the side and people would be standing at the stone wall with cameras and binoculars. He started to recognise the roads and their turns, the hills of Dunquin and he remembered the little creak that ran across the road, the cars wobbling on the cobblestones. He remembered the sheep on the hedges and the beehive huts and seagulls seeming to be frozen in time out over the ocean then falling away and down out of sight.

He turned off the road and parked his car close to the mobile homes and walked onto the sand of Ventry Strand. Where it was dry the sand was bright and powdery and he could see way up ahead it swirled in the breeze, and where the water had retreated the beach was concrete grey with minute stones running in bands across it and tiny channels of purple running through them like deltas of blood.

He walked for a few minutes on the hard sand, then turned up and sat beneath the dunes. He pulled his knees up to his chest and held them there with his arms. He wedged his chin between his knees and stared out to the water and the water barely moved. His anorak crackled a bit when the breeze blew. It was a cold breeze and the sand on which he sat was cold.

He sat there for a long time, moving only to turn his head up and down the beach or turning his head away from the sand when the breeze was strong. A man walked past with a dog and nodded at him. At times he could make out tiny figures way over where the beach curved and came back around almost parallel with itself. At other times he was sure he was alone on the whole beach. Who would come to a beach in November anyway, he mused. The beach grass behind him clicked in the wind. He picked up a fistful of sand now and again and let it drain out of the bottom of his fist and it would blow sideways as it fell like something burst free. He sat there for a long time.

He did not see her until she was quite close. When he first saw her, he looked away again, certain that it could not be her. She walked straight towards him and watched him keenly as she did. When she was close he finally looked over again. He was sure it was her then. And he was embarrassed for being found like that, sitting in the sand alone in the cold, and by her of all people. She was wearing a long black coat and blue jeans and a black scarf that was twice wrapped over the top of her head and under her jaw with the ends tucked into the top of her coat.

She smiled as she came up to him. Playfully, she said, "Hi – how are you?" Then she sat down next to him and pulled up her knees as he had his.

"As you can imagine... I'm very confused," he said.

"I'm sure you are, Michael. I don't blame you at all."

He looked at her watching the sea. After a while he said, "Okay. Go on."

"Go on, what?"

He laughed a bit. "You know."

She leaned in and nudged him with her shoulder. "Your father told me, of course. Who else?"

146

"How – you rang him?"

"Last week. Mr Nolan told me you were gone on sick leave. I was ringing your phone for two weeks. I went to the office and got your home number. Your father answered the phone. He told me you left your phone behind."

"Sure what do I want it for."

"Misanthrope."

"He gave you the address?"

"Ya. I said I'd drive down on the Saturday, see how you were. He seemed surprised by that."

"We're both surprised. And happy, of course." She looked at him and he looked away. "He say anything else?"

"He said if you weren't at that address – there'd be a good chance you'd be on Ventry Strand."

He stared out at the water and picked up another fist of sand and let it drain away out of his fist. "Why did you come, Jill?"

"Worry? Who knows."

"Did my father say anything else? Anything about why I might have taken time off school? Why I'd come down here for a few months in winter? Why I'd be sitting in the cold on Ventry Strand?"

She shook her head slowly. "No. He didn't. I asked, of course. He said he wouldn't tell me, but that you might. You don't have to of course. That's not why I'm here."

He dug his hand into the sand and lifted it out and shook it off. He did this a few times, then he wiped the grains that had stuck to his hand off the side of his pants. "We've reached the funeral stretch of our lives, I think, Jill. That long induction of looking down at coffins before we get inside one ourselves."

"That's lovely. Can I put that in the children's book I'm writing?"

"You're writing a children's book?"

"I'm joking. It's an insanely morbid thing to say, I meant."

"You writing anything?"

"Oh ya. At the weekends. Some vapid vignette that reads brilliant at night with my wine and rubbish in the morning with my Nurofens."

They looked down at the water and Jill turned her head to the hill away to the left. Michael stared out at the mountains across the bay. Then he looked up the beach. He could smell Jill's perfume and hear contentment in her breathing.

"How did he sound, my father?"

"Fine. He sounded fine. He was on his way out to the pub when I rang."

"Ah! Down to his buddy, John."

"He was meeting John?"

"Oh, they're very pally these days. Sometimes when I'm heading down to meet John, he'll come down with me. Sometimes he'll go without me."

"That's good for your Dad."

"Ya, it is. I watch them talking sometimes. John is good for my father in a way I never would've imagined. Just his frivolity and carry-on. An outlet for him. I'd imagine there's nothing he doesn't know about my mother now. And that bothered me before."

He looked out across the bay to where the plum mountains and plum sky were close to touching. She flicked the sand with her finger, made a little heap and stuck a piece of dry grass on the top, then knocked it away with the back of her hand.

"You're wondering what's to know about my mother, Jill."

"You don't have to tell me, Michael. Keep it, don't go against your instincts."

"They're wrong. My father was right to... to open up. I spent my childhood hearing people say my mother was nuts. She certainly sounded it. She told me some horrific things. I spent my life trying to forget them and there they were one day on the news as I ate a sandwich. One afternoon she came downstairs in her dressing gown. She had a sort of static in her voice, I can still hear it, like she wasn't used to talking. She told

148

me the whole story. We put her in a mental home. She killed herself in 1981. I was twelve." He picked up a fist of sand and dropped it and wiped his hands theatrically. "Well – now you know everything," he said. "On with our lives."

"I'm sorry."

"I remember the day she told me. I'll never forget it. You put it down to the drugs or the drink or the depression. You're sat watching TV one day in your forties – you find out it's real. Convent grounds are getting dug up thirty years after she said they should be."

She slid her hand down his shin and held it over his hands that were clasped above his ankles. When she pulled her hand away to wipe her nose, he felt a cold.

"I look down that beach now, maybe three hundred meters away it was. We met a man there once. His ball ran across our path as the three of us walked. This was 1977. I think there was something in that. I think they may have known each other, or recognised each other from years before, he and my mother. I think that may have been the setting-off down the road she took. Her deciding to go back. Back to Bessborough Mother and Baby Home. Take us back with her."

"Jesus, Michael."

"'Help me, Michael,' she said. 'We'll tell them all. We'll write another letter, we'll make a sign. Help me Michael. You will, won't you?'

"That was three years of my childhood. And then it was all over. And you're left with nothing. Nothing but the silence and the years to think it over. Twice she stood outside the church gates with a sign. We came out of midday Mass and saw her there. Everyone saw her. I remember the voices on the church steps behind me as we came out that first time. They were gasps really, not words. Some mouthed the syllables on her board, then trailed off. I couldn't breathe. My father turned around and went back inside. People walked off and stayed watching her to the road and parents shepherded children away, arching over them and throwing looks back over their shoulders like she might have been a pox that could ride the breeze.

"The country is with her now, down there with her sign, glowering righteously over her shoulder the way they had over mine. But my father and I cannot. We who sectioned her. The people who had to listen to her crying all night cannot. She looked up at us with tears in her eyes and all we did is go back inside and ask Father Dan, 'What will we do?' The Guards came and threw her sign in the boot. She screamed our names as they put her in the car. Shame. Shame is such a turncoat. It was with me then looking down at her. Now it points at me. I'm stuck on those church steps, I've never left them.

"The second time was terrible. She spat in Father Dan's face when he walked down the same steps to confront her. All the intakes of breath… I can hear them even now. It's a loud thing. Then they went for her. Men caught her and snapped her sign and ripped it up and held her on the ground until the Guards came. You don't forget the sight of men wrestling your mother to the ground. You beg for some mind-glaucoma to come and close it away. Someone called her a cunt in the struggle. Women shooed their children in other directions. 'Don't look, don't look.' She went back up to the psych unit in the new Regional Hospital the next day. In and out of there she was, just like she'd been in Our Lady's.

"It all just came falling out after that day we walked here on this sand in 1977, and we tossed a man a ball. 'Nothing's unrelated,' you once said to me. We get this doctor who said she needed to 'talk'. Well, she did. Told the whole village those two times outside Mass."

They sat there and listened to the wind. It put running dents out on the water and then the water was flat again.

"Michael," Jill whispered. "I just don't know what to say. I-I… I just don't."

He stared out across the water with a tear on his right cheek which she could not see. He supposed she might have cried herself but did not, for it wasn't her past nor her crime and her sympathies lay not next to her on the sand but elsewhere.

"Michael?"

"Yeah?"

"Can I ask something?"

"I've no problem with that, Jill. I've no problem with people asking anymore. I might have realised that, watching my father skip down to the pub, or just since sitting here on the sand talking to you. Not that people asked. But I'm gonna talk if they do."

"What did she write on the signs?"

He brought his head straight and narrowed his eyes like he was reading them a distance away or the distance from which he'd once seen them. "*They killed my baby in Bessborough.*"

"They both said that?"

He nodded. "Different signs, of course. One was the cardboard from our new television. One was the back of a For Sale sign for a house. Don't know where she got that. Probably pulled it off a pole in some garden."

"Needs must."

"Yeah."

He looked down to where the water tipped lowly onto the sand and when it retreated the shingle clicked and rolled. He remembered his mother somewhere there, that last day, holding her shoes and tiptoeing on the shingle. She came onto the dry sand close to where they sat now, and she slowed and straightened and turned her face back to the sea a last time, then up to the mountains and then about the sky and she gave a small smile with her lips closed that dimpled her left cheek and was gone.

He pressed his hand into the sand and watched his fingers slowly disappear and he pulled them out and did it again.

"She used to say, 'You push hard and long enough against the dirt, it'll rise between your fingers.'"

They stared out to the sea for a long time and did not speak and way out the whites of water flashed and vanished like dissents against the coming dark and when the night came they rose and brushed their clothes and walked away and in that dark they reached for each other's hands.

IV

1

She was eighteen years old, walking up Barrack Street, holding a rolled page of newspaper at her chest, looking up and around like a tourist with an ice cream, then she'd pause at a doorway and unroll the page and poke her finger about it for a moment then move off up the hill again and roll the paper back up and tap it against her thigh or into the palm of her hand. Her shoes clopped on the footpath for they were oversized and belonged to another girl in another time.

She stopped at the top of the street and faced down the hill, then began zig-zagging the paper over and back from the doors of the houses. Most had no numbers; the occupants knew the number, and the postman, and who else was there? The paper came to a halt at the door right next to her. She turned and looked across the street to the dark window of a pub. She unrolled the paper and looked down to it: *Three storey premises with a room to let*. She counted out the houses again, then turned back across the street, holding the paper limply outward like a jaded swordsman. It didn't even have the right number. Above the dark window was a big emerald 32.

She walked across to the other footpath and stood at the doorway like she was waiting for a bus. Someone up the street was laughing. She hunched her shoulders against it and touched her forehead to bless herself but her hand dropped away. She'd been doing it the four miles there, with children playing and women garrulous in their doorways. She'd jump at the sound, then trail looks across the road to them from the corner of her eye, like they were something obscene. Cork was happy in 1948. She nervously tapped her leg with the paper and went inside.

A man was talking to other men at the bar counter. Their heads tilted back and aslant like the words warranted deep contemplation.

"The little fucker – there he was standing upright in the middle of the room, looking at me like – *Who the fuck are you?*"

"Ya, ya, I know it," another man said.

"And was that the first time, Joesy?" said another.

"What – seein' him? 'Twas, 'twas. But sure we knew he was around. You'd see the shite. Black things, like slugs." He held up a space between thumb and forefinger and the men looked and nodded shallowly.

"Ya, ya."

"What did ya do, Joesy?"

"I went out the back and got the hurley. He went over towards the youngfella's bed. I come in and stand there holding the hurley. The fucker turns back to me, stands up on his hinds, and hisses at me. I walk over anyway – bate the fucker with the edge of the bas. Scooped him up, fucked him out inta the lane for the cats. Useless fuckers."

"Throw out that hurley, Joesy."

"Me bollix. What'll I kill the next one with? Sure they're all over the lane now."

"Ya, ya. They are. They are."

"We're to be gettin' a place over in Ballyphehane. They're clearing out the lanes up and down Barracka. There's three houses empty in our lane sure. All got a lovely house from the council over along in Ballyphehane. Half a Barracka's over there. S'why the fuckin' rats are bad. The empty houses in the lanes."

"'Tis, 'tis."

"Ya ya ya,"

They nodded into their pints of Beamish.

They did not hear her come in behind them. The door banged, but no more than the draft had done to it all day. A big man rested on his elbows at the end of the counter. He held a bottle of stout into his body and curled his hand around it and tapped the top of it gently on his chin. He watched her as the men spoke. He flicked his eyes to the men down the bar and flicked them back at her like he was sure she was mistaken, standing there, that he didn't need to move or talk, that she'd see plain as day that she had walked into the wrong place and would walk straight out again. So he'd look away to the men and look back at her and seem irritated each time, that she was bringing him close to having to say something.

Her hair was black and boyish and there were two pins either side that seemed unneeded. She wore an oversized green wool dress that an older woman would wear and a sky blue cardigan that gathered under her armpits and pulled only halfway to her wrists, her head was slung low as though to counter the heel in her shoes, and in the dull and dark of her sockets that ran to her cheekbones, her pale blue eyes seemed to shift and bob like a vibrant water in a turbid earth.

"What?" the man said.

She stood inside the door and held up the paper. "Room," she said. "It said it." She dropped the paper to her side.

The men at the bar turned around and saw her and stopped talking.

"Room?"

She twitched the paper out from her leg. "It said it."

The man came off his elbows and stood up straight and pushed his bottle away and beckoned her with his head. She walked over to him. The men at the bar rotated back in their stools and picked her up again on the other side.

"So – a room?"

"Yes."

"Where you from?" He waited and watched her face.

Finally she said, "In Cork."

"Right," he said.

He reached in behind the bar and took up another bottle of stout and took a long gulp and set it back on the counter. Then he picked it up again and took another one. He swivelled the bottle at the base with his forefinger and thumb. He pointed at the bottle and looked at her.

"No," she said. Her head twitched to the left where the men sat.

"Don't mind them. They'd be cribbing about a girl in the bar for two days – spend the next hundred remembering it fondly."

She did not move.

"So where ya really from?"

Her eyes roamed about the space in front of her, unfixed, seeming to not really see.

"I'm from Cork," she said.

"Why are ya looking for a room?"

"My parents went off to England. And I couldn't go 'cause there wasn't enough money."

"I see. Where are your belongings?"

"I don't have belong—"

"You've no clothes with you?"

She shook her head.

He looked down her body to her toes and returned up to her face.

"Have ya money?" he said, and he looked down the bar at the men and smiled.

She pulled her hand from the pocket of the dress and opened it out.

"One pound?"

Her head twitched left and she looked at the floor.

"How long are you hoping to stay?"

She shook her head and shrugged one shoulder. "I need to find work."

"You do, girl." He dipped his head to the money. "If that's all you have in this world."

She closed her fist around the money and folded her arms and nodded at the knuckles that encased it. They were bony and tartaned with creases that ran to her fingers.

"I do," she said.

"What's your name?"

"Marjorie. No – Elaine."

He dipped his head and stared at her out of one eye as though peering into the stem of a pipe. "'Marjorie. No – Elaine?'"

"Just Elaine."

"Why did you say Marjorie?"

"I used be called that. I forgot."

He looked at her a long time. Then he reached down to the shelf behind him and took up two bottles of stout and opened them and placed one gently in front of her. She watched it and she felt the face of one of the men down the bar; when she turned to him he turned away and began swirling the dregs of his glass then holding it up for inspection with a face of love and loathing for what remained.

She looked back to the bottle. "No. Sorry."

"You could do cleaning in the bar."

"Yes," she said.

He licked his teeth and dipped his head and peered out under his brow with a sluggish self-certainty she'd only seen in men and in some women when they were alone.

"It's a nice room," he said.

"Thank you."

"People've liked it. Christ, I stayed there meself for two years. And sure you work here now."

"I do?" she asked, and looked up at him.

"Ha?" he said, slightly irritated.

"I'm working here?"

The men at the bar sniggered.

With his thumb he scraped some skin from the knuckle of his index finger then flicked it away. She thought of her father, the times he brought back a loaf and her mother found mould in it, or the face of the Jew cobbler Mr Goldsmith when she was collecting her shoes, the look on his face if a hardshaw straightened himself off the reflection in his window, the look of a boy in Blackpool who tore his Mass clothes. The chastened male was a pitiable sight.

He took another long sup from his bottle like he was mulling it one last time and belched softly into his fist and looked down the bar to the men.

"Yes – you are," he said.

"Thank you so much," she said and cast a tiny smile around the little shelves, then out past the faces of the men to the banging door like she was taking reconnaissance of her future out there in the light and perhaps it wouldn't be so bad and hadn't she it coming after all, hadn't she saved up every scrap of good that was due to her in this world, and every piece of luck and every kind word and anything else the good Lord could abide her? It was like He had finally turned back to her the way the light had suddenly swollen at the window and the voices at the bar rose in a dull chorus with the zest of pub in her nostrils, like the world was returning in all its wondrous confusion; she would take it, she would take it all.

She heard them shouting on the floor above her.

"We don't need anyone for the pub."

"Ah, Frances – it's only short-term. She's a pound to her name. Her parents are gone to England."

"So you're going to take the rent with one hand and give it back as wages with the other? I tell ya – I don't know how ye took over anything."

"Ah, Frances – it's short-term. We'll get her on her feet, and then we'll have a long-term tenant."

She could hear feet on the ceiling. In a moment the door was flung open and a woman stood staring at her. The man from the bar came and stood out in the hall twisting his finger in his ear.

She lay on the bed with her feet resting on the windowsill to cool the blisters. Her mouth hung open, she looked like a boy who had got into his mother's wardrobe.

"I'm sorry. It's just my feet are killing me," she said.

The man gave a sympathetic slow-motion blink. The woman stared at her in silence until she removed her feet from the windowsill, then she asked her name and where she was from and why she needed the room.

"I'm Mrs Holmes," she said. "This fella here is Mr Holmes."

She stepped through the doorway into the room and stood aside and lay open her hand to the man standing in the hall.

"Mr Steven Holmes," she declared. "If only there were money given for figurin' ways to lighten your load – I swear he'd be the richest man in Cork. My poor father says to me on my wedding day, he says, 'Marrying an unmoneyed Protestant is like kissing a child for his consumption.'"

The two women looked out to the man in the hall, gently bobbing his head as though in agreement. Then he walked away.

His wife turned to the girl on the bed with perhaps a near grin. She began to walk after her husband, then she turned back.

"We'll see," she said. "That's all."

She'd come down at 7.30am and open the door for the early starters, get the five or six of them a pint and a chaser and they'd walk off down the hill to the brewery or wherever they were going and she'd see them again in the evening after tea, three or four pints and a chaser and they'd head home before last call, see them bright and early again in the morning; the working men; bottlers in the brewery, masons, a lorry driver, a plasterer; men of means and status and their initials on the tin of their cigarette cases. They had something in the world, enough for it to name them: they became 'Jimmy the Mason' and 'Pa the Plasterer' and the other men looked around at them leaving and said, "'Tis fine for 'em, workin'."

The other men walked in after their dinner around 1pm and swung a leg over the bar stool and sat there until the bar closed at 10pm. All they seemed to own was the drink in their hands and the cigarette they smoked and their mark on the world was no more than the ink on their birth certs and the finger-stains on the peak of their caps and they did not care for God had made them and His plans were written out in the littleness of their lives.

She started off sweeping the cigarette butts off the floor and wiping the tables in the little square of lounge where the couches were laid out in a U and some men liked to sit and play cards and thought themselves some way removed from the bar counter and the career drinkers that resided there. She cleaned the windows and swept the curtains and washed the glasses as Mr Holmes leaned his fat shoulder into a conversation at the end of the bar and poured porter for the patrons and for himself, but it wasn't long at all before she herself was serving porter to the men and the men would eye her circumspect and shy as she pulled the wooden lever on the wooden barrel below the counter, for she was close on another species, being young and woman and employed.

At the end of the night Mrs Holmes would come down cranky from upstairs and take out the till drawer and study the figure of her husband to gauge his inebriation, then point them both to some glasses or ashtray and return upstairs with the takings. When they'd finished the clean-up, Mr Holmes would lean at his place at the end of the bar with another drink and she would sip her orange cordial and disguise her yawns. For three weeks she wore the same green dress she'd walked in there wearing until his wife gave her a few of her old dresses and odd blouses and cardigans she'd been holding onto for patches and repairs. They'd talk at the end of the counter for a while and Mr Holmes might suddenly point at her and say, "I remember that," or "God – that dress takes me back," and she'd nod and be embarrassed and rub the material in gratitude.

She worked hard and paid her rent before it was asked for and she brushed her bosses' daughters' hair and gave them French plaits that they liked and she taught them how to sew. They said, "Goodness – where did you get so good at sewing, Elaine?" and she said, "Don't know."

Mrs Holmes asked her about her family sometimes and she got very little in reply, and so she took an interest in asking and an interest in the famished answers. Elaine spent less time with the girls just to avoid their mother and when Mrs Holmes walked in behind the bar, she looked for something to do in the lounge. The two women walked about the premises and watched each other when their backs were turned.

Mrs Holmes said to her one night, taking out the till drawer, "If I was to write to your parents, Elaine – would they tell the same story you do?" She looked at her husband after saying it, then walked upstairs. So when Mrs Holmes asked their tenant questions about her past or her family and she got no kind of an answer at all or some ambiguity, it only fed a suspicion that Mrs Holmes had from the day her husband came upstairs and told her they had a new tenant and employee. And the more their tenant and employee withdrew from nearly any conversation relating to herself, the more her employer began to ask, all that reticence and reservation was simply spread across the bad logic of employing her in the first place.

On Sundays she walked around the pub collecting glasses and wiping tables and emptying ashtrays and she'd go up to Mr Holmes at the bar and give him an order and he'd ask her brusquely and out of earshot of the men whether they had legs at all, then he'd pour the porter and lay it on the counter to settle. She'd stand there waiting and when he topped up the pints she'd take them down to the men in the lounge and he'd watch her all the way and watch her talk to the men and watch the light in their faces. She had a tray she'd hold with her inner wrist against her hip and standing at the bar waiting for the pints to be topped up she'd randomly roll it to the front edge of her pelvis around to the small of her back in a collaboration of hip and arm that set her torso moving out in one direction and then back in the other that pressed her flesh full against her clothes and set the men watching her through the smoke and the dim light and the unmarried men would call her over for every small thing and the married men would watch them then turn away.

Mr Holmes would lean on the counter with both elbows the way he did that first day when he called her over and he'd take another bottle of stout and he'd drink it without lifting his elbow and when they sat after closing he'd watch her drink her orange cordial, her swallow and lip-licking, the tautness of her flesh, the pep of youth in her movements. She saw him watch her as she walked about and he was cranky on Saturday afternoons when football boys would come in and sit at a table with their wages and buy people a drink like they were well-to-do and they'd touch her hip and talk to her for she was the only girl in all the pubs of Barrack Street save for the odd wrinkled hand poking a shilling out from a snug-hatch, and when she walked away smiling she'd look up and Mr Holmes would scowl behind the bar.

She felt it was coming; those long, leery looks he'd give his wife's dress as it sat there drinking orange like he was reminiscing about the times inside it and aching to get back there. The rapacious prod, she knew all about them. Heard and read at least. She'd never spoken to a Protestant until the day she walked into his bar. And it was true, she could see it in his eyes. The lascivious, red-eyed looks he'd give her. He'd tilt his head sometimes when they sat alone, like he was gauging her from a different angle. A nice man, she thought. But the devil swimming in his blood and thoughts like she'd always known of them, for wasn't it written on his face and uttered in his own wife's words and certified in the jowls and paunch and intemperance. Protestants went to hell for the manner in which they defiled their flesh with the poisons of the world and with the poison of other flesh. *They'll take you with them*, she was told in school. And he was, he was taking her with him. For she liked him. And that's what she was told would happen for as long as she had memory. You'd start to think them normal, nice, if you ever got close. And she didn't know what to do, but she knew something was coming; most likely he'd whiskey-up one night and knock on her door, and what would she do, this man who took her off the street and gave her a job he hadn't needed and fed her every evening with the food out of his family's cupboard, sat over soup and bread every Sunday when his wife and daughters were at Mass, what would she do when he came looking for some *recompense*?

They drank their drinks one night at the end of the counter and smoked. She looked around the walls and floors and stopped at the photo of a man standing on Barrack Street. It was on the head-high shelf behind the bar. She had seen it the very first day she walked in and every day since and never bothered herself with it. It was next to a picture of Padraig Pearse and both were between a row of empty brown stout bottles and on the other side a row of empty whiskey bottles from the Midleton distillery.

"Who's that, Mr Holmes?"

He looked up and back over his shoulder. Then turned back and sank into his seat like he was exhausted.

"Mr Kelly."

"Mr Kelly?"

"Mrs Holmes' father. That's him in front of the pub... Jesus – years ago. Not long after he got it. He lived here. His parents lived here. This was all one house. Three floors. His father died when he was young. He went away fighting with Liam Lynch for five years in the 1919–1923 wars. He was caught with him in the Knockmealdown mountains, I heard. Got a few years for it in prison. When he came out he went home to Barrack Street with his wife and daughter. He opened The 32 and they ran it together. I come along in 1937, I think. He hated me. He'd been burning out Prods for five years from Bandon to

Fermoy. He's washing glasses one day behind that counter and one comes walking in with his daughter. 'Holmes?' he says to me. I'll never forget it. 'That's your name?' He stares at me like I was turning his family out in the street. He pointed up at Padraig Pearse there and stared back at me and went back to washing glasses. Barely said two words to me after. Barely spoke to me on our wedding day. Mrs Holmes told you already what he said to her. Fuckin' bastard. On her wedding day. Wouldn't speak to me when we moved in here after. I went down and stayed in that room you're in now. Three years later – he's gone. Doesn't wake up. And do I think sometimes, was it me? I think my wife thinks it was. But it wasn't. It was his hate. In all my years, I've never seen anything like it. The power and strength of it; the blinding blaze of a Catholic's hate. They'll turn it on themselves if they have to."

He looked up and back over his shoulder again to the photo above the bar of his father-in-law. Then he turned back and took a long drink from his bottle and settled it down on his thigh and wobbled the flesh there with it. He shook his head gently.

"You don't go to Mass," he said.

"No," she said. She took a drink from her glass and he watched her.

"You gonna leave it at that?"

"Yes," she said.

She took another drink, then rose and walked behind the bar and washed her glass in the basin of water and set it on the shelf and said goodnight to him and walked up the stairs to the first floor where her room was. He was completely still as she left him, the bottle on one thigh and his hand on the other with his head bent down over them. She undressed in her room and put on her nightdress and climbed into bed. Men were talking outside on the street. Then it was quiet. She thought of him down there sitting on the seat alone. Sometime in the night she opened her eyes and heard his lumbering footsteps on the lower stairs and then on the floorboards overhead.

In the morning she heard Mrs Holmes screaming at her daughters and their footsteps over and back across the ceiling. Then she heard them on the stairs and then outside her door. They did not knock immediately and when they did it was light and the knocks were spaced out like they were unsure. She threw over her blanket and climbed out of the bed and walked to the door. His younger daughter stood in the hall with her hands clasped and trembling at her chest.

"Anne," she said. "Are you alright?"

"Daddy won't wake up," she said.

Mrs Holmes told her the day of her husband's funeral that she had a week to find somewhere else to live. She was given her wages on the last day. She said to Mrs Holmes that she had nowhere to go and she'd have to sleep under a bridge. And Mrs Holmes said calmly: "There's something behind those eyes of yours, Elaine." To which she replied: "Yes, there is, but not your husband." She walked out onto Barrack Street and headed down the hill towards the city, content to have delivered unto her former employer some bedtime thinking of her own. That she could've – if she wanted. The little she had in this world; the power to have touched her husband – and to not have. She walked down Barrack Street towards the bridge. There was a sign in a window at the corner of French's Quay: *Room for rent.* She went in and asked about it.

She got a job with Quality Cleaners and for eighteen years she swept and mopped and wiped and washed before they began losing business to contractors with electric Hoovers and one day her employer packed it in and bought a liner ticket and headed off to America the following week with the last payroll.

She picked up a few days a week with Ryan's Cleaners in the summer of 1967 and walked into the offices of the City Hall one day with a mop and bucket and silently walked down a corridor and started off again the slow rhythmic back-and-forth of her elbows and arms and feet, the inexorable ceaseless dance she deemed her charge, her fate in the world. A man looked up from his papers and watched her for a while, the business of floor-mopping, its arid mission. She knew he watched. *He thinks me a widow, working at my age.* She mopped differently to other girls. They stabbed the mop forward and drew it back in straight lines across the linoleum. She mopped horizontally in a continual tapestried S that implied some dance or pleasure in the action.

He pities me. The monotony of this. The tragedy of cleaning. I could take you, good sir, I could drop this mop and take you out the road to tragedy. But you won't. You wouldn't dare. Better to block your eyes than hate them.

2

The cleaning girls came into the offices of the City Hall in the evenings: three or four of them came in at 5pm on Wednesdays and Fridays and the sight of their navy uniforms stirred the men at their desks to banter and yawning. They checked their watches and said hello and the girls wondered whether someday in a hotel foyer their timekeeping wouldn't be passed on to Mr Ryan himself as his children bounced on furniture, for didn't everyone who worked with a biro know each other? So they were always on time, meticulous and energetic; quiet, unsmiling, for the men of biros and paperclips and sleeve garters could be watching.

The first time Martin Connolly saw her, she came walking in behind the younger girls and looking over their shoulders and around the room like a mother viewing her daughters' workplace. One of them pointed down a corridor and she followed on down with her mop and bucket. She was thirty-seven then. Other girls came and went in the passing months, got married or emigrated and were replaced with teenagers who'd left school and were sent out to bring something home to the family before they too joined another, but Elaine Dillon remained, silent, pointing down corridors to new girls. She was there a year when he asked her to the pictures.

She knew he watched her from his desk. He watched her that first day. Perhaps a curiosity at first. He seemed lonely at his desk. She rarely saw him talking to his colleagues. She supposed he was not married, though she had not seen his ring finger. Unmarried men of his age had a nervousness about them, a pre-beaten quietness that grew year by year until it was thrown off when they walked up the aisle. She had a feeling he was working towards something day by day, week by week, that he might ask her to go with him to a dance or the pictures. He walked up to her one Friday evening and nearly tripped over her Hoover cord.

"Elaine, is it?"

"Yes."

"I've heard the other girls call you."

"Elaine, yes," she said.

"Elaine – would you come to the pictures with me – if you'd like?"

"I don't like the pictures."

"Oh, okay," he said. "That's fine. Not to worry."

"Not the pictures. But we could do something else – if you want."

"Oh, okay. Grand."

"I just don't like the pictures." She shrugged her shoulders and they both stood there waiting for the other to proffer an activity.

"A walk?" he said.

"Grand," she said.

He picked her up the next day outside her door on French's Quay and they drove out to Curraghbinny Woods and went walking. She had black hair to her shoulders and a dimple on one cheek and glacial blue eyes that would show up vampirish in the sunlight. She was short and thin, she chain-smoked and when she lifted the cigarette to her lips or when she walked her clothes would dangle and sway from her bones. In the woods she bent down and plucked some bluebells from their stalks and walked up to trees and peeled some moss from them and sifted it in her fingers and brought it to her nose.

"I love the smell of moss." She held it out to him and he looked at her and furrowed his brow and smiled and poked it with his finger.

"It's moss," he said.

"Yes," she said, and she smelled it again.

He talked mostly, she nodded and smiled with her lips closed.

They went to Killarney the following Sunday. They spent the whole day there. They walked up to Torc waterfall and stood there in its spray and he reached out and held her hand. They took a jaunting car around the lakes and up to Muckross House and out to the abbey. A man selling photos took their picture in front of the jaunting car with Muckross House in the background. They stood not thoroughly arm in arm, nor shoulder to shoulder; he leaned towards the camera and smiled roguishly and she stood with her shoulders hunched and her hands tucked under her armpits, laughing. She had a missing front tooth that put an asymmetry to her face, like a dark door in an empty white room.

They went for a walk every Sunday after. Martin picked her up from her door on French's Quay and they headed off for the day somewhere. He packed a lunch and an umbrella and kissed his aged mother and headed out of the family home in Ballyredmond village and he did not come home until the late evening; his mother sitting by the fire, crosswording on the armrest and stroking the cat on her lap with the bottom of a brandy glass.

He'd sit with her a while and make himself something small to eat and iron his shirt for the morning. He nodded at Elaine on a Wednesday in the office the way the others did and on a Friday he walked down to the Market Tavern Bar and nursed two pints before she walked in around seven from her mopping. There'd be a Friday verve in his voice and he'd rush to meet her as she came walking in, swivelling her head about the place and he'd hand her the Club Orange he'd taken a habit of ordering in the minutes before she came in; "I don't drink," she'd said on that first walk around Curraghbinny.

He collected her from a school she cleaned on her own on Saturdays in Ballinlough and they parked in Friar's Walk and talked for a while before she got out and walked down Barrack Street onto the quay. They held hands over the handbrake and when he leaned diffidently over to give her a kiss, she leaned in and kissed him back, and she knew that was all he needed, shy as he was, reciprocation, a halfway hand, a meeting of mouths; she licked the inside of his upper lip one day when they'd stopped along a path in Farran Woods and they walked on and pressed each other's hands and he brought up her hand to his mouth and kissed it tenderly.

One Sunday they drove to Dungarvan in Waterford. They came home in the late evening and Martin stopped off at the house in Ballyredmond.

"My mother was born in this house," he said. "She's never lived anywhere else. Nor me, actually."

His mother was sitting listening to the radio when they walked in.

"Mother, this is Elaine."

"Oh, hello, Elaine. Martin has told me all about you."

"Hello, Mrs Connolly," she said.

"Come and sit, come and sit."

Elaine went over and sat on the armchair across from Mrs Connolly and Martin went into the kitchen and put on the kettle. Elaine held her purse on her lap with both hands and her feet were together and in her shoes she coiled her toes.

Mrs Connolly was slim for her age and tall with grey hair that was parted in the middle and came down over her ears and was cut away at the cheek. Though it was small, her nose was thin and pointed and Elaine thought it quite elegant, along with the clothes she wore. A dark cardigan over a grey blouse with a dark skirt to the bottoms of her calves. She had golden stud earrings. Perhaps these were her Sunday clothes or perhaps such people dressed no other way, birth and environment giving their diktats for Mrs Connolly as they had for her and everyone else.

"Martin says you grew up in Blackpool."

"Yes, I did. Yes."

172

"Oh. Nice?"

"Yes."

"I knew someone from Blackpool once."

Elaine nodded and gave a half-smile and put her tongue in the socket of her tooth.

"You're an only child, Martin tells me."

"Yes."

"Like Martin himself. Ye're well suited. That's very rare."

"Yes."

"Poor Martin. I remember when he was in school. He'd come home and cry for not having brothers and sisters. I suppose by the time he was a teenager, he was delighted. We spoiled him, in a way. I heard that only children are the loudest people or the quietest. Our Martin is quiet. Are you quiet, dear?"

"I suppose I am quiet, yes."

"And I know your parents went to England when you were young. Martin was telling me. That must've been hard, I was sorry to hear that."

"I was eighteen, Mrs Connolly, so... they went away on the boat."

"Where did they go?"

"Cobh. Yes."

"No, where in England did they go?"

She shallowly jerked her shoulders and twitched her head to one side.

"London, I think."

"You're not sure?"

"No."

"Did they not write to you and tell you? I assume they write?"

She half nodded and half shook her head and shrugged her shoulders at the same time, like she was giving three answers at once or not giving an answer at all but rather shaking loose of the question.

There was no talk for a while, just the sound of Mrs Connolly sucking on her false teeth and swallowing her saliva.

"So you stayed in Blackpool, Elaine?"

"No. I left."

"Oh, you left?"

"Yes."

"And?"

"I just didn't want to be in Blackpool anymore—"

"I can imagine."

Martin came back into the room and stood behind his mother's chair and placed his hands on the backrest.

"So I came across to the southside. And I rented a place on Barracka."

"Where?"

"On Barrack Street. They call it 'Barracka'."

"I see."

Martin smiled at her as she spoke. He left again and came back in with a plate of salad and cold meat for them both. He handed Elaine a tray and then gave her the plate and she ate on her lap with the cutlery in the wrong hands and when she looked up now and again, mother and son looked back at her and at her food. When she finished, she wiped her mouth with a knuckle and then Martin rose and came back with a cloth napkin. She wiped her hands with it and put it on her plate.

"Would you like a brandy, dear?"

"No, thank you. I don't drink."

When Martin had finished his own food, he walked his mother out to the hall and up the stairs.

"Goodnight, Elaine. Nice to've met you."

"Nice to meet you Mrs Connolly," she said.

They did not fully close the door and she could hear their slow careful steps on the stairs and Martin going *hup* every few steps. Then she heard his mother.

"A Northside non-drinker – now that's something, Martin."

On their wedding day his cousin walked her up the aisle. She had not a single friend or relative to sit on her side of the church

174

so Martin instructed some of his relatives to fill in the other side and his mother gave explanations as to why not so much as an aunt or uncle existed of hers to attend, no friend parent or sibling or distant cousin. "Sure she's quiet out." That was the explanation he was used to giving himself. Quiet people don't accrue the social accoutrements. That's what he told his fiancée in the days before the wedding. That she wasn't to worry that the guests were all his. She told him she wasn't worried about that, but rather that she did not go to Mass, hadn't been inside a church for twenty years or more and perhaps it would be written on her walking up the aisle that she was a con, a non-believer and non-attender and the priest would run her out of there before she got to the top of the church. But her fears were allayed when she met Father Dan. She found him to be a lovely man. Gentle, with a warmth in his eyes and he'd touch them both as he spoke to them about the sacraments and how the ceremony would go and what their responses should be. Martin drove her home that night.

"I hope you'll be attending Mass when we're married," he said.

"Why?"

"Because – that's what people do. Aren't you afraid?"

"Of what?"

"Beyond here. Judgement Day. What you'll say to Jesus."

"I know what I'll say."

"We'll be the talk of the place, Elaine."

"I'd go. I nearly would. But all those words, the praying. I can't. If Jesus is who ye say he is – he'll have no problem with me. The reverse if anything. I might have a problem with him. I'll walk through the pearly gates and start pointing people out."

"I don't understand."

"I think I'll be fine on Judgement Day, if heaven is the place I'm told it is. If it's something else – if it's something else – maybe I don't want to get in. I'm going inside a church for the first time in twenty years and I'm doing that for you. There is no other way to be married and that's what I want to be. But that's it."

"Don't tell Father Dan that."

"Of course."

"Nice man."

"He is."

She walked up the aisle a week later in a single-breasted navy jacket and white blouse and a white skirt just below her knees and white shoes and there was silence in the church aside from the organ playing above her. She saw her husband-to-be standing there in his pressed suit with an uncomfortable smile on his face and he'd look at people in the pews as she approached. She heard her heels on the church tiles. Nothing echoes in the world like a church, she thought. It put a solemnity and gravity to every damn thing. Every step, every word. Forgive me, Jesus, she thought. I don't belong here in your house. I do it for him. For *him*.

She walked to Martin and took his hand and they both faced the altar.

"She's not eating, Martin."

"Mother, look – just leave it."

"Leave it?"

"Yes, just leave it be now awhile."

"Okay. Grand."

"It's fine."

"I'll leave it so."

"Thanks."

He went back to his newspaper and she went back to writing her letter. But he read nothing further nor did she write another word. A couple of minutes passed.

"It's just—" she said.

He dropped the paper on his lap and slapped it with the back of his hand.

"It's not like she can be losing weight."

"She's not well, mother, God almighty."

"Don't bother raising your voice now, Martin!" she said sternly.

"But it's always something, mother. 'She's still working, Martin'; 'She's very quiet, Martin'; 'What did she say, Martin?'; 'Why doesn't she go to Mass, Martin?' And who cares that she still cleans a school on a Saturday? She likes to get out of the house, she had to stop her old job once we married – which she liked. And so what if she's quiet? And I know you understand what she says. Making her repeat things – it's just a little dig – and don't think she doesn't know that. And now it's: 'She's not eating, Martin.'"

"She likes cleaning?"

"God almighty."

"Watch the tone, Martin."

"Maybe she grew to like it, yes. It might be satisfying – a bit – I suppose. Don't women naturally have a grá for such things?"

"Well, yes, but..."

"But?"

"But it's usually their own homes. Not for the love of cleaning itself."

"And Mass?"

"What about it?"

"She doesn't go."

"I asked her about that. I didn't know until we moved in here. I assumed she went on a Sunday before we went away for the day."

"Why doesn't she go?"

"I asked her. She said she just doesn't. She won't."

"She *won't*. Oh, that's brazen out! And yet she barely opens her mouth."

He nodded gently at his mother and the newspaper rustled when he crossed then uncrossed his legs under it.

"We look like eejits walking into Mass – just the two of us."

He nodded gently.

"They're thinking she's Protestant, Martin."

He held the newspaper with one hand and with the other he rubbed the side of his face and brought it across his lips and over the other side and out across his ear, then rubbed gently his earlobe.

"Well, better Protestant than…"

"Go on…" she said.

"You know – than just not going to Mass."

"Maybe. Maybe, Martin."

Eventually he lifted the newspaper from his lap and his mother's arm rested back on the table with the biro point hovering above the last word. She cleared her throat and wiped a hand across the pages and began blithely whispering the words of previous sentences.

"And Father Dan has noticed, of course," she said.

They had one or two more of those conversations. They started off about his wife not eating and veered off into all the other things she was or wasn't doing. In one of them he told his mother that every day his wife walks up behind the village to the new estate under construction to see how far along Number 11 was, so aching was she to get out from under the present roof, and his mother wouldn't talk to him for two days after. His wife would put on her coat to walk down the village to get a loaf of bread and her mother-in-law would be sitting in her chair and say, "Don't worry, Elaine, you're nearly free."

But she had stopped eating, almost entirely, and she'd never eaten much before. She'd stopped smoking as well. She might go the whole day on a slice of buttered bread and a couple of glasses of water and maybe a cigarette before she turned in for bed. And then the vomiting started, one afternoon when her husband was at work and she was putting on her coat to go, as her mother-in-law put it, 'checking when to pack'.

She ran to the kitchen sink and stood over it vomiting for a few minutes. Her mother-in law walked slowly to the sink and began rubbing her back, and when she was finished she lay her on the couch in the next room and turned on the kettle for some tea and walked out to the hall and phoned the doctor.

Martin came in from work and the two women were sitting at the kitchen table, drinking tea with a plate of buttered biscuits between them. Elaine could see the nervousness on her husband's face. She looked up to him through a sickly smile and he looked in her face and lay out his hands so that she might speak.

"Elaine."

"Martin," the two women said together, then exchanged glances and giggled a bit.

He reached for a buttered biscuit and walked over to the kettle and filled it with water then put it on the ring and turned it on.

He pulled up a chair and his wife looked at his mother. His wife's chin trembled the way it had when he asked her to marry him. The way it had when she walked to him on their wedding day. He stared at his mother. She stared back at him and smiled slightly, she gave little weaves of her head as though in resolution, or triumph. He looked over to his wife and she smiled again through the ardent retch-water of her eyes. His mother lay her hand across the table, as though giving her daughter-in-law the floor. But there was nothing.

"Go on, Elaine. Go on dear," his mother said.

His head flitted between the two women.

"What?" he said. "'Go on, what?"

"Go on, Elaine," she said again. They both smiled again.

"I'm pregnant," she whispered.

3

He was born in St Finbarr's Hospital on the 11th of August 1969, Michael Martin Connolly. His mother wanted to walk out of there the next day, stitches and all, but they kept her in for another week and told her to relax and enjoy the baby and the week off. A big, cheery, country nurse came and took her temperature and checked the baby and checked the mother's suture and told her as she stuffed another pillow behind her back that there was a saying from out her way: *You'd forget your name before any second of your first labour.* And of course she told her, as the midwives had, as every nurse she'd spoken to had, just how lucky she was: "Only ten minutes of pushing! That's unheard of for your first."

She walked down to the pay phone by the shop in the foyer and rang her husband and demanded to be taken home.

She'd spend the whole day in the nursery holding her baby and putting him down for a sleep and she'd stay watching him over the rim of his chrome basket until he woke a few hours later for a feed. On her ward she was the only woman who breastfed her baby. The nurse would ask her to go back to the ward for a sleep of her own and she'd head off and turn and stand at the doorway looking back to her baby and begin crying and the other mothers who sat in chairs and fed their babies their bottles would watch her warily, for who did she think she was, denying herself sleep only to watch her sleeping child, and as though they were only half interested in their babies just because they could walk away from the cradle for an hour or two to get some sleep.

One nurse remarked to her in the nursery, "Is it *me* you're watching, Elaine?"

She'd go down to the mother's ward and sit up in her bed crying silently and the other mothers would break off from their chat and watch her and turn to each other again in whispers. They were glad when she left; she could see it in their faces when she waved goodbye to them. The nurse told her husband some women were just 'prone to a bit of crying' after the baby came but it wouldn't last long and a nurse would be calling round in a fortnight to see how everything was.

But the crying stopped once she left the hospital, like she'd promised it would. Martin drove home and his wife cradled her baby in the backseat and Martin watched her in the rear-view mirror smiling down at her son and gently pushing her little finger through his tiny fist, touching her lips to his lips to breathe him in, to wear him on her lungs, in her blood, as before.

"God, I've never seen someone hate a coddling like you, Ellie."

She looked up from the baby and into the rear-view mirror but said nothing and looked down again.

"Hmm?" he said, awaiting a response.

"I just don't like hospitals. All the beds in a line. And... and the... babies, crying."

She looked down again at her son and dipped her lips onto his. A tear rolled off her cheek and fell onto her baby's closed eyelid and his eyelid flinched and she licked it away and dried it with ethereal dabs of her nose.

A month before her son was born they'd moved into Number 11 The Orchard, a four-bed semi in a development of four-bed semis a few fields and a copse of trees to the rear of the derelict Somerville House, named after its orchard which they'd cut down and torn out to build those very houses. The Orchard was the first estate built up there, but others would follow down the years; Somerville View in the eighties which was set further back and across the road on slightly higher ground, allowing it the

View of the house's chimney pots which looked like blackened chess pawns poking out of the trees. The Willows would come in the nineties and Oakwood in the early noughties.

Her mother-in-law wanted to stay in her own house down in the village but her husband wouldn't listen. "No, mother," he said. "All the Connollys live together. That's what family is," and he shipped her up to The Orchard and gave her the second biggest bedroom and the back dining room to decorate as she saw fit which amounted to a cushioned armchair and a foot pouffe and a painting of a mountain and a picture of the Sacred Heart that had been over her own mantelpiece for sixty years and the clock her husband had received on his retirement.

The baby's crying came one day, close to summer; piecemeal and slight at first, like memos slipped under the door, but it grew and grew, longer and louder by the night until it was honed to a murderous tinny rasp in the deep night that set her whimpering in the dark with her hands clasped at her chest like she was praying to god for sleep. Sometimes she'd spend the night walking him across her room and somewhere near daylight the room would go silent and she'd lay him gently in the bassinette and collapse in her clothes on top of the mattress and five minutes in he'd start up that jittery new-lung bawl. Her mother-in-law told her about a woman back in her day, it was in the papers, a woman over in Glasheen; she hadn't slept in three weeks, she'd said. Didn't know what she was doing, she'd said. Couldn't take anymore crying. That's what she told the Gardaí: *I couldn't take any more crying.*

"Her own child, Mrs Connolly?"

"By accident."

"How?"

"Don't know, dear. Shaking, maybe. The poor creature. But a screaming baby – day in and day out. The child could have acid pain. Desperate. You wouldn't be right in the head from it."

"Was Martin like that?"

"No. His cousin was, though. My sister's son. Desperate. She was demented from it."

When her husband returned from work in the evening he'd sit with his wife and baby and his mother would tell him he was the lucky one, being able to leave. He'd walk in around six in the evening and his wife might be scraping the infant's faeces from the cloth napkins with a butter knife then wiping the knife with toilet paper and flushing the paper down the toilet. She soaked the dirty napkins in the plastic basin he'd bought her in Roches Stores for that very purpose and scrub them on the washboard then hang them on the clotheshorse she'd pushed up next to the radiator in their bedroom. She doused his behind with baby powder and wrapped him in cellular blankets and breastfed him on the edge of her bed with muslin under his chin, listening to the alternate cadences of swallow and breath and the gluttonous hums of a feeding baby and she'd rub his hair with her thumb.

Her mother-in-law walked into the house one day leaning on the outstretched arm of a cab man and under her armpit she carried something like orange juice or a loaf of bread wrapped in a plastic bag. She walked up and placed it on the kitchen table and turned around and paid the cab man. She turned back to the table as the cab man walked out to the hall. She pulled off the plastic bag and tapped the top of the bottle and stroked the glass with her finger.

"Milk of magnesia, Elaine." She tapped the top again. "Maybe. We'll see."

When her baby cried in the night and his hiccups echoed in the room like a recurring sleep deprivation nightmare she gave him the milk of magnesia that his grandmother had bought from the chemist and she rubbed his hair until he fell off to sleep again and sometimes she put him down and he wouldn't stop crying until he was picked up again and she knew it was going to be one of those nights. But he was getting better; she went herself down to the chemist when the milk of magnesia had run low and the lady behind the counter gave her some baby rice, so she went home and gave the child a few spoons of it that evening. He didn't stir again until her husband closed the cupboard door the following morning. So he got it every evening, and then every afternoon, and the crying drifted away like it had never been but somewhere in her dreams.

Her mother-in-law died when her son was two years old. They had grown close by then. Her son would walk around the downstairs clanking pots and pans together and hammering the lids against the floors and the two women would take turns to watch him so the other could escape for a while; the relieving supervisor would pick up the pack of cigarettes where the other had left them and sit back amidst the mayhem. His grandmother bought him a plastic play kitchen set for his second birthday and he cried because the utensils were so small and the pots and pans didn't make the noise of steel ones.

She had a stroke a few weeks later. She fell off the side of her chair and Elaine ran out to the hall and phoned for the ambulance, then ran back and held her head in her lap. She was up in hospital for a week, unconscious. Then she died.

Michael was an only child when he started school. His house was a quiet house, as his mother was. On the odd occasion she stepped into someone else's doorway, perhaps to collect Michael from a birthday party, she would block her ears against the noise and she'd stand at her windows sometimes and watch the other children in the estate playing and fighting. She watched her son amongst them. She watched him crying out there sometimes and turn away towards his own gate and she'd rush out to meet him and carry him into the house. In time, that's all anyone would ever see of her. Standing at the window watching her son. The other children would sometimes look back at her and move away. They chanted at him one day, *The devil's fork's in Michael's ass, 'cause his mother won't go to Mass!* He went home and asked his mother why she didn't go to Mass and she said nothing and rubbed his hair and carried on polishing the mahogany.

For a while after her mother-in-law died, it seemed to her like she was still somehow living there with them, like some night worker who came and went when they weren't looking, for the back room had remained as it was the day she had the stroke, and it smelled like her still, for no one went back there, and lacked reason to, so the back dining room remained a silent, untelevisioned room with ghost-odours of tobacco and urine and perfume, a bed and a commode being back there for her last year when the stairs were too much. They called it 'mother's room.'

Elaine gradually began to go down there; she'd lean against the headrest of the bed with a book or magazine, usually after dinner and for longer spells on a Saturday when Michael would walk in the door having been out all day in the park or down the GAA pitches. He'd come in and ask his father where his mother was, saying he was hungry. His father would say she was back in 'mother's room' and Michael would say, "Still?" and his father would just say airily, "Yeah" or playfully "Yessiree", like they did in those cowboy shows he watched at the weekend. They eventually took out the bed and put in a two-seater couch and she would be sitting on it with a blanket over her legs when her six-year-old would walk in and find her there in the silence. She'd look up to him when he walked in. "Michael," she'd say, and she'd slide a finger into her book and close it and tap the couch for him to come and sit. He'd look about the room and inhale through his nose and scrunch his face.

"Nah," he'd say.

He'd walk out and she would pick up her book and continue reading. There was something about the room she liked. Detached from the rest of the house, unused and yet older-looking, some kind of domestic anachronism that the rest of the house had somehow attached itself to; the odours of age and the old clock and old painting and the Sacred Heart that was older than them all; the sun-faded Jesus had turned near to the beige of the background and the heart a dull pink and the blue of his eyes had bleached to the glacial blue of her own. And what was wrong with it? she thought. What was wrong with a woman finally using the dining room of her house for the first time since she moved in six years before, what was wrong with her taking time away from her cleaning for some moments alone with a novel after dinner? Nothing; there was nothing at all wrong with it.

They drove up to Nenagh in Tipperary to her husband's old uncle and his wife in the old family farmhouse. The Connollys had bought the land from the Land Commission way back in 1911. Uncle Joe was given the farm in 1937 and the rest were cast unto the world; one son went and fought for the Brits in the second war and died somewhere in North Africa and another went off to America and was never heard from again, and another, Martin's father, went south to Cork and nuzzled his way into the civil service.

They went up one September morning and arrived in the farmyard in the afternoon and the dogs came up to the car as they pulled in and walked around the car smelling the tyres. There were no children on the farm for Uncle Joe didn't marry until he was in his fifties and his bride was the same age; two old things had walked down the aisle without a parent either side and the locals had wondered whether it was worth his while at all taking a wife when she was past bearing age. Some farmers did and some did not. Some old farmers sat around the bars at night with fellow virgins with veined faces and seemed each other's brides.

When the drink driving laws came in, they stopped going out for a pint in the evening and a lot of the old country bars closed down. Gleeson, with 140 acres across the way from Uncle Joe, walked a few times all the way into town for a pint until his hip got sore, then he stopped going; sat around in the old farmhouse in the silence and went out one day and took the rope from the gate up the fields and went into the hayshed he'd put up with his father sixty years before.

"Takin' a few pints from a man in the evenin'll do a lot worse – believe me – than what he'd do behind any feckin' wheel."

That's what Uncle Joe said about it; he'd look out across the fields in the direction of Gleeson's place and drop his head sideways to whatever he was doing like he was gauging something.

She watched her son watch him, this man of the earth and grass and cow shit and all three camped under his fingernails and in the breath he breathed; a different order, the culchie; dirty and coarse and half-feral and seeming both to celebrate and be oblivious to it, like Norries with money, she thought, and she laughed to herself. Uncle Joe put his elbows on the table and drank his tea and pulled on his eyebrows and moaned about his piss-broken sleep and the pains in his fingers and the soap rashes he'd been getting and he pulled away his collar to show them. The four of them went walking across the land after dinner out to some fence he'd been putting up with some young lad from the town and off over to the fields he was letting out to someone else and she lagged behind the men with her son and they watched the two men walking across the land together. In his ninth decade Uncle Joe was still shearing hedges and arguing with the Co-Op man and digging post holes with a hand-held auger; she watched them and thought them not so distant in age and she turned over the backs of her hands and studied them for she did not wish to see age on her husband alone.

"You're some man for one man, Joe," his nephew said.

"Erra sure, I've no child to be worrying about. A child will be the death of you. Sure I've always said that."

He turned back and pointed at Michael and winked and put up his giant fists to mimic a boxer. Elaine watched him and thought there was something in that, that you poured some of your own years into your child's. Perhaps it was true, that the childless lived longer. She had never known a parent without pain. No, she thought. For the love and torment cancel each other. The childless experience neither. She could tell Uncle Joe, she thought. She could tap him on the shoulder and she could tell him. A child would not be the death of you. The death of you would be the child's death. She turned over her hands again and walked on across the fields with her son.

After he showed them the fence, they walked over to some tarpaulin he'd been using to clear up the wood detritus of a storm the week before; they helped him load on some branches and Joe perused them and picked up a few and walked to a hedge close by and dropped them there and kicked them parallel, came back and said, "No good". They went up and came back to the yard twice or three times, the four of them pulling the tarp across the grass. They came back and had dinner and when they sat into the car in the evening the sun was dying way off at the rim of the great green and the clouds in the west had vermillion edges.

It was close to eleven when they got home. They got out of the car and Martin put the key in the front door. The hall was in total darkness as were the stairs and the landing above it. The door to the kitchen was shut. Martin went in first and then Michael and then his mother. Martin dropped his keys carefully on the hall table and walked over and turned on the light. He walked down towards the kitchen, and Michael stepped into the hall and followed him. She stood in the hall for a while. The kitchen light was off, as was the light in the back room. She walked into the kitchen and went out into her mother-in-law's backroom and sat on the couch for a while with her feet tucked up under her and her coat still on.

She could hear her husband and son talking. She heard the kettle being filled and the fridge opening and cupboards closing.

"Elaine," her husband called. "Elaine."

She heard his feet on the kitchen tiles and then the abrupt quiet when he reached the carpet.

"Ellie?"

"Yes," she said.

"Some toast?"

"No, thank you."

"Are you alright?"

"I'm fine."

"Grand."

She rose and walked past him pulling off her coat and she went upstairs and took off her clothes and put on her nightdress and dressing gown and went back down the stairs again and walked past them and back out to the room where she'd sat before.

After a while, her son came in to her in his pyjamas.

"Goodnight, Mammy," he said.

She was in the brown dressing gown that she'd bought for St Finbarr's six years before but it rose on her legs now and stretched tighter across her shoulders and was faded to close on the tobacco tint of her fingers. She held the sides of her wedding ring with her thumbs and fingers and turned it softly as if it were a tiny steering wheel. She looked over at him.

"Come sit," she said, and she tapped the couch beside her.

He stood for a moment, then walked over and sat down next to her. She leaned back and put her legs on the floor and slipped her ring back on her finger and wedged it at her knuckle, then she put her left arm around the shoulder of her son and brought it down so her hand held his side.

"Mammy," he said. "Are you a different sort of Mammy?"

"Why do you say that?"

"You don't talk to other Mammies. You don't talk like them. You don't really talk. You like to just stay at your house and do cleaning."

"But I talk to you, don't I?"

"Yes."

"And Daddy."

"Yes."

"Well – who else is there?"

"Teacher asked me if you were sick."

"When?"

"Ages ago."

"Why did he say that?"

"'Cause Daddy went to see him for the parent-teacher meeting."

She stared ahead and nodded gently.

"I never liked schools, Michael. Those corridors that echo. Virgin statues and crosses every two feet. I sent your father. I find them – schools – just awful. Not that you should."

"Sometimes..."

"Sometimes," she said.

"Sometimes... I think you might cry."

"When?"

"Just sometimes. I hate that."

She lifted him wholly onto her lap and she wrapped her arms around him and began kissing his face and ear and the side of his head.

"No," she said.

She rocked him gently and gave approximate little looks about the room and her head weaved gently like grass in the wind.

"Mammy," he said.

"Yes?"

"Where's the Sacred Heart?"

He pointed above the mantelpiece and she took her face from his face and looked up there. Then she looked away to a space of carpet.

"Gone," she said. "I took it down a while back."

She let her hand fall down the back of his head and onto his neck and she rubbed his neck with the backs of her fingers. They did not speak and she could hear his breathing change after a while and she let his head down on her lap and she ran her fingers through his hair and over his ear and caressed his face with her thumb and she watched his eyelids close and flicker and capillaries shape out of them like river systems in some minute landscape. She sat in the silence for a long time, stroking his hair. She leaned over and slipped her ring from her knuckle and read the inscription on the inside, then pressed it to her lips.

"My darling baby," she whispered.

She thought of her first-born and wept silently, for he had died on this day thirty years before and she looked down at her second-born breathing in his sleep and she could feel his heat and the oil of his hair on her fingertips and she thought of the man he would be and she thought of a man who never was.

4

S he sat up in bed and tapped a cigarette over the saucer that lay in the valley between her legs and she looked down to it and took it up and shook it gently like she was panning for gold. The ash drew in towards the centre and she set the saucer down and pulled on her cigarette and tapped away again.

It was late afternoon and some clouds had come in and dulled the blankets. The curtains were pulled back and tied and a vase of daffodils was pushed to one side as though to better the light and the view, and she figured her husband had done that while she slept. The doctors had told him to let in the air, to leave out the smoke, to let in the day, to block out the night; like there was some arcane balance between air and light and cure, a gravity to every sight, to the very yellowness of the daffodils and drift of the dust motes. She could tell the time of day by the shadows in the folds of the blankets and the dimness of the wall in front of her. She stared at the wall for a long, long time, like there was cure in its whiteness, a cure from the things she said, the things she'd seen. They were going to put her in an asylum for those things now. Cure the land of the likes of her. Nothing changes, she thought. The mouths and legs of women. Dangerous things when they're open.

When she was twelve years old, she walked with her mother into town two days before Christmas. They held hands on the thronged footpaths so they would not lose each other and she felt the hardness of her mother's hand and when she squeezed it slightly, she could feel the strength of it. There was a smell of mothballs and snuff and when a motorcar went by the fumes would linger amidst the coats on the footpath and she'd breathe deep and loud and her mother would giggle and wag their hands.

They stood at the crib on St Patrick's Street and lit a candle and said a prayer and her mother handed the nuns a penny and they went on up to Roches Stores and her mother had a tea and warm scone and butter and she bought Elaine a cup of warm milk and she'd break off bits of scone and hand them to her. Her mother went through the contents of her bag on the table; she had bought cloves and tinsel and fruit for the stockings, a pair of socks for her husband, some hairpins for herself and her daughter.

She watched people at the table next to her watch the fruit and she was proud, proud of the orange and the bright redness of the apples. Her mother bought another tea and began to look at her watch when she put the cup down. Her daughter watched her and grew nervous.

"What time we meeting Daddy, Mammy?"

Her mother looked at her watch again. "Six."

"At Cash's, Mammy?"

"Yes, love."

"Is Daddy finished his porter?"

She looked at her watch again. "Nearly."

They walked out of Roches Stores and went down St Patrick's Street and her father was standing outside the doors of Cash's, leaning on one foot and looking about and nodding at people who passed by. He had the droopy lower lip that he got every Christmas and the porter glaze in his eyes. When he saw them, he straightened up and walked briskly up to them and he kissed his wife on both cheeks and she brushed him off and looked around her. He bent down and did the same to his daughter and his daughter giggled and her mother scolded them both.

"Stop, Christy," she said. "You're not in Paris. Every Christmas it's the same."

She turned and walked up St Patrick's Street and father and daughter smiled at each other and walked after her. They walked over Patrick's Bridge and headed down Coburg Street and Devonshire Street onto Lower John Street and all the way up Watercourse road to Number 18 Madden's Buildings. Her mother was cranky for a while when they got home and her father was quiet and he'd wink at his daughter and glance in the way of her mother and roll his eyes and she'd laugh quietly behind her hand.

He said eventually, "Erra Christ, woman – once a year a fella has a drink. Would ya rather be down the way?" and he gestured over his shoulder with his thumb. "Or across there, la? Or up in 28 or would ya rather be Mrs Forde or Mrs McCarthy? No – ya wouldn't. A man goes for a drink at Christmas and he'll hear about it for twelve months."

He looked at his daughter who had come and sat on the rug in front of the fire. She hated when they fought. It only happened at Christmas when he drank. And he was right. Other fathers were worse. She knew things. Children didn't look away. There was nowhere to look sometimes in the lane but in a window; you look up from your ballahs or glassy-alleys or hopscotch and there was always something happening inside a window. A newspaper being read, dinner being cooked, rosaries said, fists thrown. She heard about it if she didn't see it: who got a day's work in Murphy's Brewery, whose mother was pregnant again, who was coughing more than usual, who got trounced in school, who got trounced at home, who was half starved, who got help from the priest, who drank all his wages, who bought their house off the Corpo. A Christmas drunkenness she would take gratefully. Her father was the best of the fathers. Children in the lane knew things, and they knew the standing of their parents there.

After her tea she got up from the table and with her parents still eating she walked by the sideboard and there she saw a glass of red lemonade next to the bottle. She picked up the glass and looked over her shoulder at her parents then threw it back in two big swallows. She felt sick immediately. A nauseous burn in her throat and stomach. She ran to the front door and opened it and rushed out and vomited in the lane. She stayed there on her hands and knees for five minutes, vomiting and retching and she could hear doors opening up and down the lane and zealous foreheads pressed and squeaking on the windows and giddy murmurs of children and parents shushing them to better hear the regurgitant pitch.

Her mother knelt at her side and rubbed her back in circles and called aloud, "Oh Sacred Heart, Elaine, you drank your father's whiskey and red! Ya poor thing. You weren't to know. You weren't to know."

When she got her off her knees, she wiped her mouth and they went inside. Her father sat in his chair with his arms folded high on his chest and her mother stood looking at her with tears in her eyes and there was no sound across the stone floor except when the coal shifted and the flame flapped and settled.

"Elaine," her mother said finally, drawing her fingers slowly down her cheeks until they touched prayer-like under her chin. "Your pledge."

It was a Wednesday, 23rd of June 1943. Not the greatest night for Bonfire Night but she supposed a Wednesday night would drain the mothers and fathers away faster and they would take the small ones with them and all that would be left would be the older kids who had neither a job nor school to be worried about in the morning.

She heard the boys behind her in the lesser light, sniggering and play-fighting and they'd momentarily gather in circles, as though for a pep talk, and break off again and one or two would occasionally come through the crowd rolling a tyre or carrying a pallet or furze bush and cast it into the flames and slink back through the crowd out to the deeper shadows and turn around to the towering flame again and give parental nods to it, like it was born of them – a fire-child they'd raised up and unfurled upon the people of Blackpool who'd come to watch and clap and compare it to other years, other children.

And she was right. The mothers and fathers and young children all disappeared by ten o'clock, and nearly all at once, like some bell had gone off calling them home. Those who remained, older children and teenagers and the odd old bachelor, they moved closer to the fire and stared into it like their lives were patterned out in the flames and when a wind picked up they'd turn their faces away and step back for a while, then inch towards it again. Some smoked and drank from whiskey bottles they kept in their jackets.

An old man stood alone on the other side of the fire. There were bits of food and tobacco paper in his beard which was grey except where it matted at the sides of his mouth and condensed to the colour of rust and dirt. He looked at the boys nearby and edged closer, then asked each of them for a cigarette and a nip from their bottles and she watched them wave him away or turn their heads out and look past him to the fire like he wasn't there. A boy gave him a cigarette and the old man thanked him and called him 'sir' and he put it in the breast pocket of his shirt and pulled the grotty lapel of his jacket across it in some custodial impulse like it was everything he owned and he walked back to where he'd stood before and he looked back into the fire as though newly worthy of it. He waited a while, then took out the cigarette and smoked it with rhapsodic quivers in his hand. He flicked the end into the fire and stood and stared after it for a time, then began edging back towards the boys.

She could smell the whiskey. She thought of Christmas, six months ago now. She'd never got sick like that before. Her stomach lurching. Her mother down with her on her knees. She could taste the whiskey for hours after. She watched the boys reach into their jackets and pull out their bottles and drink and wince and return them. They laughed and shoved each other towards the fire. Some fell and lay on the grass laughing.

A boy came up to her and asked her for a cigarette and walked away and laughed with his friends and they looked over at her and laughed some more and she stuck up two fingers at them and they went quiet. Another boy came over and stood next to her. They talked for a while, then he opened his coat and pulled out a bottle of whiskey and drank from it. He was putting it away and then he stopped and held it out in front of her and she looked at it and shook her head. He took the cap off and jigged the bottle.

"G'on," he said. He looked down at her bare legs. "It'll warm ya."

She stood for a while and just looked at it. Then she reached out slowly and took hold of the bottle and she held it out from her as though to keep it distant or to take it in more fully. She brought her nose to the top of the bottle.

"Don't do that," the boy said. "You won't touch it if you smell it."

She put the bottle to her mouth and watched the boys watch her from across the fire. She raised it up and took a mouthful of whiskey and held it in her mouth for a moment and dropped her head down and pressed her eyes closed and clenched her fist. Then she swallowed it and coughed and handed the bottle back and some of the boys chuckled. No red lemonade this time, just whiskey. She was different now. Just turned thirteen. Tough-as-nails Elaine Dillon. Twelve years old she broke her pledge – eight months into it. She wasn't to know, but in the end, what did it matter? The days of our lives unfurl like the blooms of spring, she thought. All different and similar and irrevocable.

The boy drank again from the bottle and handed it to her and she lifted it to her mouth again and took another drink. It was Bonna Night and there was whiskey and the world was beautiful.

She woke from the cold when the fire had died and she was alone and there was no light. She did not move. She stared into the black sky. The remnant smoke trickled on up and greyed out batches of stars. She could hear the fire squeak and snap like it was bemoaning its end. She figured someone must have dragged her there for whatever warmth was left in it. She sat up and looked around her and said "Hello?" but there was no sound. She pulled up her dress and looked down between her legs, then drew them up and hugged them and rocked back and forth.

"Mother of Jesus – please – no," she said.

She could feel the heat of the chafe inside her and the cold of the track of discharge down her thigh. On the other thigh was a biscuit-sized patch of blood from which a single drop had run towards her knee and dried and cracked now in her movements. She climbed slowly to her feet and pulled up her knickers and straightened them on her hips then she pulled down her dress to her knees then pulled it even at her shoulders. She whimpered as she brushed the grass from her dress and wiped the backs of her legs. She walked away and felt a warmth drip into her knickers.

"Mother of Jesus, no," she said.

Her mother walked out the big North Infirmary gates and she followed behind at a distance and she wondered for a while about all the gates and walls that were going up around the place. She felt that she was dreaming. That she'd surely wake from the dream with her mother patting her forehead and none of it, none of it would have been remotely real. And as she walked behind her mother she let her mind wander to where it wandered, half-presuming everything pointless anyway for she was sure to wake soon, and so she brazenly rubbed her belly and thought of her bastard child in there and the pretty dress of a passer-by and the gates going up all over. Half the country seemed to be put to work at some wall or other. Schools and convents and churches and hospitals and the decent with a few bob spare. One of those big places over in St Luke's, they had three men on ladders mounting a wrought iron fence atop a wall with all the spikey railheads sticking out, things that would pass right through you if you had the notion of climbing over. The decent were all walls and gates nowadays, she thought. In the lane, it was a number for your door if your father was working. Bright, brass numbers shined up daily like the postman had gone near blind and could only tell one door from another by the glint coming off it.

Her mother looked back over her shoulder and then kept walking and a dog straddled her for a while and her mother slowed and shooed it away and walked on and when a fellow pedestrian walked with her awhile she came back and caught her daughter's hand and pulled her up the road without saying a word.

She'd sat in the examination room in the hospital and she'd watched the doctor walk outside and call her mother. She'd heard the click of her mother's knitting needles as she collected them in one hand and stood up.

"Mrs Dillon?"

"Yes."

"In here, please."

"Is she alright, doctor?"

He'd closed the door behind her mother and brought her over to where she sat upright on the padded table with her clothes on.

"Is she alright, doctor?"

He'd seemed to be close to tears or rage.

"Mrs Dillon... she's with child."

When they'd walked out of the examination room her mother had looked away from the people waiting and when they'd walked out the door of the hospital she could see by the tiny jumps in her mother's back and the back of her head that she was most probably weeping and she'd watched her pull her handkerchief from her bag and wipe her face with it then hold it over her mouth. She never spoke.

The doctor had not spoken to her as she left. He'd said only "Up," and gestured at the door. She'd seen the doctor bless himself over at his table. She'd seen the look on his face as she was leaving. It reminded her of faces in the Warsaw Ghetto; she'd seen pictures on the footpath in town at the feet of the paperboy, the confusion and horror in the eyes.

As she walked, she knew there would be no waking. She'd already woken: that night by the bonfire, the first cramp, the first late day. She'd probably have to leave the lane. She might have to stay at her auntie's in Limerick. She'd get a clatter off her as well. That was the least she'd get when she went home, she thought. A clatter from her mother. Her father never put a hand on her. Some men just don't have that streak, the need to reach out and hurt, and withdraw sated. The doctor had looked like he would have if he could. He'd looked like he was trembling under his coat, like he was holding off throttling her or fainting. You know you're in it when you've sickened a doctor. But she would tell them. She knew what she was going to say to her father: *Daddy, I didn't know. It was Bonna Night. I had a drink of whiskey. I don't remember…*

She walked and she rolled the sentences through her mind; I didn't know, I don't remember, I didn't see a thing, I was barely there. I didn't do it. It was done to me. Yes, yes, *it was done to me.* A mile from home her mother began to near run, a light jig in her stride that she'd never seen before.

When she eventually turned in to the lane, she could see halfway down that her mother had left their door open. There was a small comfort in that. She'd walk in and sit them down and start off with: *I'm innocent. I didn't do this.*

She walked up to the door and walked through it into the dark and closed it behind her. Her father stood facing the fire with his head dipped and blowing his smoke down towards the flames. The door of her parents' bedroom was closed. She supposed her mother was somewhere behind it. She could hear the hum of the fire and the blithe whistle of the wind in the chimney chamber, like some trivial agony. She stood in the dark by the door and she did not speak and her father did not speak and they stayed like that for a long time.

When her legs began to tire, she leaned against the door. As though suddenly aware of her, her father broke from the fire and walked up to her and paused. He looked back at the fire. He turned back to his daughter and he looked into her face. He had tears in his eyes and she had an urge to kiss him. He drove his fist hard into her mouth and she fell up against the door and hit her head, then he dragged her into the fire's light. He kneeled over her and caught her jaw and pulled her face up to his.

"No, daughter," he said. "You didn't!"

Then he slammed his fist into her mouth again and a tooth clicked on the floor. He rose to his feet, patted his hair at the door, and walked out.

She lay on the floor in a silent concussive reverie, rhythmically swallowing her blood and gazing up at the ceiling. She thought, what did I do, Jesus? Oh God of mercy, what did I do? It's gone. The Christmas child on St Patrick's Street is gone.

She slowly got to her knees. "Sorry," she wept. She looked at her mother's door and said, "Sorry, Mammy." She held her belly with one hand and she cupped the other under her gushing mouth. "Sorry, Mammy," she said. "It wasn't... I didn't..."

Her blood pooled in her hand like an infernal black lake and a chink of light from the fire put a crimson to its edges and her tears dripped down off her nose and vanished into it. She knee-walked to the fire and tipped her hand into the flames and placed it back under her mouth. She stroked her belly with her thumb and looked back towards her mother's door.

"Sorry, Mammy," she cried.

Her father stood out in the lane looking up towards the road but the light was young and the mist was down and he could not see much beyond the few cottages either side but he looked on up to the gap anyway like he was mapping a path up there. He gouged his palate with his tongue and clenched his eyes and drove his fingers through his hair and he'd look back at his own door as though he might just go back inside, forget the whole thing.

"We could leave," she'd heard him say to her mother in the night. They could all leave. They could go to Cobh and buy a family-fare and never come back. "Tell them all... tell them all nothing. Just disappear."

The door opened and she came out and closed the door behind her. She stood there with her head bowed, zipping her long coat over her Mass clothes. She held a piece of bread in her hand. He walked up the lane and disappeared into the mist. She walked after him.

They walked into town and crossed over Patrick's Bridge and went down St Patrick's Street and through Winthrop Street, across Oliver Plunkett Street and onto the South Mall. He walked ahead of her as his wife had done the day before and, as with his wife, he would look back at her and find her face in the crowd and carry on. They never spoke.

They went down Anglesea Street and she saw up ahead some chatty nurses coming out a doorway and her father step sideways through them and pull his jacket straight and carry on. She stepped onto the road to read the words over the door: Victoria Hospital. She'd heard of such a place, some childhood telling of the places in this world where the skin scorches on your shoulder should you ever dare to cross the threshold for they were Protestant buildings and as doomed as all within, as were any of the true faith who poked a face in to glean how they cursed and mocked the Virgin Mary and the body and blood of her son. She watched the nurses cross the road like they were of another world and she shook her head at their mirth and pitied them for what lay ahead, for their not knowing what was coming. They disappeared into a tea shop on the other side of the road and she returned her gaze to her father's back. He headed up Southern Road and when he got to the top he turned and lit a cigarette and stood watching her for a while. When she got close enough to see the lick of sweat on his face and the bloodshot in his eyes, he turned and walked on.

They walked passed St Finbarr's Hospital and she remembered hearing somewhere that it was once the workhouse for the people of Cork during the famine and a lot of people died in there and the Brits deserved all the Kilmichael ambushes in the world for what happened in there alone. It was a hospital now, for southside babies among other things. Her baby wouldn't be in there. They don't put Norries in southside hospitals. They don't line up the bastards alongside the wedlocked cradles. The unwed don't lie in wards with the wed.

Pascal Moore came back from the war with shrapnel in his knee to his mother's in the lane. They said he was seen down the quays one night with one of the women that'd be down there. The kids chanted at him *Pascal Moore, where's the whoore! Pascal Moore, where's the whoore!* He'd turn and limp after them like some fool in a three-legged race with himself, but he'd never catch them. They'd laugh and chant it some more as he hobbled away. He's still there with his mother in Number 62. He doesn't chase the children anymore. Doesn't come out his mother's front door, and he only twenty-odd years of age.

But she was no whoore. She was not one of those women down the quays. This was done to her. She may not be St Finbarr's – but she was as far from the quays. After this journey, wherever it led, after today, she would know; like a wandering water, she would eventually steady and stop, at her place, at her level.

They walked down the Douglas Road and out into the countryside where blackberries and briars reached over the wall and fields of sheep and cows were edged with nettles and the odd great tree stood adamant out in the expanse and a gentry house was dying on a hill way off and a motor car came along and set the animals nervous and looking out to the road. They walked up a low rise and when she got to the top the road sloped away to the village of Douglas below and she saw a steeple rising up out of some trees and she walked on down, figuring she had it worked out, she knew where she was going. He'd walk on out to where he'd never been and would never go again and he would walk her into a church and a priest and she would give her confession and no one but some distant Douglas priest would ever know a thing. The priest could cast her to hell all he wanted, he could give her penance of a thousand Hail Marys and be more sickened than the doctor in the North Infirmary and they would walk back those roads and back over the river and that would be that. She would go to her auntie's in Limerick and have her baby and that would be that. Madden's Buildings would never know. You dump the bodies in a hole outside of town. That's what she heard they did with the workhouse dead long ago. Took them up Carr's Hill on a cart and tipped them in. You walk far enough so's the putrid wind can't follow, walk back across the river cleaner than a Christmas bath. It was thinking like that had her father with a job since he was thirteen.

But they did not walk into Douglas Village. Just before, they turned up left onto the Well Road. It was then he seemed to lose his breath and she began to catch up with him and he would look behind to her and notice her close and push on again as best he could, then slow again.

When she was close behind she could hear him wheeze and he would gather up some phlegm and spit it on the ground and take his handkerchief from his pocket and wipe his mouth and then his brow and return it to his pocket. He looked back and saw her right there behind him. Now that they had looked in each other's eyes, she dared to speak.

"Where we going, Daddy?"

He turned and walked up the road in silence with the fields of Blackrock rolling away to a sudden rise like a hiccup in the land the way of those hills up behind Blackpool and the clouds dropped low as though remembering the dawn and she thought: Blackpool or Blackrock, the wind doesn't know where it blows nor the clouds where they ride low or the river what's on either side. Or the baby that it's base-born. Someone goes and tells them.

He carried on with those shorter steps he'd taken up since turning up the Well Road and he looked around more now as though looking for a signpost or someone to ask and when a man came towards him on the path he faced into the hedging until the last moment and as they passed the man said, "Hello to you," and her father just nodded into his chest and wiped his hair into its crease with the flat of his hand, then he walked on and turned back and watched the man as he passed and said the same to his daughter.

He came to a right turn off the main road and she saw him stop there and face up the road to a cottage half nudged out of the fog with a red tin corrugated roof and pitchfork standing upright in the soil at its front window and a dog barking somewhere unseen up there and he turned back over his shoulder to her for a moment, then returned fully to the cottage. He looked manically at his watch, then up to the sky as though incredulous of the hour, then he spun back to the cottage, then back to her, then he rolled a pebble with the sole of his shoe then kicked it away and dropped down to one knee and untied his shoelace, then tied it again. All the while, his head flicked between his advancing daughter and the cottage with the standing pitchfork. As she approached, he stood up, brushed his trousers, took a last look up to the cottage and hurried right off the main road.

He could see the gates, there was a gentle collaborative sloping down to them and as he approached he could see that they were not the forbidding black that he had first discerned but a welcoming cast-iron white with two outlying ornamental pillars and two inner ones, above which stretched the words, themselves in cast-iron, *The Sacred Hearts of Jesus and Mary* and the trees either side caressed and canopied overhead as though giving the words shelter; he stood there for a while looking back up the slope with his hand on the latch of the gate, waiting for her to shape out of the fog. A gate-lodge stood just inside. As she approached, he turned, slid the latch across and attempted to walk through, but the gate didn't open.

A figure came and stood at the window of the lodge. As his daughter made her way towards him, he shook the gates repeatedly and pressed the latch up and down then he walked out to the wider pillars looking for a pedestrian entrance in the railing and came back and shook the gates again. The door of the lodge opened slowly and he looked up and saw a man of his own age walking towards him. The man wore a shirt and tie inside his brown cardigan and big brown coat that wasn't buttoned. His hair was uncombed and there were crumbs on his cardigan like he'd been at his breakfast.

"Yes, sir?" he said.

"I'm here with my daughter." He pulled at the gates again and the man just watched with a blank face but high eyes of pride or amusement.

"Is that her?" He tilted his head to one side.

Her father looked back and saw her standing there behind him. "Yes."

The men stood facing each other. Then the man dipped his chin onto his chest and looked down and then into the face of her father.

"Do you know where you are?"

"Yes."

He tilted his head past him to his daughter and then looked back. The men stared into each other's eyes. They may have given the merest nod. The man broke off and walked back to the gate-lodge. He returned with a short wooden mallet and walked over to the pillar and knelt. He struck a lower section of gate with the mallet a number of times and a wedge of wood fell out on the other side. Her father walked over and picked it up and handed it back over the gate.

"Thank you, sir."

He walked over to the latch and slid it across and pulled open the gate. "Straight up the avenue," he said.

Her father said nothing. He looked back to his daughter then he carried on up the avenue. She stood for a moment and watched him fade in the fog. She looked up and read the words above her.

A convent, she thought.

The man stood holding the gate and staring at a spot on the ground. She walked through the gate and said, "Thank you," and the man said nothing but closed the gate and walked over and knelt by the pillar and began tapping the wedge back into place. She dabbed her tongue in the empty tooth socket and followed up the avenue after her father.

Yes, they were becoming a country of walls, she thought, and like the browning of the leaves she couldn't give a day or a week as to when it started and the southside seemed to have them all the more, for this one that skirted the avenue she'd never seen the likes of. It must have cost a pretty penny and there was many a father in the lane would've given his eyeteeth for the weeks of work this wall would've given. Couldn't even see its end; she only saw its top where the fog thinned over it, like it was fraying on the alpine shards of brown and green and clear glass set into the top. It would be a brave blaggard putting his hand up there, she thought.

But she was nervous now. Since the moment she'd been told that morning to put on her Mass clothes and coat and come out to the lane, she'd known there was a destination and she never dared to ask where she was going, not until they turned up Well Road. But now she knew, and she was scared.

She left the nuns of St Vincent's after her Confirmation one April, went picking spuds up the fields behind Gurannabraher. She never went back after that. It must have been two years now. She washed trays in Thompson's Bakery in town for a summer; the following year she was back picking spuds from June to November. Now, she was going back to nuns. And the religious were not all the same. She'd have taken a priest over a nun any day. Priests smiled and came to your house and had tea; priests bounced around the altar like they were happy with their lot or like they were anxious to push on with the rest of their day, like there was a life to lead. Father Mulcahy fell asleep one day in the confessional, they could hear him snoring outside in the pews. Father Dineen got so drunk after a Stations of the Cross he was said to have fondled the hair of the hostess, a Mrs Flannery, not long widowed. They walked around with the swagger of those knowing they were first in heaven's queue, like there was nothing left to do but wait and smile and have a drink and dangle that cross off their necks like it was the very key to paradise.

Nuns didn't smile. In seven years at St Vincent's she'd never seen such a thing. They seemed to bristle with hate; the gaudy light each morning, the cuddling couples beyond the convent wall, the lady and pram at the school gate, the stockinged leg, the lice-ridden urchin at a desk that doesn't know her three times tables. These were the ceaseless stings of a chosen purgatory, and what kind of a life was it at all that a father could choose for his daughter that had her waiting out this world for a death-dividend since she was fifteen? Priests lived. Nuns seethed like jilted brides and lusted for redress with other people's children; veined wet eyes, splayed nostrils, grey trembling lips, spittled hate lathering in the corners of their mouths. She'd been beaten up and down the classroom for yawning once, another time for misspelling 'Gaeilge' in her copybook. Now she'd given them a reason to hate. Here was God's gift to a southside convent – the fallen Norrie with her burgeoning bastard. Second thought: better in the end – a nun. Let them gorge, she thought. And then she'd go home. Nuns didn't follow. Nuns stayed behind their walls. Nuns didn't cross rivers. Clever Daddy. 'Brains trust', Mammy called him.

She walked past a red-bricked chapel on her left and the avenue curved around it and there the convent stood with a great sunroom out its near side and the convent steps rising to a massive green door with a giant brass knocker. Her father stood at the bottom of the steps, looking back at her as she came out from the bend. His shoulders were slumped and he might have been crying before he saw her but she wasn't sure in the mist and when he saw her he shot his shoulders back and cocked his chin in the air like she might've been coming to inspect him. Then he walked up the steps and knocked on the door. And she walked up and stood behind him.

No one answered.

They waited in silence.

Nothing.

Her father stood breathing loudly through his nose and flitting his eyes about various parts of the door.

She eventually turned and looked out over the brilliant lawn that stretched from the avenue's tar out across the vast front to a grove of trees away to the left. There was a little black gate before the trees and it was closed. A grotto stood to the right of the gate and some flowers were laid there. Mary's head tilted sorrowfully and her eyes were cast mournfully out towards the avenue. Beyond the glass-garnished wall the grey mudflats of Lough Mahon slid into the mist in some dismal confluence of earth and air.

The door opened behind her, and she turned back around. A large middle-aged nun in a white habit stood in the doorway. She looked at the man first and then lifted her jaw over his shoulder and peered for a moment at his daughter behind. His daughter dropped her eyes onto her shoes. No one spoke. Then her father too dropped his head and stared at the granite slate at his feet. The nun finally said, clipped and hard, "Yes?"

Her father looked up to the gold cross at her centre. He flicked his head sideways. He whispered, "This is my daughter."

"Yes?"

"She has... sinned."

The nun looked hard at the top of his head, and then to his trembling hands at his side.

"Step aside, please."

Her father moved a step to the right. The nun stared at his daughter. His daughter stared at her shoes.

"How old?"

"She's thirteen."

"How far?" the nun said.

Her father said, "We came from Blackpool."

"No – how long is she with child?"

"Oh... em... a few months... I think... since Bonfire Night. Yes... Bonfire Night was... when."

"*Bonfire Night*. And look at you now, girl," the nun said, in high-pitched sarcastic merriment. "Bonfire Night in Blackpool!"

She stared at man and daughter and nodded to herself and the man's shoulders trembled and his head seemed to bob at his chest like some bodily corroboration of the nun's words.

"Come in," she said.

The nun opened the door slightly and the man stepped through the doorway and his daughter started to follow before the nun held out her hand.

"Wait here."

Her father looked out at her through the dwindling space in the door and she looked back at her father and turned out her hands to him and he stood there and stared back with tear-brimmed eyes.

The door closed. She heard her father's shoes on the tiles inside. It was the sound she heard every Sunday when he went up for Communion, the leather-on-tile tap, the sound of work and means and earnest man. His three kisses every night on her forehead and his shoes at Mass; those were the drumbeats of a happy childhood.

She turned around and looked out across the flawless lawn to the wall that fringed it. She looked out over to the mudflats where some little birds sat hunched in a posse against the wind and an oystercatcher stalked about punching its beak into the mud like it was goading the land into some small bequeathing.

She looked over to the grotto.

"Mary – pray for me," she whispered.

She took her hands from her pockets, faced fully out to the grotto, forty yards away, and joined her hands.

Hail Mary, full of grace,
The Lord is with thee,
Blessed art thou among women,
And blessed is the fruit of thy womb, Jesus,
Holy Mary, Mother of God,
Pray for us sinners,
Now and the hour of our death
Amen.

The door opened slightly and her father walked sideways out onto the steps and passed her and descended onto the avenue and kept walking and did not look back. The door remained open and the nun in all white put her head around it.

"In," she said.

She stepped up to the open door and turned back to look at the grotto.

Mother Mary, help me, she thought. Then she walked under the doorway and the door was closed behind her.

The nun stared at her in the dark hallway and said nothing.

"Sister – I don't know where I am," she whispered.

"There's no talking here," she said.

"Where's my fath—"

"Ah! Did you hear me?"

"Yes, Sister."

"You needn't be worrying at all about your father. You're here to work and pray. And when the time comes…" She opened her hand towards the girl's body.

"Here?" she gasped.

The nun leaned close and smiled merrily. "Did you think they'd put you up in the Erinville with the doctors' daughters? Is that what you thought? Are you slow? We've plenty of you around here."

"No, Sister."

"Oh, you poor soul. Bonfire Night in Blackpool."

"I just want to know where I am, Sister," she said.

"You're in Bessborough Home," she said, calmly. "*Elaine*. Isn't that a very grand name for a Northside girl? *Elaine*. Are you grand? Are you posh? Well?"

"No, Sister."

"No. And yet ye Norries… the way ye try and name-away ye're lowness." She gave little shakes of her head, in marvel and disgust. "Aren't ye gas altogether."

"Yes, Sister."

"Your name now is Marjorie."

"Yes, Sister."

She stood with her head bowed. The religious in white stared at the top of her head. She leaned furtively to check for head-lice in the crease of the girl's hair, then straightened up again and stood in the silence. The girl stared at the tiles and her body convulsed silently.

"Norries," the nun said. "And yet ye're the most trouble when the time comes. Thinking the child is better off with ye and ye're imported names."

The girl did not speak but she had stopped crying and she raised her head to the nun's crucifix as her father had done.

"Follow me," the nun said.

She turned and walked down the hall and the girl followed. The nun's steps were staunch and nimble for her age, and made no sound at all on the tiles and the girl wasn't sure whether it was the silence of the feet that loudened the *swish-swish* of the habit or whether the habit silenced the steps. She remembered it from school, that cloth-on-cloth *whish* of the religious in motion; it had always sounded to her like a panting dog or like the whispers of children.

She thought now of those first moments in Bessborough Mother and Baby Home. In thirty-four years, the smell of the air and the simmering rhythm of the silence, the tiny hairs about the nun's mouth and the pin-prick pores on her cheeks; she'd never forgotten those things. She stuck her tongue in the gap in her teeth and left it there and reached over to her bedside table and took a cigarette from the packet. Her husband had bought her a 'bridge denture' a few weeks before they got married and she'd lost it two days before the wedding so he'd bought her another one. He called it 'the dark' in her smile. He must've bought her five or six down the years.

There must've been many weddings like hers, she thought, where no one seems to be related to the bride. She told Father Dan that her parents emigrated to England and she stayed behind. She told Martin Connolly that very thing walking around Curraghbinny Woods. It wasn't until the doctors started telling her later that her depression might well be linked to feelings of abandonment and that her 'issue' with the nuns was misplaced rage over these feelings. "Often it's vented at the ones who take the individual in." It was then she told them that her parents never went to England at all, that they never left Blackpool and were probably still there. "But they may as well have. May as well have gone to Timbuktu for all they'd say to me now. Or me to them."

The doctor said, "Well, that only exacerbates the feelings of abandonment – that they never left. Not just alone – but outcast."

She said, "Well, haven't you got all the fucking answers, doctor."

Before her wedding she went into town to the registry office to get her long-form birth certificate, and that was that. That's all she really needed to get married. She walked down the aisle on her wedding day and her eyes welled with tears and she heard the women fawn and say she was lovely and she walked to her husband-to-be and took his hands and he wiped a tear from her cheek with his thumb; the happiest day of her life and all she could think of were the echoing whispers of a religious room, the smell of candle wax and solemnity. She hadn't been in one for twenty years; she walked up the aisle to her waiting groom and somehow felt in every step like she was walking the halls of Bessborough.

When she was in there, she heard the only road was the road to Rosslare when you got out. Walk out Bessborough's door and down the steps in the grief garments some other girl arrived in and down the long avenue and out those gates and keep walking towards the city and somewhere on that hazy journey you open your hand and see the bus fare to Rosslare and the ferry fare sweaty and crushed and limp like a dead lettuce leaf in your palm and you close the hand and walk on out into the remains of your life, pitch what you can into the Irish Sea and start the post-life in England. Some had no idea where they would go. Some went straight into the laundry up there in Sunday's Well, The Good Shepherd Magdalenes. Some went up to Our Lady's and never came out. She walked into a shop and bought a newspaper instead. Walked into the city and rented a room over a pub.

She sat in her bed, flicking ash into a saucer. It looked a ghastly snow, and her breath seemed a wind, and the odd thud of a closed cupboard below a distant thunder; a little world there in one room. No one gets out, she thought. Your child lies starving in a little metal cot next to other babies starving in other cots, Sister looking in to them, like she was checking broth on a stove. You don't get out. You go to Bessborough because you aren't married and it's Bessborough you marry for the rest of your life; and it's a loyal beggar, it doesn't leave.

Sometimes she thought those women whose children survived had it worse. The mother and child might have been together for two years. Sister would come along one day and tell the mother her baby was leaving in a few hours. To have the child ready for its 'parents'.

Some of the women tried something in the days after. They drank floor cleaner or varnish or slit their wrists or jumped down the staircase in the convent. A dead child is the end. The end of them, the end of you. *He is with Jesus, he is with Jesus*, you tell yourself. A stolen child is not with Jesus. It's his very living, the theft of his living, that is agony.

Elaine had been painting one of the dormitories with two other girls one summer. A girl in her twenties came in with her child and she was crying silently and wiping her nose with her sleeve. The child was sitting on the edge of the metal-framed bed and the mother would kneel down and hug the child tight for a long time then break off and continue dressing him then stop again and pull the child into her until the child began to moan. They knew he was going.

Two nuns came in and told her to get off her knees and dress the child, then they squabbled about something and looked back to the mother and walked away looking at their watches. The mother touched and hugged the child like something malfunctioned for she seemed not to breathe at all until she took a huge inhale and retched it out and she'd pat and squeeze the child's body all over like she was putting out a fire and when she hugged the child she'd press her mouth to his face and cry against his skin. The child looked up blankly at its mother. The mother looked at the new clothes the nuns had laid out for the child on her pillow. All departing babies departed in new clothes from town. The mother put on the clothes bit by bit, then she put on a blue cardigan she'd knitted the week before for the child, it was tight-fitting over the other clothes. When the nun came in, she took it off and the mother begged her to leave it on.

"Please, Sister. I knitted it last week for him. Please, please, please. It's all he'll have of me."

They left on the blue cardigan.

Elaine could hear the child being picked up and the nun and the mother and the child walking out of the dormitory. They dropped their paint brushes and crept silently after them down the stairs and stood peeking out from behind a door at the end of the long corridor which led out to the convent. Behind the mother and child and nun, two other girls stood with their heads bowed with a mop and bucket and sponge.

"Last goodbyes now," said Sister. "Last goodbyes."

Elaine had been one of those mop girls. For six months she'd stood with a mop and watched women say goodbye to their babies. They palpitated and collapsed or got violent or some shut down and seemed indifferent. No mother ever said the word *goodbye*. They gasped, some of them, a muted pant as the nun took the child; some voided their bowels at the moment of taking. Some vomited into their hands and stood ravenously watching the last morsel images of their baby, big-bummed in new napkin, a little arm stretched up to the nun. The nuns always seemed to her like progeny of the walls, an unblemished great white that was defiled only by the flesh and blood of their faces and the colour of their eyes. One mother had turned to the wall next to her when her child was taken and pulled off the picture of the Sacred Heart and began smashing it with her fists. She was never seen again. There was a rectangular stain on the wall now, an eye-level squarish discolouration and she looked down to it now from the gap in the door.

The mother stayed in the corridor for a long time. The girls stood away down the hall in silence with their mops. Elaine and the other two painters went back up to the dormitory and picked up their brushes and turned back to the wall. A while later they could hear the mother walk in behind them. Elaine looked out the door and dropped her brush and walked over to the woman and sat next to her on the bed. She rubbed her back. She wiped her own tears with her shoulder for her own hands had spatters of paint on them. The woman was silent and stared down at her hands which were balled into fists. She'd touch them together and bring them occasionally to her mouth and lower them slowly onto her lap again. Elaine leaned closer to put her arm around the woman and it was then she saw, encased in the woman's grasp, the blue wool cardigan. They stayed on the bed for a long time and the mother never took her eyes from the clenched cadence of her hands and Elaine would look over at the two painters across the dorm who'd look back at her as they dipped their brushes and they'd nod at each other and return silently to their missions.

She could hear her down the dorm in the night, perhaps ten beds away. A hissy, seeping sound like she was wincing and breathing through her teeth. In the morning Elaine watched her at breakfast with a ghost movement in her limbs and a lobotomy face that barely blinked. She did not eat or speak but made cradlesong moans now and again and other girls flicked their eyes to her and some looked down and put their hands to their bumps and ate no more. She cried in the night and the next three nights. And then she cried no longer.

The first thing Elaine saw in Bessborough was the grotto. It was the last thing she saw when she left. She walked out onto the convent steps the last morning, the Madonna's hands still praying, head tilting. She walked down the avenue and out to the gate and she heard the lodge man close it behind her; she remembered how much she thought she was walking away.

She was fifty-one now. She'd been in bed for three years. Her child had lain unmarked in the ground over there in Blackrock for decades. She'd made signs and stood outside the church holding them under her chin. The men went for her that second time. Faces all gnarled and rosy with rage. The bracelets of bruising on her wrists were starting to fade, like the flesh was forgetting.

In the evening, the house was silent. She got out of bed and she walked downstairs and opened the front door and saw the car was gone. She went back up to her room and put on some clothes and she came down the stairs again. The house was dark and she could not find her coat in the closet. She put on her son's coat and walked into the kitchen. She went out the back door and down to the shed at the bottom of the garden. She picked up the short-handled sledgehammer her husband had put up the fence with. She tucked it inside the coat. She walked through the house and out the front door and walked up to the grotto at the top of the village. She waited for the cars to pass. Then she opened the little gate.

"He was my baby, Mary," she whispered. "He was four months, fifteen days and eight hours old."

V

1

Easter, 2016

Michael pulled off the road and drove up the avenue. There was a light upon it that he had never seen and where the limbs of trees had been severed, pale discs of wood stared out of the trunks like jarred faces and the manicured hedging ran with his car and flicked and squealed at his mirrors when he got close and he wondered had he ever really been here at all amidst the manicured gardens and the croquet lawn and the putting green. He came around the back of the house and he saw the stables had been converted and extended to a spa and he could see a sign for hot-stone therapy and he grew nervous. He proposed then that the bird in his belly was a Bessborough child itself, adopted by him but born of her, galled at his own abandonment, galled at his origins, galled at her ending.

He parked his car in the rear carpark and stayed there for a while, thinking over what he might say should someone ask for a room number or offer him a menu and whether it was alright to just wander around a five-star hotel for a look. A belt of baby spruces came out around the western edge and swung south towards the woods in the same sweep their forebears made before they were cut down and cut up and set in brass buckets by the remote control fireplaces in the Deluxe-Ultra Rooms. In the spaces between, he could see the rooftops and the backs of houses a mile away in Ballyredmond. He'd read in the newspaper recently that that was how Somerville House came to be, how Ballyredmond came to be; his lordship put down a row of cottages for some of his estate workers some two hundred and fifty years before and the whole thing went from there. And now it was a five-star hotel.

He breathed in deep and let it out and undid his seatbelt and got out of the car. He walked towards the front of the house, skirting the croquet lawn where some children had dispensed with the mallets and were kicking the ball through the hoops and shouting "Goal!" with their parents sitting with massive sunglasses on a bench up on the raised garden.

He walked with his head down, his green shirt still creased on the shoulders and back from the cardboard insert, the sleeves rolled twice back to his forearm. He watched the children playing, he smiled at them and carried on. He came around to the front of the house and saw a doorman standing up at the door in a top hat and tails, facing down the green expanse where a man some way off hunkered into his shoes and swung his golf club again and again in slow motion. When he hit the ball, it sounded like clicked fingers in an empty room.

The doorman pulled his jaw onto his shoulder. "He hit it… finally."

He turned back his head. "Sorry?" Michael said.

"Excuse me, sir?"

"Sorry, I thought you were talking to me."

"Oh no, sir. I was talking to my colleague inside."

Michael stood tapping his foot on the lowest step. He thought of the last time he sat there. He and John had stumbled down the steps that summer evening when they were both seventeen and he'd stopped on the last step and watched the rabbits run for the trees and draw meagre tracks in the dew. A lone rabbit remained. It had not moved but raised its head and stared side-on at them up at the house. Its cheeks rolled and its mouth twitched like it was talking. The two boys looked at each other then ran screaming and laughing down the land after it. At first the rabbit made a run for the trees as the others had done and then it broke down into the parkland and the boys followed it on down, still screaming and laughing. It turned again and came back up towards the house and the boys came after it. It turned towards the trees and when it came up on them, it stopped, and turned side-on again and looked at the boys. They had stopped running and had begun walking towards the house again. When they saw the rabbit stop again, they smiled and shook their heads and walked on up to the house and sat on the steps. They could see it out there, returning to the spot from which they'd first chased it. They looked at the rabbit for a time and held their flagons of cider and breathed hard from their noses when they drank from them.

"What would we have done if we'd caught it, Michael?"

Michael looked on down to the fleck of brown movement in the great green.

"Dunno," he said.

"If it tumbled or something. Or if it was lame – and that's why it never moved off with the others?"

"Dunno," he said again. "You get a momentum up behind you, you mightn't be able to back out of something."

"Ya."

"We might've walked up on a lame rabbit and killed it for the arrogance of not moving. At the balls of it for not keeping out of sight."

"Two drunks with a notion for violence."

"And that's how it would've been. And we'd have regretted it. There and then I'd say."

"Ya."

"Insects, bees. A spider – grand. But a rabbit is big. A rabbit is more living. Flesh and blood and sentience. We'd have regretted it the rest of our lives, I'd say."

"Then why d'you think we would've?"

"Would've what?"

"Killed it?"

"Dunno," Michael said. "I suppose 'cause it wouldn't have mattered if we did or not."

"Ya."

"The life has to matter before the death will."

His friend nodded and he nodded and they looked down to the rabbit and its cheeks bulged like there were marbles in it. They got up and went inside and when they came down the steps in the morning they looked down the grass and the rabbits were back again and they watched the boys head down the avenue towards the road and did not move.

He looked up now from the step and around the brilliant white of the house with his mouth wide open and shaking his head just a little and bringing up his hand to shield his eyes against the sky.

"It's a different house," he said.

"Pardon, sir?"

"It's a different house."

"Are you local, sir?"

"Yes. I used to come here."

"Used you?"

"Way back."

"Oh. What was it like then?"

He swept another look about the house's façade and back down to the step where his foot resided. "It was old. Abandoned," he said softly.

"Yes, they did a lovely job on it."

"It looks like they built it yesterday."

"Well, in many ways they did. It's ninety-nine per cent new."

"Yes, well..."

"Sir?"

"Are we looking for *new*? I mean – need everything be new?"

"Yes, I see."

"There's a refinement in a slow dying, I think."

"In a...?"

"I wonder, would it have taken a fire in 1920 over a hotel in 2016?"

The doorman stepped out from the porch and gazed up the face of the house. Then he turned back to him.

"Are you coming in, sir?"

He looked up into the room where he'd stood those nights in his youth, drinking. He would grow rowdy and run about the house and break windows and bounce on the collapsed staircase and John would stand and watch him. He'd run around sometimes on his own and destroy some cornicing or ceiling plasterwork with the glass from his naggin, then he'd sit on the windowsill beneath the tiers of cobwebs and go quiet. He'd roar sometimes out of the blue and then stand and wait for the house to call back from some far-off upper landing a few seconds later like some spirit-world mimicry. He'd sit at that window sometimes until the dawn, the leaves blowing in the hall and the nettles bobbing at the skirting boards and sometimes he'd watch his friend muttering in his dreams.

A middle-aged couple sat at the window now with their heads down, going wordless about their food. They had matching blue polo necks and beige trousers and he figured them American and he was proud of that, proud to have people come so far, pay so much to sit in that room.

"No, no. Thank you. I only came for a look. I just wanted to see what they did with the place."

"Okay, sir. No problem."

"The parade will be on shortly anyway."

"You're going to head into the parade, sir?"

"We'll head in anyway for a look, I suppose. For the day that's in it."

He pulled his green shirt out from his chest and delivered the upward half of a nod and scoffed. "Erra, you can't get away from it at the moment."

"No, sir. A hundred years. A hundred years. There's loads on in town, I hear."

"God, mobbed, I'd say. Sure, we'll have a look anyway."

He turned aslant from the house, trailed his eyes down its front and across the windows like a wary child; there was a light in them that he'd never seen, a double-glazed glint and colour like that of new coins.

"I'll see you."

"Have a good day, sir."

He looked back a last time to the house and walked back to the carpark and passed again the boys on the croquet lawn who had now stuck two mallets in the ground handle-first and measured out a length of goal and acquired a soccer ball. Their parents had vacated the table on the raised garden and a man in black trousers and waistcoat was clearing it and looking nervously down on the boys and over his shoulder and all around like he'd just stumbled upon a crime. He gathered up the cups and plates on his tray and walked briskly inside.

Michael walked on to his car. He reversed out and headed back around the house and across the front and he felt the doorman's eyes through his window and he raised his hand to him. He drove through the trees to the gates on the road. He pulled out towards Cork City. Easter 1916, Centenary Memorial Parade. He would drink and give thanks and be so happy that he was Irish.

2

When he was a child, he would go with his father into town on St Patrick's Day and they'd park the car along one of the southern quays and walk into the city and take their place among the crowds. They would stand on St Patrick's Street and watch the floats go by and he'd feel his father's hands on his shoulders and their width and weight and slow seeping warmth to his bones.

He stood now on St Patrick's Street on the centenary of the Easter Rising, with T.W. Murray's fishing and gun shop behind him and Porter's newsagents facing him across the road and he knew this was not like Paddy's Day for there were no vintage fire engines and there were no Brownie Girls or Cub Scouts or flowered floats of the Cork coat of arms or a school's papier-mâché of Shandon Steeple with the tinfoil fish painted gold and tilted back like it sought to leap free of its own sloppy rendering and St Patrick was not bringing up the rear in mitre and green vestments and the end of his staff skewering a snake with his eyes cast celestially out to the people and other worlds.

The crowds now did not cheer but were sombre and contemplative and there were banners and flags and military marching bands and colours and tricolours and badges and medals in glass cases and on blazers and on velvet cushions carried by the rebels' descendants. Dublin on Monday, Tuesday in Limerick, Cork today. He stood not so far from where he often had with his father, his new green shirt among all the other green shirts and t-shirts and jumpers and Celtic jerseys and Ireland rugby jerseys and he felt a great pride and a great kinship with these people; Patrick's people, Pearse's people, enslaved no more by myth and memory and king and Christian. They knew better now. Ireland unfree...

Here comes Plunkett, they said.

A giant Joseph Plunkett head rose above the crowd up by the old Roches Stores building which had become a Debenham's and he thought of the seven men who had signed the Proclamation of Independence and he looked up at the sky and the cranes against the clouds seemed like golden pointers to a better world and the First Southern Brigade Band passed behind the giant black and white canvas of Joseph Plunkett and he felt a warmth that rose in his stomach up to his chest, a heat that parched his mouth and wet his lower back and his eyes and blazed more with every drum, every tricolour, every patriot visage.

He looked at the faces across the road between the passing IRA flags and gold harps sewn upon green and yet another tricolour and he saw that he was not alone, there were others with wet eyes and wet backs and warm hearts, others who knew they were the greatest nation on Earth, gathered here to show respect, to give thanks to the men who made them so.

"Look, here comes Mac Diarmada," a few in the crowd said. "And I think that's Clarke a bit behind." And his eyes welled again at the sight of those giant bobbing canvas heads above the crowd.

Jesus, he thought, we'll be in an awful state by the time Pearse comes.

They delayed him. The same hundred steps between the Proclamation and six of the people who'd signed it was not there for the seventh, the man who penned it, the creator, head taker-of-the-British-hand-from-their-throat. After Connolly there was a gap and the road seemed to shimmer in the heat. He could hear them starting up by the Father Mathew statue – the rat-a-tat-tats of the snare drums going off like the crackle of machine gun fire and the pound of the bass drums in between like some deep sonorous recalling and he knew he was coming somewhere behind those drums and the Collins' Barracks Battalion that followed up behind them and every head was cast over to where the first Dunnes Stores arrived in 1944 and remained still and cut off their view and lumps grew in throats and children nestled their crotches onto their father's necks and leaned out to catch something of it and lifestyle drinkers left their glasses on Le Chateau's counter and came out squinting into the crowds and went on tip-toe like everyone else and cast their heads over to that bend and waited and waited, waiting for that giant head to come.

He thought, This is life – a gap in the parade, waiting to see what's coming. Life is the lull. Life is the waiting throng. And he was happy there, being just one in the multitude, the diminishing rigour of other people. He was a nobody amidst his countrymen, and he was happy about that. He looked on up and waited and they all waited.

A man ambled out of Le Chateau Bar and worked his way through the crowd, greeting people and thanking people; he wore a beige trench coat that was black along the collar with stout stains on the lapels and at his elbows and his remnant hair was dyed black and greased in strands across his pate with sideburns and eyebrows and nose-hair flickering in the air and he looked to where the others looked and he shook his head.

"What are we at, lads?" he said.

No one answered.

"What are we at, lads, ha?"

Some children on their fathers' shoulders turned to him then slinked their eyes away and back up the street again. Some turned around to see who would smoke in such close confines and amongst children and at what was still all in all a memorial service, and they too turned away.

Michael could hear the erosive raspy breaths behind him, wheezed little body-bios that told a tale of cigarettes and whiskey all the waking minutes of his days, and he knew that tale and he knew that smell. The nose remembers. The nose is a sentimental bugger.

It might have been his mother standing there behind him in those last years, at the bathroom sink, standing over him as he brushed his teeth, leaning in for a bedtime kiss, the whiskey wheeze over his shoulder, guiding his pencil around the dotted words on his copybook.

And then Pearse came. Fix-chinned and cheek-boned, staring off to blood and sacrifice and days such as these. The people were silent and stared on with low, reverent faces and fathers tugged on their children's arms overhead or rubbed their shoulders and some kids looked up to their fathers questioningly and their fathers pointed outward with their chins and the kids took out their iPhones and started snapping away and a few councillors from different parties pushed out to the front and looked at each other and looked at the people around them. A quiet clapping began all about him which he could not see at first and then he saw across the road the people at the front joining in and some older people blessing themselves and the politicians clapping robustly and inviting others to clap.

Two men came behind with a white banner that stretched the width of the road. It was held up with two wooden poles, the base of each planted into the cup of the men's hands and held perfectly upright with their other hand holding it at their chests. They looked straight forward and clenched their jaws and did not smile. The banner read: *Blood is a cleansing and sanctifying thing, and the nation that regards it as the final horror has lost its manhood... there are many things more horrible than bloodshed. And slavery is one of them. – Padraig Pearse.*

He felt that, most probably, his interest long ago in Tone and Connolly and Fitzgerald and Emmet and all the rest of them lay with his mother's decrying of everything Irish when she was drunk. The great patriots she'd bat away with her hand and roll her eyes and quote their words aloud, then raise her arms aloft like some inebriate Jim Larkin and say, "No English man killed my child in a convent." Then she'd most often pull out her breast and wipe her finger along the scar and lay her hand underneath as though disclosing it for the first time. Some year after she was gone, he hung a laminated copy of the Proclamation over his bed and it stayed there for twenty years. That's why, he assumed, he'd wanted to study them. That's why, he supposed, he'd wanted to teach them. That's why every time he did teach them, every time he randomly thought about some Irish patriot, watched some documentary, drove past a Celtic cross in West Cork, he felt a comforting distance from her, that she was further sealed up in the attic of his mind and would remain there always. He came third in his History degree thanks to her. Wrote a brilliant thesis called *The Imperative Reductivism of Revisionism in the Irish Nationalist Debate.*

But as the years went by, he couldn't pretend anymore. There was no negation. There was only a coalescence in his mind of all of them with his mother. When he spoke to his students of long dead martyrs, he thought of his mother. When he passed a Celtic cross on the roadside, he thought of his mother. When he heard the national anthem or saw a tricolour or heard trad music under a pub door, he thought of her. She was there in his mind with them all. But Pearse most of all; those last words of hers had so infused Padraig Pearse with his mother, he could not see that famous profile without perceiving in his ear the ribbed cartilage of her own, her lips in his, the trauma of her eyes in his one.

Then he sat one day watching the television with a sandwich on his lap. He went off to Dingle and sat in the sand of Ventry. Jill Roche came walking up the strand and sat down next to him. He told her everything and they held hands and stayed there for the longest time. They went back in the night to the cottage and they made love. She returned every weekend and they talked in the night for hours and in the day they drank and walked and she wrote when he walked alone along the roads and the beaches and they walked together across Sybil

Head over across the cliffs and back again. They lay on their chests and poked their faces over the cliff edge to the ocean far below and he felt he was the happiest man alive to have such a woman next to him, to have such a woman naked with him every night, to tell him so delicately every night about the bond of mother and child, to tell him that his mother and people like her suffered more than any patriot and they were more Irish than the peat of Connemara or the Great Blasket Island, for she was transgressed by them, by their indifference and silence. He'd walk out along the Atlantic roads and feel lighter for the things he'd told Jill and he'd apologise and she'd tell him to carry on and take hold of his hands.

It was Jill who told him to go to the parade. She told him to stand at the side and clap and be proud like everyone else. Proud of what the few could achieve against the many, the small against the great. She told him to remember that the weak have their memories and they are long and they are sharp as any blade. She told him he should think of that as Pearse went by and he said he would and he knew of what she spoke. He asked her to accompany him and she said she would not, that he should go alone. And he said he knew that, but that he was ashamed.

He sent letters to his local TDs' offices and into the newspapers about all he knew, about all his mother had told him, and when he came back from the post office Jill said she could see it in his face already; 'a colour'. He said, "Shame has no face. No colour. It beats in the body like another heart."

"No," she said. "That's sadness. For your mother, for her dead baby." She rose and walked to him and put her hand to his face and began stroking his temple with the edge of her thumb. "They're still here," she said. Then she put her hand over his heart. A tear rolled from his face and fell on her hand and she kissed it.

He could smell the man behind him as Pearse went by and he could smell him as the banner went by and he could hear him mouthing the words and he could smell the alcohol all the more as he did, it was warm against the back of his neck and his ear. Michael closed his eyes and breathed deep through his nose. He put his hands over his ears and kept his eyes closed and he stayed like that until people began to turn away from the metal barriers and the crowd began to dissipate and people bumped his elbows. The last-day trinity was alcohol breath and tobacco smoke and Padraig Pearse. The integrant dusts that rose in his eyes and ears and nostrils every time he ever took out her final words and thought of them.

He pulled away from the barrier and cut through the crowd and walked on down the pavement away from the advancing drums, past Golden Discs and on past Woodford and Sons Wine Wholesalers and onto the Coal Quay and on out to the river railing and there he turned and headed upstream along Bachelors Quay and onto Dyke Parade to Mardyke Walk and turned in the gate to Fitzgerald's Park.

He sat down on the first bench and crossed his legs and rubbed his palms along his thighs. He noticed a stain on his trousers and he spread out the material and raised it up off his skin to glean its provenance. He scratched at it with a fingernail, then left it alone.

It was thirty-five years ago now, but he remembered the whole thing: the day of the Pearse portrait. He'd been out on his bike and when he walked into the hall he stopped. He could tell by the daylight on the wall at the top of the stairs that her door was open; that she was probably there beyond the door in the kitchen. Sitting in that seat of hers. When he opened the door she was sitting in her seat with a leaf stuck on the top of her slipper and some mud along the sides with a whiskey bottle and a bottle of red lemonade peculiarly out of reach at the far side of the table like she'd pushed them there when she heard him come in or as though if there were task enough in her reaching, she may not reach at all. She turned her head to him and smiled when he came in. Her dressing gown was open but pulled up and across her thighs like a mini-skirt and her pyjama top wasn't properly fastened and he could see the limp and littleness of her breasts and the outer edge of scar under one of them and her bare legs were crossed under the chair with varicose veins bulging on her calves like tiny mountain ranges risen in her flesh. Then she returned to where she looked before. She pointed up at the wall on the far side of the French doors and said nothing for a time, just stared and pointed.

Then she said, "Ye bought a picture."

"Dad brought it home from town the other day."

She nodded slowly as she looked up at it then glanced to him then looked back again to the picture. He pitied his father; he seemed to have done so since he was born. He pictured him walking into bedlam later, the whiskey half gone, his innocent mouth agape, his wife rambling with drunk indignance.

Michael sat on the bench now and shook his head gently, then stopped abruptly for the parade was over and the park was filling up and he didn't want anyone thinking he was one of those park bench crazies who made mothers nervous sitting around and smiling all day in stained pants and intermittently nodding and shaking their heads, wrapped in some internal dialogue. They'd think, *He's for the Lee Road.* It wasn't far away; only up Mardyke Walk and over the bridge. But Our Lady's was gone now, turned into apartments, and he wondered about the kind of person who'd buy an apartment in an old asylum; only the people who were unacquainted with it, he reasoned. People unconsumed with former lives there.

His father had asked his mother to marry him in this park, on one of these benches. Perhaps this one, he thought. No. He recalled his father telling him once on one of those drives to the hospital that it was on one of the benches by the river, the Lee right there by their feet, listless and silent, waiting out those last few miles before the sea ended it all.

When his father came in that evening, she held the glass and cigarette with the same hand and was stooped over them with her knees turned in and touching, like she was crouched in pain;

she rocked faintly. He probably wouldn't have remembered it only for what came after; would've been lost, just another day in a great many like it. She stayed in bed the next day and never said a word and the day after his father came home from work and went upstairs and stuck his head around the door.

So these became the last words. Her son rose from the bench and walked out along the river and thought of them.

"Why the picture, Martin?"

Martin stood and looked at the bottle of whiskey and the plastic bottle of red lemonade at the far side of the table and he did not take his eyes off them as he spoke.

"Oh, Elaine," he said. "Ya know – long ago in Ballycotton my father would have five mackerel on the line and I'd be sat at the edge of the boat waiting for the glints of the fish. And they'd come, these glimmers of silver." He poked his head forward towards the table. "The glass and plastic of the bottles there – they sometimes, with the sun like that, they sometimes seem like the fish coming whirling up out of the gloom. I know it's strange, but they do, sometimes, remind me."

She did not speak for a long time but only sat and watched him stare at the bottles on the table. She then looked back up at the picture of Pearse on the wall.

"Where'd you get it?"

"We used to have a picture of Pearse at home above my father's armchair. So I just thought it would be nice."

She leaned back in her seat, set down the glass and outed her cigarette at arm's length in the ashtray, then took up her glass again.

"And what did we do with the freedom when we got it? Ask the penitents, the orphans, industrial school children. Ask the women whose babies were stolen. Ask the girls whose lives were stolen. Ask them. Ask them all. Go round to the asylums of Ireland and ask them all about their glorious freedom. They don't have pictures like that. They have cigarettes and rosary beads and slippers, they trudge around state hallways of piss and crucifix, replaying their lives, waiting out the end on a metal bed, chain-smoking among the schizophrenics. And no imperial Britain did it. We did it ourselves."

His father leaned against the kitchen sink and pushed his fingers up under the lenses of his glasses and rubbed his eyes.

"I'm just living, Ellie."

"You're a local in sleepy Belsen village. You look away. You look away and say, 'I know nothing.' One day they'll go digging in Bessborough. And you'll know then it isn't me, but you, sitting there beneath your Pearse picture, watching the news. It is you – it is you that has fallen."

3

Michael stood by the river and he looked up and there they all were, somewhat unexpectedly, lined up along the hill. He could see their upper windows and roofs above the trees. Where the river Lee breaks in two, they follow the north channel for a mile or more starting with Our Lady's asylum and then the red bricks of St Kevin's asylum and the old city Gaol and the Magdalene Laundry of The Good Shepherd Order and St Finbarr's Industrial School for Girls and the orphanage alongside it, all facing down onto the river and the land and the city that filled them and way up the crosses of their steeples were sparse and bent like abandoned graves in the sky.

He took off his shoes and set them down and he rolled down his socks and pulled them off and he put each of them into his shoes and left them there at the river edge. He rolled his pants to his shins and dipped his toes in the water. He looked up over the trees to all the glassless black in those buildings and he thought of all the terrible eyes that must have looked out from them once and he thought of his mother's eyes.

He stood up and walked into the river to his knees and he looked down into the water and he could not see himself for the murk and he put his hand in his pocket and took out her wedding ring and he closed his fist around it and slowly dropped his hand down into the water and he left it there for a while just looking at it. Then he opened his hand. It stayed for a moment on his open palm, then the current stood it upright and then it was gone.

He stood up and faced down to where the river ran slow and silent away behind some trees and he thought of where the river joined up again on the other side of the city and carried on out to where it started dropping silt and bodies and memory. They could find a ring out there someday, he thought. When he was gone and the yet unborn were gone. Some kids by the shore of Blackrock Castle or a man with a dog by the rocks over in Passage West. They'd wipe it clean on a shirt end and finger it on a palm and read the engraving on the inside. It would read: *My Baby. Always.* And they would not know the woman who wore it, that she'd carved him in silver and turned him over a knuckle and wore him always against her finger flesh. A child of gene and past and bone and blood. A child of man and man's god. A child of Ireland who lived and was loved and held by a mother in that country. And they would not know he had no grave, for he was bastard. And that there were many, many like him.

Leabharlanna Poiblí Chathair Baile Átha Cliath

Dublin City Public Libraries

Author's Note

Early in 2014, I was walking with my wife in the grounds of Bessborough, as we sometimes did. We were discussing a novel I was writing, or struggling to write. Passing the front steps, she looked up at the façade of the convent and said, "Why don't you write a novel about this place?" I started the following morning, those first paragraphs.

Bessborough Mother and Baby Home was opened in 1922 as an institution to house women and girls who became pregnant out of wedlock. It was owned and operated by The Congregation of the Sacred Hearts of Jesus and Mary. Once the child could be placed in foster care or adopted, the babies were taken from their mothers, weeks, months sometimes a few years after birth. The cleaving of this bond between mother and child was considered by the state, by the Catholic Church and, yes, by society at large, as the best outcome; the separation of the sinner from the sin. In the great majority of cases, mother and child would never see each other again. This was long known, Bessborough long a whispered word on the old footpaths of Cork.

Less known were the deaths there. In 1943 in Ireland, the infant mortality rate was 7%. In Bessborough Mother and Baby Home it was 75%. Successive government health inspectors attributed a great many of the deaths to "marasmus", i.e. malnutrition.

A fuller historical accounting would delve deeper into the forced and illegal adoptions, what I would call a "forced consent"; the falsification of birth certs, the drug trials on some of the children in the 1960s; the thwarting of grown-up children seeking information about their birth mothers, about themselves; of mothers seeking some small knowledge about the fates of their long-stolen babies. And of course the deaths of the babies and the mystery of their burial. But I will leave that to others. I offer here only a keyhole to those crimes.

This is a novel about a fictitious woman who was held in Bessborough Mother and Baby Home. But it is dedicated to all the real ones: to every woman and girl and baby who ever resided there. To the 923 infants who died there. To the 859 infants whose graves are unmarked there.

Mel O'Doherty
12/3/21

Acknowledgments

M Y THANKS TO: Kevin Duffy and everyone at Bluemoose Books, especially Annie Warren for her expertise and encouragement. Also, my gratitude to Fiachra McCarthy. My agent Brian Langan for his guidance, patience and longstanding support of my writing. Conall Ó Fátharta for writing about Bessborough long before any government took an interest. Catherine Coffey O'Brien and Maureen Considine of Cork Survivors and Supporters Alliance. My late friend Pearse McCarthy. My beautiful children Senan, Fiachra and Erin for their love and support. And finally, I'd like to thank my wonderful wife Elise for her never-ending faith and encouragement. This book could not have been written without her.